THE ONE WHO COULD NOT FLY

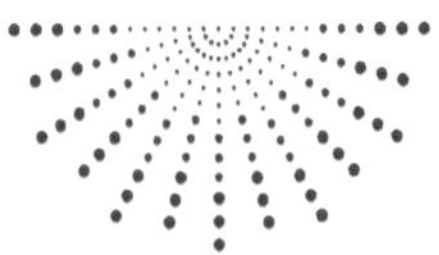

E.G. STONE

This book is a Tarney Brae Creative Endeavours production.

Edited by Vanessa Anderson

Cover design by Fay Lane Graphic Design

Paperback ISBN: 978-1-7347965-0-6

Hardback ISBN: 978-1-7347965-1-3

❀ Created with Vellum

Dedicated to Kendra,
who is still in my contacts as
The Coolest Person on the Planet...
for obvious reasons

CONTENTS

Hullgar
Salusian Empire
Mardego

So

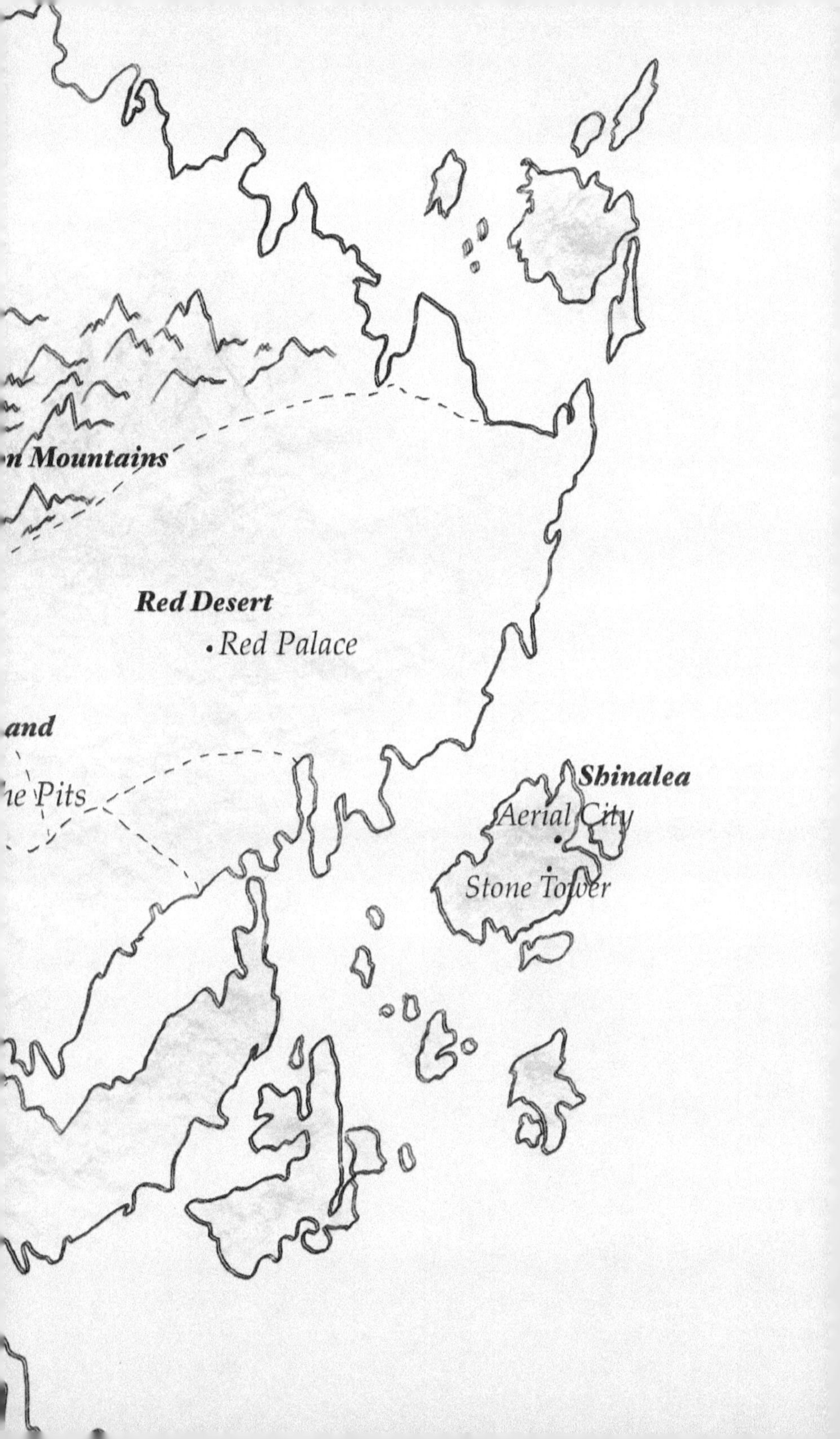

n Mountains
Red Desert
Red Palace
and
e Pits
Shinalea
Aerial City
Stone Tower

PROLOGUE

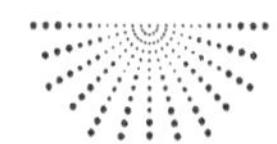

*I*f there was one thing that Dagan, Firstborn Son of the Salusian Emperor, Heir Apparent to the throne and the Scourge of the Unconquered, revelled in, it was bloodshed. He had been trained from childhood to wield a blade for the honour of the Empire. But, over the years, he found he preferred to wield it for pure pleasure. If the honour of the Empire and his own pleasure happened to coincide? Well, then, that was something to behold.

That day, Dagan led his armies to conquer a tiny nation hardly worth noticing. Their defences were weak. Those who fought against him were hardly capable enough to bother with. They probably could have been annexed with nothing more than a piece of paper and Dagan's army standing on the border. Certainly, it would be *easier* and less costly for the Empire to pursue a diplomatic alternative. But Dagan still raised his sword and led his people to their victory. And he fought for blood.

The ground was slick with the mud from blood and churned gore. The defending armies stumbled and baulked, flailing in failed attempts to fight back. They had not had time to prepare against the onslaught, nor enough time to prepare a surrender before the armies of the Empire had descended on them, eager for a fight. Dagan's armies had fought in worse battles and were simply having sport now. Dagan was in the thick of things. He roared with pleasure as his muscles swelled at the activity. His skin, normally a golden-brown glowing with health and vigour, was smeared with dirt and blood and who knows what else. Sweat dripped into his dark brown hair making it lank. And his eyes, fierce, dark, glistened with passion.

Dagan carelessly swung his sword in a needless arc, leaving his chest open for a counterstrike should his enemy chose. He supposed he should be wearing armour, but what was the fun in that? Oh, if these people had put up a fight with more than pick-axes and pole arms—that they hardly knew how to use—well, maybe he would have bothered. In the meantime, perhaps he could gather another scar to tell his father about when he returned from the campaign.

His sword bit through the soft tissues his opponents left exposed as they tried to regain balance long lost. One soldier's head severed cleanly from his shoulders and Dagan let out a bellow of victory. A quick glance around told him that his fellow soldiers were faring equally well. The defending army was all but obliterated.

Dagan leaned over and scooped up the severed head by its hair, lifting it into the air and letting out another roar.

"Victory to the Empire!" one of Dagan's soldiers cried at the sight, hefting his battle axe into the air. The cry was picked up and echoed around the battlefield.

"Victory! Victory! Victory!"

Dagan looked a dead soldier in the eyes and laughed before tossing the head aside.

The few left alive in the defending army slowly sank to their knees. Surrender. Unconditional.

Dagan's men walked up to them and raised their weapons.

"Well, my lord?" Dagan's Captain asked, a ruthless woman

who wore her hair cropped to her skull and had kept up with Dagan since childhood.

One day, he thought, he was going to tempt her into his bed and then they'd see who could keep up. For now, though, she was a valued asset and kept his armies going. Dagan considered the small, squirrelly man at her feet, eyes wide and pleading.

"You!" Dagan pointed his sword at the man and grinned when he received a tremble in return. Dagan took a few squelching steps towards the kneeling man. Blood dripped down his face into his mouth and Dagan spit it out, the globule landing on the soldier's armour.

The man closed his eyes and gulped.

Dagan levelled his sword, resting the tip at the spot where neck met open air.

"You," Dagan repeated, lower now. A demand.

"Yes, m-my liege?" the soldier said, the words falling from his tongue like lead.

Dagan smiled. Another nation conquered. Another people to bring into the fold of the Salusian Empire. It would be beautiful when Dagan returned to his father with the map of the Emperor's new territories. He would be forever remembered as the Conqueror of the World. He would be legendary. And, one day, he would gain enough power to be a god.

"Where is the nearest village?" Dagan asked, his sword point digging into the fragile skin of the fallen soldier's neck.

The soldier's trembling increased.

Dagan's Captain held him still, as did all of the other soldiers with their captives. It was up to Dagan to decide what to do with them.

"O…o-ver the hill," the soldier flashed his eyes to a hill some short distance from the churned battlefield.

Dagan turned and considered.

"About half-an-hour's march," the soldier continued.

Dagan raised his eyebrows. "Good. We won't have to make camp here."

"N-no," the soldier said.

In agreement or defiance, Dagan did not know. He did not really care. Lifting his sword from the man's neck, he wiped it on his dirty breeches, then sheathed the curved blade into the worn leather at his back and turned to walk away, stepping indiscriminately over bodies and mud puddles as he went.

The soldier slumped in relief, only the Captain's strong grip keeping him upright.

"Kill them all," Dagan said dismissively. By the time the screaming ended, he was moving towards the top of the hill and his army was following behind him. No one bothered to bury the bodies or set them aflame. That was a task for the villagers... When Dagan was done with them.

* * *

The village had not liked being overrun by a conquering army. After a few complaints from older men and women who hadn't been on the battlefield—women who had been home tending to the village and the children, and anyone who had not been there to see Dagan's decisive victory—who were forced to feel the bite of his fists, the protests quieted. They gave him anything—or anyone—he demanded.

Most of the army was camped around the village in tents set up by haggard servants. Those bold enough took the choicest beds from the villagers. Many were bold enough. Dagan's tent had been set up in the centre of the town, all of its gild and elaborate hangings just as bright as the day they had begun their campaign.

Dagan may have thrived in the gore of the battlefield, but he was not unimpressed by luxury and had no qualms about taking what he wanted. He was Heir Apparent to the most powerful nation anyone had ever known. He was used to having every-thing he wanted at his fingertips. He spent money indiscriminately. The peoples and nations he conquered were enough for him to justify the pinched expressions of the bureaucrats back home in response to his admittedly high demands. His tent and the belongings his servants were required to drag with him echoed that.

"To Dagan the Conqueror!" his Captain cheered, raising a flagon of the choicest ale the village could offer. The soldiers gathered around her cheered, some of the precious liquid spilling onto the bonfire. Dagan laughed as one woman hissed and retreated from the surging flames.

"Is there anything like it?" Dagan asked his captain, liquid gold sliding down his throat.

Instead of answering him, she drank and grinned wolfishly in the firelight. "What are you going to do when there are no more lands but the vast Wastelands and desert to conquer?" she asked.

"I'll search for the dragons and other magical beings rumoured to exist in the north," Dagan announced. "And when I have taken their magic for my own, I will return to rule the Empire."

"You want to be a sorcerer?" she asked incredulously, raising her brow, then dragged her arm across her lips dripping with ale.

Dagan laughed at the shocked look on her face. "I want to be immortal!" He bared his teeth. There was a pause between the captain and himself and then both burst out laughing, good moods buoyed by the alcohol and the rush of having beaten yet another people into submission.

Little did she know, Dagan was truly thinking about how it could be done. Magic had supposedly been lost for generations. It was nothing more than a myth to tell hopeful children. But Dagan knew there must be a way. The legends would not exist otherwise. He never wanted to be as frail and old as his father. He wanted to fight and drink and revel forever.

Dagan finished off his ale and threw the flagon into the bonfire, making the fire crackle and spit. His people let out a raucous cheer. Dagan grinned and stumbled towards his tent, where he knew his servants would have one of the beautiful women of the town waiting for him.

The heavy drapery closed behind him, dampening the sounds of his people's celebrations. Dagan did not like the quiet. He had never liked the quiet, even when it was in the form of well-deserved rest. He preferred to go until he dropped into sleep as black as night and just as empty. Or, like tonight, to fight a wildcat in his bed.

"Come out, come out, wherever you are," Dagan murmured, stumbling towards the enormous bed and its wrought iron frame. He expected to see a woman tied to its posts, eyes blazing with anger or fear. What he saw instead was a body. Dagan paused, his mind spinning as he tried to piece that into his vision of the night.

Her face was bruised, bloody, as if Dagan himself had beaten her. Had he? Earlier that day, maybe? But, no, he would have remembered her. Underneath the bruises, she was lovely. But she was also dead. Her throat had been cut with one swift slice, just like what he himself would have done. That was silly, though. Why would he do that when he hadn't even had his pleasure for the night?

Someone must be playing a joke on him, Dagan decided. Maybe his Captain had gotten tired of the women he took to bed after his days on his campaign. Maybe one of his soldiers. *How annoying.*

Well, there was nothing for it. Dagan would have to demand another woman. He would figure out the why and the who later. Right now, he was in the mood for—

"Hello, Brother."

Dagan spun around, shock passing over his features. A figure stepped out from behind the changing screen. Unlike Dagan, he wore padded leather armour over his chest and carried not the single curved sword, but two shorter and thicker blades at either side. His hair was cropped short and would never be a temptation for an enemy in battle, as Dagan's was. But the man shared the same golden-brown skin, the same dark hair, his eyes just as shadowed. Only, there was a wall of steel that kept his thoughts from showing in those depths.

"Davorin!" Dagan held out his arms wide, his drink-addled thoughts moving straight into joy at the unexpected surprise. "You must be responsible for ruining my fun." Dagan pointed to the dead woman on his bed and chuckled.

Davorin did not smile.

"No, Dagan, you were," Davorin said, stepping forwards.

Dagan frowned. Maybe he'd had more to drink than he should have.

"I don't understand." Dagan drew his brows together.

"Of course not," Davorin said with a sigh. "I always have to explain these things to you."

"What are you doing here?" Dagan asked, just now realising that perhaps his brother shouldn't be there.

"Me?" Davorin took another step forwards. Dagan swayed on his feet. "I'm here to kill you, brother."

Before Dagan could laugh at the absurdity, Davorin surged forwards—the final step between the two, plunging a dagger into Dagan's chest and then twisting. Dagan choked and looked up at his brother for a glimpse of explanation, of anything. Davorin's features were perfectly impassive, as if he were no more interested in what was happening than if he were listening to a boring speech. Dagan stumbled backward. Davorin pulled the dagger out of his brother. He reached forwards to slip an arm under the staggering warrior.

"Come on," Davorin said calmly. "Let's get you on the bed. I have to make it look like you fought back."

Dagan understood, now, why the woman was dead. She was supposed to have fought him. To have gotten his dagger away from him and stabbed him. Dagan would have fought back, might have even killed her with an efficient cut to her throat. And then, choking on his own blood as he was now, he would have bled out.

Davorin stood over his brother until the last breath fell from Dagan's throat. He put the dagger on the bed between the two bodies. He wiped his hands of blood on Dagan's shirt. Then, he slipped out the back of the tent with no one the wiser.

Dagan the Firstborn was dead.

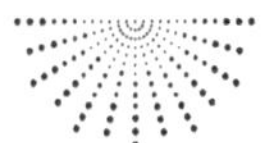

CHAPTER ONE

*R*avenna was born squalling into the night where no one but her sobbing mother and the scholar, Tacitus, could hear. Her mother's wings hung limply at her side, their golden feathers matching her sweat-sheened skin. Her amber fire eyes were wide with tears as she stared at her daughter.

Tacitus, his own golden wings tucked neatly behind him, put out a charcoal-dark hand. "My dear lady, it will be alright."

Her mother turned her head away from the baby that was offered her, her jaw flexing with unspoken emotion. Tacitus tried again, nudging her arms with the baby's flailing fists, but the sylph woman refused to even acknowledge her daughter beyond sobbing harder. The scholar's heart broke and he pulled Ravenna to his own chest, staring at her mother in pity.

"So what if she does not look like—"

"No," the woman snarled. "Don't you dare try to tell me about my daughter."

"My lady, surely it will be alrigh—"

"No!" She was screaming now, repeating the word over and over again until Tacitus nodded his assent. She settled back against the low cot, moaning and sobbing. Her dark hair was still damp with sweat and she clutched at the ruined sheets with desperation.

Tacitus tucked the tiny child to his chest and backed away from the woman, his head bowed. "I will take her, then," he murmured. The woman jerked her head in a nod. Tacitus sighed and turned to walk away, his own amber eyes fixed on the crying child. She did not look like any sylph he had known, in recent memory or in history. No sylph in the Aerial City had pale-as-moon skin and black wings and hair. No, they were golden skinned like her mother or charcoal-ash skinned like Tacitus, each prized for their beauty. Their eyes were amber or brown and their wings were golden and brown feathers. All strong.

Tacitus turned back to her mother one last time. "Do you want to give her a name?" he asked, throat thick.

She said nothing.

"Very well." The scholar turned and left the room. The bent healer was standing outside the room, his own wings nearly white-feathered with age. The healer looked up at Tacitus, eyes questing. "We will raise the child here."

"I see," the healer said in a low voice. He reached out a gnarled hand and stroked the black hair away from her face. She quieted slightly, her tiny black wings folding around her shoulders as much as they could manage, the down feathers hardly enough to warm her. "She will be ostracised, you know, for her looks as much as for the fact that her mother abandoned her. Abandoned her *here*, no less."

"Her family will know her," Tacitus said. Yes, the older sister to the one he cradled and her grandmother, they would know her even if the mother would not. At least the child was not sisterless or without female relatives. She would know them, if nothing else. That was the way of things. "She will have that."

"I wish it would be so simple," the healer sighed. He gestured with his fingers and Tacitus reluctantly released the child. With expert hands, the old healer examined her from every angle, even grabbing her by her ankles and holding her upside down. Her wings flapped furiously as she squalled louder. The healer shook his head and returned the child to Tacitus.

"She will have a normal life here," Tacitus insisted. "It's not the first time this order has raised a child away from the city. Even if the Intellecti are…separate."

"She will never be normal," the healer said. "Her colouring forbids it. But worse than that, or the burden of the Intellecti, I fear she will never be as other sylphs."

"What do you mean?"

The healer stroked the child's black downy wings and she twitched, cooing and pulling away. Her squalling had stopped, and she was yawning in Tacitus' arms, stealing his heart and breaking it simultaneously. "Her wings should be twice the size they are now," the healer murmured. "At birth, she should be able to wrap them around her to keep warm. They barely meet in front of her chest."

"She's…deformed?" Tacitus breathed. His wings fluttered nervously behind him.

"Not deformed, just…small," the healer said. He took a deep breath through his nose and let it out just as slowly. "It is possible they may grow. That her colouring and the smallness of her wings may be unrelated. But I fear otherwise."

Tacitus hugged her closer, wanting to tuck his own wings around the child. "She will have a normal childhood," he insisted. "As normal as we can give her. She will play with the other children. She will take the lessons. Learn the Dalketh. She will know what it is to be a sylph. And if her mother does not want her, then we will have to love her instead, no matter that we are male and Intellecti."

The healer shook his head, tightening his aged wings against his back. He pushed towards the chamber Tacitus had abandoned. "I will check on the mother. And, for her sake, Tacitus, I hope that it turns out as you believe. The alternative would be difficult."

Tacitus nodded and stepped away from the chamber so he could climb the winding stairs back to his own chambers. He would take the child and care for her. It was far outside his normal duties as Keeper of the Tomes, but surely, he could learn to care for the child. Some of the other Intellecti could help him. She would be raised in the Tower and she would grow well. Tacitus had no doubt.

"Tacitus!" the healer's sharp voice called him back. Hope bloomed for a moment that the child's mother would want her back, but the stricken look in the healer's eyes told him otherwise. "She's dead."

"What?!" Tacitus flew forwards, his wings parting the air with a single thought. He slowed in the chamber where he had recently left the woman crying and denying her child with vehemence. She lay there, her wings limp and her mouth hanging open, the tears still wet on her cheeks. But there was an emptiness about her that left no doubt. She was dead.

The scholar staggered back to lean against the stone wall, hardly feeling its coolness through his feathers. The child in his arms seemed to sense his emotions because she began waving her hands again, a cry building in her throat. "Hush, little one," Tacitus said in a shaking voice, drawing his fingers over her forehead, soothing her as best he could. "It will be alright," he crooned. To the healer, he said, "What happened? She was fine!"

"I don't know," the healer said. "I would say that there was some internal tearing. She bled profusely during the birth as well. But it could just as easily be that she died of grief and shame."

"The Queen will have to be told," Tacitus said. The healer nodded. "But not tonight," he continued, brushing dark whorls of hair back from the child's forehead. The healer nodded again.

Tacitus turned away from the dead sylph and carried the child back to his chambers. Warm milk and some blankets were already waiting. Sighing, the scholar sank onto his simple wood-frame cot, spreading his wings and cocooning them over his head. At the warmth and change in light, the child hiccoughed and wriggled. She stilled, then opened her eyes, and Tacitus had to fight not to reel back in shock.

Instead of the fiery amber that all sylphs had, her eyes were icy blue. Her pale skin and dark wings could have been put down to a one in a million trick of nature. But the blue eyes spoke so much more than that. Her blood-father must…but that was a question impossible to answer. Not only did their society not acknowledge such things as fathers, but her mother was dead. Tacitus pressed his lips to the child's forehead before she could sense his alarm and start crying again. His resolve strengthened. He would take care of her. He would do his best to raise her and to teach her to be a sylph, despite whatever problems her wings gave her or how the others treated her. She would be his heart-daughter.

"It will be alright, dear child," Tacitus said. He scoured the records in his mind to find a suitable name, hoping it would give her strength when his own faltered. "You will be a great sylph, my Ravenna. And you are going to stand this world on its head."

Ravenna cooed and wriggled in his arms.

* * *

"Dalketh is more than a means of learning how to control your limbs and your wings," Kratos instructed, pacing back and forth before the line of sylph children. He held himself straight despite his impressive girth, his golden skin gleaming and healthy. Two sylph children of about seven cycles at the end of the line, a girl with golden colouring and a boy with the charcoal skin and golden wings, snickered between one another when the older sylph was at the other end of the line. "It's a way to achieve the inner peace necessary to fly."

"He can't even get off the ground, he's so fat," the boy whispered to the girl.

She widened her eyes and shrieked in glee, earning a scolding glance from Kratos.

"Desarra! Crispinus!" Kratos snapped, striding over to the two of them.

Crispinus straightened, his golden-brown wings flaring out slightly.

"Sorry, Kratos," he said contritely, though his hands shook with suppressed laughter. "We just didn't think Ravenna was going to make it through the Owl Swooping Down motion."

Ravenna, next in line to her sister and the bane of her existence, glowered at the ground. She tightened her black wings in close to her tunic and hoped that Kratos would not call her out like Crispin had. She was trying, really, but she was two years younger than Desarra and her wings were not as strong. Tacitus had told her she might not be able to keep up with the other children, but Ravenna was determined to try.

Kratos took a breath in through the nose and let it out before shaking his head. "None of you made it through the Owl Swooping Down motion," he informed the class. The several sylph children grumbled in annoyance. "Now do it again. The whole exercise, mind. And I want not one word between you, or I'll assign another lesson before you can even *think* about flying."

There was a collective groan, but the children dutifully began the Dalketh exercises again. Ravenna glared at the two next to her. Desarra was having a hard time controlling her giggles as Crispin made his way through the exercises with funny faces for each new stance. At least Ravenna *knew* the entire set. She had even been praised once by Kratos for being able to do the movements with the proper breathing. It was the only reason they let her train with the other children, given her age.

Ravenna took a breath from her stomach and tried to ignore the others. If she could make it through the Dalketh lessons every child had to take with the Intellecti, then she would be permitted to learn how to fly. Her wings stretched eagerly at the thought, almost throwing her off balance. Ravenna set her jaw and focused. One breath in from the stomach, step out to the side. Arms up and then down. Another breath.

The other children were being alternately praised or scolded by Kratos, their stances corrected or observed silently. Ravenna held in a smirk when the scholar told her sister that her wings were inches away from dragging on the ground. Desarra squeaked and immediately lifted her wings, a blush tingeing her golden cheeks a ruddy orange. Ravenna received neither correction nor comment from Kratos but did not mind. She knew her stance was perfect, her wings positioned correctly. The gentle smile on the scholar's face told her so.

After another half-hour of Dalketh, the children were released from their exercises to go play until the adult sylphs came to fly them back to the Aerial City. Ravenna was the only one who lived in the Tower on the ground with the Intellecti, but she did not mind. She got to play with the other children when they came for their lessons and, occasionally, Tacitus flew her up to the stone aerie that was the city so she could see her grandmother, the current Chosen Queen.

That day, the children ran from the stone courtyard to the forest with gleeful abandon. Ravenna always marked the moment her thinly clad feet moved from the moss and stone to the undergrowth of the forest. The pine trees lay down light blankets of needles and the hardwood trees covered that blanket with their leaves. A few ferns and grasses poked up from between the layers, but mostly it was clear for the young sylphs to run.

Crispin and Desarra ran to the gully that bordered the creek separating the Tower from the path to the Aerial City.

Ravenna, desperate to be included, followed.

Crispin's longer legs meant he got to the edge of the gully first, sliding to a stop, using his wings to back flap and keep him from going over the edge.

Desarra was less graceful and stumbled towards the edge, giggling wildly as Crispin pulled her back.

"Geez, Des, you have to be careful," Crispin teased.

Ravenna came up behind them, taking great lungfuls of air.

Crispin turned and sneered at her. "Oh, look, the runt followed us."

"Why can't you just stay away, Ravenna?" Desarra pouted, flaring her wings. Ravenna's own black feathers tightened behind her. The older sylph glared at her sister. "You ruin all the fun."

"I just want to play," Ravenna said.

Crispin and Desarra exchanged a glance and the unspoken words between them seemed to amuse them both.

Crispin stepped forwards and fisted his hands on his hips. "We weren't going to *play*," he said. He, too, flared his wings and took a few experimental flaps. "We were going to practise flying."

Ravenna's jaw dropped open. "You can't!" she protested. "Kratos says we're not supposed to start flying until next moon!"

Crispin tossed his head, "Yeah, well, that old bird wouldn't be able to tell that we're ready if we were flying right in front of him."

Ravenna burned inwardly at the insult to her friend and caretaker. She wished Tacitus were here to tell them off. Kratos was a good sylph, a good teacher. He was living on the ground in the Tower with the other Intellecti because he chose that life, not because his weight kept him from flying, or some sort of punishment that forced him to separate from the other sylphs, as Crispin and Desarra seemed to believe. Furious, Ravenna folded her arms. "Yeah, well, prove it."

Desarra faltered, looking at her friend. Crispinus laughed and folded his arms, mimicking Ravenna. "I don't need to prove anything to a pipsqueak like you," he said slowly. He tossed his head and the sun caught his hair, turning his streaks a copper gold. "We're not going to do anything until you can prove that you're worthy of practicing with us. Isn't that right, Des?"

Desarra nodded eagerly, grinning at Crispin. "Exactly. We don't want you making a fool of us."

Ravenna bristled, "I can too practise flying!"

Crispin stepped closer to the edge of the gully. "Oh, yeah? Prove it."

The black-haired sylph gulped and inched closer to the edge of the gully. It was not a sheer drop, but it was sloped enough that falling without flying would hurt. A lot. At least the rocks were covered in moss and didn't look too sharp. But she had wings. She was a sylph. All it would take was a few powerful down strokes and she would fly gently to the bottom. Sylphs were meant to fly.

Ravenna steeled herself and nodded. She inched closer. Her heart started hammering in her throat and a voice in the back of her mind told her, desperately, not to do this. Ravenna was just about to turn and beg that Crispin or Desarra show her how to do it when something hit her in the centre of her back, right between her wings. Hard.

Ravenna did not have time to scream before she was falling down the gully. Her arms wheeled and her wings strained. She flapped instinctively, the muscles in her back straining as she tried to gather the air as Kratos had said. Ravenna moved into the Dalketh motion he'd said was the best for flying: Eagle Catching Prey. She angled her wings just as she did during practise. She beat the air. Once. Twice. The air caught beneath her wings. She could feel it!

And then, it did not matter how hard Ravenna tried to fly. Her wings strained and her back ached. Still she fell. The sides of the gully were sharper than she had thought; they sliced into her fragile skin with ease. Ravenna managed to stay upright and keep from crushing her wings beneath her, but barely. All she knew was that she was falling, not flying. That she should have been catching the wind and flying gently to the ground, but she was not.

Finally, Ravenna's foot caught on a particularly large boulder. Her frantic wingbeats couldn't compensate, and she tumbled head over heel, landing on her wings in the stream at the bottom of the gully. The cold water startled her into sitting upright and she let out a cry of pain. It hurt everywhere. But that was immaterial. What Ravenna could not get out of her head was that she had not flown even though she should have. Maybe Tacitus was right: she was just too young. But she knew the Dalketh!

"Desarra?" Ravenna called, looking back up at the path she came down. Tears were starting to fall down her cheeks and she desperately tried to wipe them away. Her sister was nowhere to be seen. "Crispin?" Ravenna yelled louder. Nothing. Maybe they'd gone to get help. Tacitus would make it here in a short flight and carry Ravenna back to the Tower where they would heal her and figure out why her wings had not caught the air. No, she shook her head. Desarra or Crispin had pushed her. *Why would they help her after that?*

Wincing, and rubbing more tears from her eyes with a child's trembling fist, Ravenna pulled herself into a standing position. She stretched her wings experimentally. They were sore—as was her back—but whole. She shook the feathers to dispel the water, wishing that she could do the same thing with her linen tunic and breeches. Even her thin leather shoes were soaked through. She sniffed and finally held back her tears. Tears wouldn't help her. Tacitus would help her.

Ravenna managed to scramble up the creek, knowing that if she followed the bed a few hundred more metres, the gully would become a gentle bank that she could climb to get back to the Tower. She did so, flapping her wings a few times in the hope that maybe she would fly up. Maybe it was a fluke, her blind panic making her think that she was doing the Dalketh motions correctly when, really, she was not. But her wings did little more than give her an extra boost to climb the bank, just as they had always done.

Ravenna was swallowing down more tears than she could contain. She ran towards the Tower, terror making her stumble more than once. But there! The comforting stone walls of the Tower rose just before her and the courtyard opened up to greet her.

Tacitus, tall and proud, was standing with fury written on his features. His fiery eyes flared as he saw Ravenna. She froze in shock at Crispin, his wing held in Tacitus' hands. The young sylph glared up at his captor and glared harder at Ravenna. "See? There she is!" he protested, struggling mightily.

"I did not ask where she was," Tacitus said in a calm voice, though his brows furrowed in a rare showing of anger. "I asked what you had done to her."

"Nothing!" Crispin shouted. "Ask Desarra!"

"I have already done so," Tacitus said in a low voice. Ravenna wilted, knowing full well that her heart-father was inches away from snapping. And that was never a good thing. Ravenna slid her feet forwards to approach Tacitus. He sighed as she got close enough to be just out of reach.

"Here I am," Ravenna murmured.

"I can see that," Tacitus replied. He shook Crispin. "Did he hurt you?"

Ravenna searched the face of the older boy. He was looking

at her with undisguised loathing. Ravenna knew that if she ever wanted to play with him and Desarra again, that she should say nothing. The other children would ostracise her—even more than normal—if she tattled. It was hard enough given that she lived in the Tower and not the Aerial City. And if she told the truth, then Crispin would know that her wings had not worked. If she did not, then maybe he would think she just stumbled with her landing amongst the rocks in the creek. Ravenna wanted today to be over.

"No," she said, looking at her water-soaked shoes. Tacitus blinked.

"Are you certain, Ravenna?" he asked carefully. Ravenna nodded, her brilliant blue eyes hidden behind her dark hair. Tacitus released Crispin, who immediately yelled and ran off to the other end of the courtyard. The young sylph glared back at Tacitus and Ravenna and she knew, suddenly, that it wouldn't matter whether or not she had lied to protect him. He would never want to play with her again. Him or Desarra.

Tacitus saw the tears sprouting once more in Ravenna's eyes and knelt next to her, his wings folding around them in a cocoon of warmth and golden light. "Ravenna, child, what happened?" Tacitus said, his hands hovering a hair's breadth over her skin so he wouldn't bump her bruises or cuts. She opened her mouth to speak. "And I would like the truth, please. Not whatever you were going to say to protect your sister and her friend."

Ravenna scuffed her shoes on the stone and hunched her shoulders. "I fell," she said.

"Yes, I gathered that," Tacitus said drily, a wry smile curling the corners of his mouth. "What else."

"We were playing at the gully," Ravenna said slowly, watching her heart-father from under hooded eyes. "Crispin and Des were saying that they were going to practise flying."

Tacitus remained silent, but his wings tightened closer

around them. Ravenna was glad for the warmth and the secrecy. Her face flushed at what she had yet to say. She hoped that she would never have to say it. Maybe it was just because she was not ready, yet. Maybe in a moon…

"Ravenna," Tacitus reached out to brush her hair away from her face. "Look at me, child."

Ravenna lifted her eyes. She had expected to see the usual warmth there, surrounded by his calm expression that could soothe her no matter how bad the nightmares or her struggles with the Intellecti tomes. She saw, instead, sadness.

"Why couldn't I fly?" Ravenna demanded, doing her best to flare her wings threateningly. Tacitus ran his fingers over her black feathers, so different from the normal golden ones of the other sylphs. Not for the first time, Ravenna was conscious of the difference. She wished for gold.

"Ravenna, child," Tacitus said. "I had hoped that I was wrong."

"Wrong about what?"

He closed his eyes and shook his head. "When you were born, your colouring was apparent and a shock."

She *knew* this already. No one *cared* about a sylph's colouring except when it was her. Why would he not tell her what she wanted to know?

"But there was something else. Your wings…they were smaller than they should have been. They've always been smaller than they should be." Tacitus smoothed a ruffled feather and looked at Ravenna again. She pulled her wings back from his hands. "I hoped that with time, they would grow. Or, perhaps, their size wouldn't matter as you became stronger. You already use them to help you move faster down the stairs, to climb, to run. Just like every other sylph. Even your Dalketh is impeccable. But…it seems that I was wrong."

Tears streamed down Ravenna's face as she took in what Tacitus was saying. She did not want to believe it. She wanted him to be wrong. But he was so much older than her. So much wiser. Why would he be wrong about this? Ravenna waited in silence for Tacitus to finish what he was saying. He *had* to say it.

"I don't know that you will ever fly," Tacitus murmured.

Ravenna let out a sob.

The older sylph opened his dark arms, so different from her own pale ones.

Ravenna knew that she could move forwards and find comfort in them as she had before. Instead, she pulled away, pushing through Tacitus' feathers and running as fast as she could to the woods.

The trees loomed overhead, taunting her. Once they had seemed only to demand patience, that one day she would conquer them when she learned to fly. Now, they mocked her. She would never fly. She would never burst through the tree-tops and skim them with her wings. Ravenna let out a scream of defiance and rage at the trees. They merely stood there, laughing and enduring.

Ravenna ran farther, the tears blurring her vision. She reached a clearing far from the Tower and sank to her bruised knees. The pain throbbed through her, the only truth in a world torn to pieces. "No," Ravenna begged the sky, hoping that someone would hear her and help her. All she felt was pain.

Her wings seemed to wrap themselves around her without her volition. Screaming again, Ravenna grabbed her feathers and tore them from the wing. If they would not help her fly, then they were worthless. She was worthless. The pain was immediate, blinding, and put a knot of satisfaction deep in her belly. Ravenna reached for another handful and tore them out, too, flinging the useless black feathers as far from her as they would go. She kept pulling, kept pushing through the pain until her tears turned to lung-wracking sobs and her head fell forwards on the bed of feathers.

She cried herself to sleep, her throbbing, bleeding wings limp at her sides.

Ravenna did not know how long she had slept there when she was woken by a cool hand on her burning wings. She woke with a weak cry and turned to find Tacitus standing over her, eyes wide with horror.

"Ravenna!" he breathed. "What have you done?"

"I wish I didn't have wings at all!" Ravenna yelled, sitting up and pounding her small fists at Tacitus' chest. "I wish I'd never been born!"

Tacitus lunged forwards and pulled Ravenna to his chest, as much a hug as keeping her from struggling and doing more damage. He breathed hot, furious words into her ear, and she felt his tears brush her skin. "Don't you *ever* say that again, Ravenna! You are *not* worthless. You are *not* incapable just because your wings will not hold you in the air. You can still do everything that anyone else can do. Do you think that I would have bothered putting all of my time and energy into you and your education, your life, your care—do you think I would have *loved you* if I thought that you were never going to be worthwhile?"

Ravenna sniffled, burying her face in Tacitus' linen tunic. "N-no," she hiccoughed.

"Then you don't believe it, either," Tacitus snapped. "If you cannot fly, then find a different way. If you want to live in the Aerial City, use what you can to jump, to glide, to climb. If you want to be an Intellecti, then learn. But don't you ever, *ever* give up on yourself again."

Ravenna nodded. She did not protest when Tacitus lifted her into the air, her pain-filled wings hanging limp from her back. She glared up at the trees from Tacitus' arms as he carried her back to the Tower. She promised them silently, defiantly, that they would not conquer her. She would conquer them.

CHAPTER TWO

*R*avenna held in her sigh as she turned the page of the ancient text with the utmost care. She did not want to disturb the other Intellecti in the reading room, where nothing less than complete silence was allowed. It had been rumoured that sylphs had been removed for thinking too loudly. It was also where most of the older texts housed in the Tower were stored.

Ravenna shifted her wings, the slight rustle of feathers garnering her a few unhappy looks from the others around her. She winced an apology and took in a breath. Stillness. Silence. She needed both to control herself. A moment later, she let the breath out just as slowly and silently and returned her attention to her book on early sylph mythology.

Nearly one hundred generations ago, sylphs were not the winged beings we are now. Sylphs were beings of air, elemental mages who could only become corporeal in rare instances when their magic manifested itself enough. Our closest cousins were the elves, both dark and light varieties, and it was from them that the sylphs understood what it was to have a physical existence.

Some of the sylphs craved this existence and worked their magics as best they could to bring it about. It worked well enough to allow them to couple with the elves and produce offspring that were physical in body and strong in magic. These half-breeds longed to taste the air that their pure sylph cousins drank and tried to work their air elemental magic to fly. It was only partly successful and ended up in the death of many of these half-sylphs. Those sylphs that had not given up their incorporeal form watched with disdain, scorning everything to do with these half-breed scions of their own foolish kind. So, the half-sylphs searched for a better solution, their blood becoming more diluted the more generations they were removed from their ancestors.

Eventually, the sylphs approached Qiaseri, the great dragon who had survived the Fire Wars. He said that he would give the sylphs what they desired, but that the consequences would be great. Desperate to taste the wind again, the half-sylphs agreed to Qiaseri's bargain, though the price was indeed greater than they could anticipate. They were given wings, the great feathered wings that we have today, but their air magic was drained in the process, leaving them both magicless and mortal. The sylphs who remained as air elementals were so horrified, they refused to even communicate with their mortal kin. These beings disappeared into the mists of history, either dying out or vanishing from living memory.

The mortal sylphs removed themselves from the mainland to learn how to fly and live as mortals. Their progeny populated Shinalea and built the Aerial City, where sylphs live today. The Tower where the Intellecti live...

TACITUS TOUCHED RAVENNA'S SHOULDER, making her jump and sending her chair clattering backwards. Her wings flared defensively. Tacitus raised his eyebrows, a slight frown marring the corner of his mouth. Ravenna winced and bowed an apology to the other scowling scholars before replacing her tome and slipping out of the reading room. Ravenna rubbed away the blush that covered her cheeks as she closed the door behind her. Tacitus was waiting for her.

"What had you so engrossed?" he asked wryly, leading Ravenna away from the reading room and towards the central spiral of the Tower. "I've never been able to sneak up on you like that. Not since you were a child."

"I was reading mythology," Ravenna said, almost scoffing at the word. She had studied other mythologies, and they all talked about mystical beginnings and beings of such great power that they were called gods. The Intellecti never bothered with such trite nonsense, instead focusing on fact and knowledge as much as they could. Sometimes, though, Tacitus would tell her stories of the great battles of the past and stories that were so ridiculous they could only be true legends, like how the stars got their patterns in the sky.

"An interesting pursuit, considering I asked you to read the Wing Cycle and map out possible sites of first settlement on Shinalea," Tacitus said.

Ravenna wilted a little. "I'm sorry," she murmured. "I got distracted."

"I can see that," Tacitus said. He shook out his wings. "No matter. The Wing Cycle can wait. Your grandmother has asked that you come up to the Aerial City today for luncheon with her."

Ravenna perked up a bit. "Really? I'd better leave, then, if I want to make it up the stairs in time."

"Desarra will also be there," Tacitus said casually, as if he were making observations about the weather. Ravenna bit her tongue to keep from growling in annoyance. She had burdened Tacitus for cycles with her hopeless desire to be closer to her sister. Desarra tolerated Ravenna and that was only at the request of their grandmother. Ravenna had given up on reconciling with her sister some time ago. Desarra would never be comfortable with Ravenna around. Ravenna would not burden someone else with hopes of something that would never happen, especially not someone who had been so kind and loving to her over the cycles.

"I had still better leave, then," Ravenna said, trying to sound cheerful. Tacitus eyed her with his amber eyes and nodded.

"Be careful on the stair," was all he said, turning towards a quiet corridor that led to the interior of the Tower. Ravenna turned to the great wooden door that led to the path between the Tower and the Aerial City. "Last time you went, you returned with bruises on your shins."

Ravenna had neglected to tell him that was because Crispinus had been waiting in the middle of the stair to trip her. He had soared out of the window in the stair before Ravenna could do more than gasp and fall to her shins. Even grown up, Crispin did his best to undermine her. Ravenna did her best to ignore him.

"I'll be careful," she assured Tacitus. He nodded and walked away. Ravenna pushed open the doors and started through the woods at a light jog. She swallowed the anticipation and fear that filled her throat in favour of focusing on the path before her. Ravenna's muscles loosened and she quickened her pace, angling her wings.

She ran through the woods, leaping over fallen trees and roots that rose out of the path, scaling and leaping off of boulders. Her wings let her twist and turn in the air with no more effort than it took to run. Ravenna reached up to grab branches above her and a flap of her wings had her easily climbing onto the lowest branches. She leaped through the trees like a squirrel, landing as lightly as the birds she had studied to understand their flight. After about ten minutes of acrobatics and using all of her muscles, Ravenna smiled.

This, this was freedom. Motion unencumbered by expectations. Dalketh exercises put to uses that none of her teachers would have approved. She was not flying by any means, but she was capable enough to move as swiftly through the forest as any sylph. Faster, even, as she had a smaller wingspan and was not dodging branches and trees, but using them to her advantage.

Running through the forest was one of the few times that Ravenna felt whole.

Then, it all came crashing down. A squirrel, startled by her presence a branch away, jumped directly in the path of Ravenna's next jump. She tried to change direction midair, but her wings had already been twisted for the next jump and she did not have the control to stop what came next. She fell. The ground was moving towards her too quickly to be stopped. Had she actually been able to fly, not just do clever acrobatics, Ravenna would have been able to save herself. Instead, she fell wing first onto the ground.

The ferns and pine needles mostly cushioned her fall. A rock, though, cut through that defence and jabbed her right in the back between her wings. Ravenna barely managed to suck in a breath before pain splintered her vision into bright stars. She struggled for a moment, trying to breathe, trying to move. All she could do was tremble and hold perfectly still.

"Ow," Ravenna finally managed. She let out her breath slowly and, groaning, got her legs underneath her so she could sit, then stand. She had to lean against a tree for support. "Wings," Ravenna murmured, stretching each in turn. They ached, but there wasn't any serious damage beyond a few feathers bent out of place. "Legs, arms, all okay," she continued, taking stock of each limb in turn. Her back hurt, but she did not think anything serious had happened. At least, the stone had not managed to pierce her skin and her back was not broken. She was going to have one beautiful bruise, though.

"And now I'm going to be late for lunch," Ravenna sighed. She stretched her wings out again, taking a few experimental flaps to stretch her back and test the ache. It was...passable.

Wincing, she started into a jog again and nearly sighed in relief when the Stone Stair opened up before her.

The Aerial City had been built straight out of a series of cliffs that rose from the forest without any warning whatsoever. The buildings were carved into the cliffs and most had windows and balconies open to the sky. Some were recessed deep into the cliffs, honeycombing it and giving the city more size than the beautiful stone carvings would have allowed. The sylphs could just fly up, so there was not really a need to have any of the buildings close to the ground. And since the cliffs were all but inaccessible from all sides, it was a perfectly defensible spot.

Unfortunately, for the elderly, and children, and those whose wings were broken or ruined in whatever form, like some of the Intellecti who lived in the Tower, getting up to the City was almost impossible. Unless, that is, another sylph flew them up or, like Ravenna often did, they took the Stone Stair.

It was a winding, curving stair carved into the interior of the cliff, the only visible sign of its existence the entrance at the very bottom. The stairs were made of the same reddish cream stone of the cliffs. It, though, was not decorated with the beautiful bass reliefs and carvings that the rest of the city boasted. It was plain and purely functional, made for those who could not fly and who were somewhat separate from sylph society.

It was also killer on the calves. Ravenna sighed. She started up the steps, her wings tucked in close so they would not run into the walls on either side and get dusty. Desarra would never let her live it down if that happened. Once, Ravenna had tried counting the stairs going up to the city and given up at two hundred and sixty-seven. Now, she just counted her breaths.

By the time Ravenna made it to the top of the stair, she was panting, and her abused limbs were thinking about trembling. She emerged into the great hall and spread her wings, her hands on her hips to give her lungs the room to expand and gasp in air. Ravenna paced the hall while her heart calmed and tried to take in the details so she wouldn't pass out.

The hall floor was smooth, with geometric designs in different coloured stone sprawling over the entire space. The walls seemed to grow organically from the floor, the designs climbing up the walls until they turned into carvings of sylphs or birds or, Ravenna's favourite, a battle scene where dragons and sylphs fought against what looked like elves and something out of a nightmare: horned and hulking and roaring with power. Windows on the far side of the hall revealed an expanse of sky that was slowly turning grey with promised rain. And next to one of those windows, her golden wings arching high over her head, her shining copper-gold hair twined into a cascade of curls, her eyes sharp and blazing, stood Desarra.

"Ravenna," she said flatly, bowing her head in acknowledgement of her sister.

Ravenna tucked a strand of her black curls behind her ear and took in the formal blue tunic and billowing trousers that cinched at her ankles. With her golden skin and high, aristocratic features, Desarra had always been lovely. Ravenna had the same features, but no one would have mistaken her for the beauty that was her sister.

"You look beautiful," Ravenna said honestly. Desarra blinked and a slight blush coloured her cheeks. A moment later, the expression was gone, replaced by disapproval.

"You have leaves in your hair and your feathers," Desarra sniffed.

Ravenna turned and, sure enough, there were fern fronds mixed in with her feathers. She imagined her hair was not much better.

"I don't suppose there's time for a bath?" Ravenna hoped.

Desarra's scowl deepened.

"Perhaps if you had arrived earlier, we could have at least made you presentable," she said. In a single, smooth motion,

Desarra glided to Ravenna and began brushing the debris from her wings. Ravenna knew better than to imagine the action was a result of any sisterly affection. More likely it was born from the fear that Ravenna's appearance would reflect poorly on Desarra. Desarra was aiming for the High Courts and needed all the societal approval she could get. Having a useless sister did not help.

Ravenna helped as best she could, even giving her feathers a little fluff when Desarra ordered. Finally, Desarra sighed and deemed Ravenna acceptable. The two of them walked through the great hall towards the passage that would take them to the Queen's private quarters.

"How's Crispinus?" Ravenna asked softly, wondering if it would ever be possible to get on her sister's good side. "I would have thought he'd escort you."

"He's on a hunt," Desarra said, her tone somehow managing to be both scolding and proud at the same time. "He was picked by the Lords of the Wind to join them and see if he could match their prowess. Of course, he will."

"Pass on my congratulations," Ravenna murmured. She did not actually care about the social clique, the Lords of the Wind, but Desarra did. They were a pompous group of sylphs who took pride in their aerial skill and their ability to hunt. A bunch of show-offs, in Ravenna's opinion. But their prestige made them the most admired set in sylph society. They had almost as much influence over public opinion as the High Council did.

Desarra strode to a graceful stop just outside the doors to the Chosen Queen's private quarters. A guard, her own golden skin seeming somehow less radiant than Desarra's, nodded at the two. "We're here for luncheon," Desarra said.

"Of course, milady," the guard swept a wing back in an indication for them to enter. "The Queen is expecting you."

Desarra nodded her head regally. Ravenna tried to copy her sister's motion, but the distaste the guard displayed was enough to be certain it did not work. Ravenna fought the urge to pull her wings in against her body, instead making sure her shoulders were square. They entered the chambers and Ravenna almost let out a sigh of relief.

The Chosen Queen was Ravenna's grandmother, Mariala, and she was one of the few sylphs that Ravenna had never felt at odds with. Perhaps it was something to do with the fact that she was happy to be herself, that she never let the High Council bully her into a decision that she did not fully back, or perhaps it was the fact that her personality was as colourful as the tapestries and rugs that bedecked every surface of the stone chambers. Ravenna rather thought it had something to do with the fact that her grandmother had never seen fit to look down on Ravenna for something beyond her control.

"Ah, there are my beautiful granddaughters today." Mariala's voice was pure honey, rich and deep. Ravenna smiled at the figure already seated at the low table. She was dressed in similar court finery to Desarra, with a flowing red and gold billowy tunic and trousers that were cut tight at the ankles. Her skin was mostly dusty charcoal, but there were a few splotches of gold where her skin tone had never been even. Ravenna thought it made her look fascinating, while Desarra had often praised her own perfectly smooth colouring. Mariala's wings were the standard gold with a few feathers showing their age with a flash of white. Her skin was wrinkled and her face kind. Her amber eyes, though, were as strong as the West Wind.

"Grandmother," Desarra curtsied gracefully, her wings sweeping the floor with a pleasant whisper. Ravenna did not bother with such formalities here, instead bounding forwards and touching wings with the bent figure.

"Hello, Grandmother," Ravenna whispered. Mariala smiled and patted Ravenna's shoulders, their feathers mingling together in a wing-touch.

Desarra shot Ravenna a furious look as admonishment for her affectionate behaviour.

"Look at you both," Mariala said, pulling back and gesturing for Ravenna and Desarra to sit. They did, letting their wings relax into the notches carved into the chairs.

"Thank you for having us to luncheon," Desarra said demurely.

Mariala flapped a dismissive hand.

"If I am not allowed to have my granddaughters for lunch, then I would have stepped down from my position!"

"You tease us," Desarra said, though the flush in her cheeks betrayed her alarm.

"Bah," Mariala said. A couple of sylphs brought in the dishes of roasted vegetables and the braised sea bird. Ravenna found her mouth watering. "You are too important to ignore," Mariala said firmly.

"Thank you," Ravenna murmured.

Mariala grinned and Desarra's flush deepened.

"Go ahead, eat! Eat! And then I will tell you why I called you here," Mariala said.

Desarra, in the middle of serving herself vegetables and a sliver of sea bird, nearly dropped the utensils.

The old Queen laughed, the sound rough and cheerful. "Oh, that caught your attention, did it, my dear? Yes, I called you here for a reason, though I am always glad to see you."

"Grandmother..." Desarra began, before clamping her mouth shut over her curiosity.

Ravenna just kept silent, serving herself a larger portion of food than her sister would ever have taken.

"I suppose you may as well know. Don't blame me if it throws off your appetite!" Mariala pointed her knife at Desarra. The golden sylph's feathers rustled, the only sign betraying her discomfort.

"I'm sure we can handle whatever news you have to give," Ravenna said.

Desarra glared at her sister, eyes flashing dangerously.

"Hmph. We'll see about that. Though it doesn't affect *you* so much, Ravenna," Mariala stabbed a piece of sea bird with her knife and brought it to her mouth. She took her time chewing and Ravenna imagined she could hear Desarra's heart beat faster as the moments passed. Finally, Mariala swallowed and nodded firmly. "In half a cycle's time, I will be stepping down as Queen and call a Choosing."

The silence that filled the room was palpable. It snaked its way down Ravenna's spine and settled in the spot where she had fallen earlier. Shock.

Desarra's spine snapped straight and her eyes widened.

Ravenna saw a flash of desire there, as well as a good deal of fear.

The monarchy of the sylphs was unlike that of other species that Ravenna had studied in the tomes of the Intellecti. Those, she knew, were often hereditary. Sylphs, she thought, were far cleverer and chose their monarchs from amongst the best in their society. Once the position was granted, it was life-long and only death or a unanimous vote by the members of the High Council and the Intellecti could remove the monarch, unless they stepped down and called a Choosing.

The Choosing was a series of tests, both intellectual and physical, that would serve to weed out the best of the sylphs from others until only one remained. The next monarch. Theoretically, anyone could participate, but Ravenna knew she would never be allowed to even try. Many of the tasks involved flying.

Ravenna wondered if she would have even tried for the monarchy had she been able to participate in the Choosing. It startled her to realise that she did not know.

"Grandmother," Desarra whispered.

Ravenna flicked her blue eyes up to her sister. Desarra would definitely want to participate in the Choosing. As would her mate, Crispin. Ravenna felt a knot forming in her chest. She looked at her grandmother, trying to sort out what was happening.

"Yes, Desarra, a Choosing. And you will be a viable candidate. Very viable," Mariala said.

Desarra's mouth opened and closed like a gull, though no sound came out.

Ravenna nodded.

The older sylph turned to Ravenna, frowning.

"I am well aware of my position in the matter, Grandmother," Ravenna murmured.

Desarra jerked and turned towards her sister, a suppressed grin curling the corners of her mouth. "Yes, I suppose you won't be participating," she said casually. "You wouldn't be qualified."

"Desarra!" Mariala snapped. It was half-hearted, though. The Queen knew her granddaughters, and she knew the truth that would never change. Ravenna would never fly. Desarra, for all that she could be kinder to her sister, was not wrong.

"Don't worry, Grandmother," Ravenna said, expression perfectly calm as she carved into a piece of her sea bird. "Desarra is right. I am not qualified. And besides, I have my own work to attend to. Tacitus has assigned me the task of mapping early sylph settlements on Shinalea."

"You are well suited for the role of Intellecti," Mariala said, not unkindly. Ravenna felt the sting anyway. "Though I fear that Tacitus wronged you when he took you in as a child. Concessions might have been made for your flightless state, but not, I fear, for the fact that you are an Intellecti."

Ravenna's feathers fluttered quietly. She made certain it did not show on her face. She was far from stupid and knew, precisely, what her grandmother referred to. The Intellecti were an organization that focused on learning as much as possible in order to apply their knowledge and improve the lives of all the sylphs. Though they were isolated, they had as much influence as the High Council. Only, most sylphs feared the Intellecti. Perhaps because they were the closest thing to a religion in a society that scorned such things. Flightless and an Intellecti, Ravenna was, indeed, alone. She focused on her food and on quietly murmuring assent at Desarra's discussion of the Choosing for the rest of the luncheon.

Ravenna showed no emotion during her long descent of the stair, nor when she walked—sans acrobatics—through the forest back to the Tower. She did no more than smile softly at Tacitus when he acknowledged her return and handed her an unmarked map of the island for her to fill out on her cartographic journey. Ravenna kept perfectly calm until she made it to her own quarters, small and stone and perfectly isolated at the top of the Tower. There, she allowed her wings to flare in anger and punched the pillow on her bed into submission.

RAVENNA LEFT EARLY the next morning to map the settlements on Shinalea. She had packed a spare set of clothes, a parcel of dried fish, some apples from the small orchard next to the Tower and hoped she would not have to go back to the Tower anytime soon. Tacitus had given her an all-too-knowing look that morning when she had relayed the general details of her lunch with Mariala and Desarra. He had probably seen right through her, but she did not want to burden him with any of her own problems. He was busy enough as it was.

Thankfully, her heart-father had not pressed her. Instead, he just handed her a set of charcoal pencils and a copy of the Wing Cycle before telling her to go off and do a proper job, instead of just doing slipshod research—the likes of which she hadn't done since she could barely write.

Ravenna stretched her arms in the early morning light. The trees were beginning to buzz and hum with bird and insect life. A few squirrels jumped on the ground, burying and digging up morsels of food they had found and forgotten about. Ravenna thought about practicing her wing-running, as she called it, but the faint ache in her back made her reconsider.

"Alright, Rav," she murmured to herself. "Where to first?"

The answer was obvious. Tacitus would not expect her back for at least a week, and she had no intention of starting on her mapping project until after lunch. Until then, she would go and see the only thing that was her solace when she felt trapped by her differences.

Ravenna jogged lightly through the woods, her leather slippers making almost no sound on the cushioning undergrowth. She did not stretch her muscles too hard, choosing instead to let her worries fall away with each thump of her foot on the ground. Her black hair had been tied back in a braid and bounced gently against her back.

So what if she could not participate in the Choosing? She would never have been picked anyway. Who wanted a sylph to rule them who had never lived amongst the others? She had been raised by the Intellecti, and while they were a cornerstone of their society, they were also isolated and preferred facts above any social dance. They were equally admired, feared, and scorned by the sylphs living in the Aerial City. They were healers and thinkers, mappers, studiers of the past. They were all that Ravenna had known, excepting the few visits with her grandmother and the couple days spent doing research in the City. No one wanted an Intellecti as Chosen Queen.

She would not have been wanted as a ruler, regardless of her flight capabilities.

Ravenna did not entertain any thoughts of her desires on the matter, as it was completely pointless. Wishes were for dreamers who had a chance. She would only ever run on the ground and amongst the tree branches. She was no fool.

Ravenna broke through the trees and stopped at the top of a low cliff that marked the edge of the island Shinalea. The sea crashed against the rocks below, unapologetically aggressive. The sound roared and subdued. Sea birds flew above the water, occasionally diving down to catch a morsel of fish or to harry other birds. The smell of salt and brine filled Ravenna's nose and, if she looked hard enough, she could just make out the shore of the distant mainland through the sun.

The cliff sloped down to a gentle beach a few hundred metres to either side of where Ravenna stood. She considered going down and testing the warmth of the water. It was still early enough in the growing season that the water might be too cold for swimming. But there might be something interesting that washed up on the beach. Like…*what was that?*

Ravenna shielded her eyes against the sun. She gasped and fell to the ground without a second thought, desperate not to be seen. That was a *ship*. On the beach. She had only ever seen drawings of them in the tomes. They were meant to be used by humans.

Cruel humans. Dangerous humans. *Wingless* humans.

Desire filled Ravenna's belly and she risked crawling closer to the edge of the cliff so she could see down to the beach. Her wings steadied her on the ground as she peered down. The ship was long and flatter than she would have expected. It did not look much like the drawings she had seen. But what else could it possibly be? *Could humans have really come here?* Maybe it was a child's game, putting boards together to play in the water. There was no one on the beach, but the white sand was scuffed up where someone—many someones—had walked. The tracks were larger and heavier than any sylph child's step. But humans were…well, they were a *myth*.

Ravenna got to her feet, looking about. She bit the inside of her lip, wondering. Should she go and tell Tacitus? They would have to know about the ship at some point. It was a potential threat to the safety of the sylphs. All the stories Ravenna had ever heard about humans were stories of blood and death and war. But they were just stories, right? Like dragons?

"Idiot," Ravenna muttered, already moving through the trees as silently as she could. She angled not towards the Tower, but the beach. And, once there, she followed the tracks.

Humans were supposed to be flightless. Wingless. They could no more fly than she could. Less, even, because she could use her wings to jump and twist and run through the trees and over boulders. How did they manage? Did they have some sort of magic that made things easier for them? Magic was supposed to be a myth as well. But surely, if the humans existed then magic did, too. None of the stories Ravenna had studied told her of these things.

Ravenna easily followed the tracks through the trees. There were three or four of them, all blundering and obvious in the trail that they left. Their steps were heavy, heedless of the undergrowth they trampled or the tracks left in their wake. Occasionally, one would break away to go inspect something, or another would double back and make the trail deeper. They were not moving towards the Tower or the Aerial City, but the uninhabited and wild parts of the island. Ravenna's guilt over not telling Tacitus lessened the farther they went. Maybe they were not humans at all.

After an hour of tracking them, Ravenna stilled. Voices. She heard voices winding through the trees.

Carefully, she flapped her wings and jumped into the low branches of a towering oak tree. A sparrow squawked angrily at her and fluttered off. Ravenna froze, listening. No, the voices continued. She let out a low sigh and jumped to the next tree, closer to the voices. Two more trees and Ravenna stopped.

She was at the edge of their camp, made obvious by the fire

that crackled in a ring of stones. Ravenna gaped at the sight that met her. Humans. There were four of them, all male, arrayed about the fire. They were not only human, but their skins were not golden or charcoal coloured. The darkest amongst them was a dark, muddy brown with a shaved head. The lightest had a pale, pinkish colour that was almost as light as Ravenna's own skin and hair of a yellow-brown. The others were sort of a light tan that could, maybe, have been the colour of stained oak wood. Their hair was a tawny brown. And, best of all, they were wingless, their clothes solid pieces of fabric across their backs instead of laced around wings.

They did not *look* like they had magic, like the stories said. In fact, they looked like they were probably quite ordinary. They had tools—daggers and axes such as Ravenna had only ever seen in ancient drawings—hung on their packs. They stoked the fire with long sticks. They had a rabbit turning on a spit that was crudely fashioned out of some broken branches and twigs.

And their voices! They spoke in the same deep tones that many of the male sylphs did, the dark one having the deepest voice. Their words, though, were like a strange music that Ravenna could not quite decipher. It was almost as if they were speaking her language, her tongue, and every now and again she would catch a familiar word. But it was also different, foreign.

Ravenna had seen some old scrolls that the elder Intellecti guarded viciously, with words that were almost like modern Sylph, but not quite. You could figure out what they were saying, but only after a good deal of thought and translation, because the language had evolved since then. This was like that, but with ears not eyes.

It was beautiful.

Ravenna was not foolish enough to step into the humans' camp while they were awake. Shinalea had been an island shrouded in secrecy for so long that she hadn't even known humans existed. Ravenna doubted the humans knew that sylphs existed, either. Sylphs were expressly forbidden from going to the mainland and there were ancient laws to protect them against sylphs who strayed. But then the sun dropped behind the trees and darkness fell but for the fire in their camp, and the humans slept. Ravenna could conceal her curiosity no longer.

She jumped lightly down from her tree, wincing as her feet crunched on the pine needles beneath her. One of the humans snorted. Ravenna tensed and he stilled again. She tucked her wings in close and crept forwards, feeling a little like she was a child again, sneaking up on Crispin and Desarra.

Then, she was amongst them, their faces shrouded by the shadows cast from the fire. Ravenna crouched next to the lightest one's pack, fingering the dagger with interest. It was a fine blade, the steel shining sharper and brighter than any made by sylph hands. Weapons crafting was a lost art for a people that never fought, except with wings and words, Ravenna thought. This, though, proved that the humans were at least more advanced than the sylphs in that area. This was what they used to hunt. It could also be that they fought, that they drew blood.

A sliver of unease needled its way into Ravenna's stomach. Her feathers fluffed up slightly. She shook it off. They had not done anything more dangerous than kill and eat a rabbit so far, and she had done that before. Ravenna put the dagger aside and opened the straps on the pack, eager to see what else the humans brought with them from wherever they came. She wanted to know whether they matched the myths.

She had her hands deep in the pack, rummaging through the rough fabric, when Ravenna felt something sharp press in the centre of her back where her bruise bloomed. She froze. Another point touched her throat.

Ravenna turned her head to see one of the tan males, his hair short and a horrid scar running along his cheek, sneering down at her with a long dagger in his hand. The other end was just under her chin. He growled something and Ravenna risked a quick glance towards the others. The light skinned one had a pointed arrow trained on her. The dark skinned one held a rope weighted on each end with a metal ball.

Ravenna dropped the pack and rose to her feet before they could stop her. She was about to strike out with a leg, an arm, a wing, when the long dagger cut across Ravenna's arm. She let out a cry.

"Don't," the scarred male said. She understood that much. Ravenna pulled her wings in close, terror making her heart beat faster, making sweat pool at the base of her spine. She lifted her hands in surrender, blood slipping down her cut arm. The dark-skinned male lunged forwards and wrapped the rope around her hands before she could protest.

The fear Ravenna had felt earlier gave way to something she had not felt since she was a child pulling out her own feathers. Despair. Given the blood dripping down her arm and her bound wrists, already chafing under the tight rope, Ravenna was certain of one thing:

Humans were as dangerous and terrible as the stories had led her to believe. And now she was their prisoner.

CHAPTER THREE

*D*avorin rode his horse with his back straight, expression suitably grim. His short hair had been neatly trimmed and he had shaved so his tan skin was smooth. Coupled with the black shirt embroidered with gold and copper threads in some suitably impressive pattern, Davorin looked every bit the Prince of the Empire. He even had finery on his weapons, normally carried to be practical, not beautiful. But in the last processional displaying the coffin that carried his brother's body, it was imperative that he looked his best.

Besides, the seven-month mourning period was almost over. Just this last parade through the streets of the capital city, Mardego, and life could get on as it should. Davorin would take control of his brother's armies and would make the Empire great. Surely his father would approve of such a motion, now that Davorin was the only son left.

"My dear Davorin, you look as though someone put a burr in your breeches," a woman purred, gilded metal and fabric adorning every inch of her as she sat just as straight as Davorin on her black horse.

"Sister," Davorin said, dipping his head slightly to acknowledge Seraphina. She tossed her head, her ridiculous beaded headdress jingling with the motions. It covered the top of her wavy brown hair, the rest of the locks hanging down her back, the tips either tied off with beads or wrapped in gild of silver and gold. Frankly, Davorin was amazed that she could sit up straight with that much weight on her head. But it was her prerogative, as wife to the Warlord Baldur, Independent Lord of Southron—the land that a collection of loosely allied tribes called a kingdom—directly south of the Empire. Southron had managed to avoid being annexed into the Empire by virtue of the fact that the various tribes' armies almost matched the might of the Empire. Almost. That and Seraphina would not allow her husband's home to be claimed.

"What will it take to get you to laugh?" Seraphina asked, tapping her fingers against the reins. They were tipped with wrought claws, delicate and whorled and probably far more dangerous than they looked.

"More than you, flashing in the sun," Davorin said, giving his sister a slight smile. He had always liked Seraphina. She was as ambitious as he was, but more cunning. And she had never bothered to contest his desire to lead the Empire, instead wooing and trapping Baldur in marriage. Davorin still pitied the man.

"Oh, please," Seraphina shook her head. "This is all for show. So those desperate people watching us march past will have something to talk about and awe over, rather than the fact that the heir to the Empire is dead and the economy is in tatters as a result."

Davorin rolled his eyes. "Former heir," he corrected. "And the mourning period is almost over. It's not like they haven't been aware of Dagan's death for months."

"Yes." Seraphina tilted her head like a watchful falcon. "But before now, they didn't have the coffin paraded before them like some gruesome relic."

Davorin kept silent, though he was inclined to agree. When a member of the royal family died, it was tradition to parade their body through every major city of the Empire, making certain that the people not only knew of the death but also of the might and wealth of the Empire. To suspend almost all normal activities for the amount of time it took to orchestrate every parade showed a great power—or a great stupidity and carelessness. Frankly, Davorin thought it the latter.

Then, Davorin had been the one to kill Dagan.

"I think it interesting how difficult this has been for poor father," Seraphina said after a moment of prolonged contemplation. She grinned a fox smile at the sideways glance Davorin threw her. He wanted to curl his lip and leave her to her conniving. Surely, she could tempt her husband into conversation. Davorin just wanted to get to the Mardego palace and move on to the final feast, a last celebration of the dead. It was to be one of the most impressive displays of wealth the people would ever see. Meat on every table. Wine and ale flowing. And it was there that Davorin would announce his intentions to his father.

"We all know Dagan was his favourite," Davorin allowed the words to fall from his tongue, though he regretted them almost immediately. Seraphina laughed, the sound tinkling as much as her metal accoutrements did. The subjects on either side of the cobbled path looked a little alarmed. Davorin curled his lip and looked away from their shabbiness. They were a bane on the image of the Empire. He intended to fix that.

"Who else would revel in brutality like Dagan?" Seraphina asked with a smile. "Who else would lead the armies to expand the borders of the Empire almost to the whispering Iron Mountains and the Red Desert? Dagan was a very capable, loud, bloodthirsty, blunt instrument to further the Empire's glory without caring about the cost. I think he probably skipped out on lessons of trade and politics to go practise at fighting three times a week."

Davorin inclined his head. She was not wrong. Dagan had never bothered with lessons and books, thinking them a waste of time when it was obvious his skills lay in fighting, as did the future glory of the Empire. Dagan had only ever been interested in the stories of dragons and magic and battles of the past.

Davorin, on the other hand, had gladly spent as much time devouring books as he did practicing to fight. He was not quite the warrior that Dagan was, but he also did not need to bathe in the blood of his enemies. He was perfectly content to starve them out and walk in after they were all dead.

"It doesn't matter," Davorin said. "Father will have to get on with the normal business of the Empire. And he will need me to do that."

"Indeed?" Seraphina crooned, running her claw-tipped fingers through the black mane of her horse. It tossed its head and Seraphina comforted it with more gentleness than Davorin had ever seen from her. She turned back to him. "Father is completely distraught over the loss of his firstborn son. I have heard that he was bemoaning the fact that there would be no one left to work for the future of the Empire. After all, I am married to the Lord of Southron. And you... well." Seraphina smiled.

Davorin frowned. "I will work for the Empire just as well as Dagan. More successfully, even, as I won't need to conquer every mewling peasant in my path. The fool was already stretching our resources to their limits, the way he carried on wasting soldiers and supplies on the most insignificant of causes. Not to mention every person in the conquered lands hated him, rather than seeing the Empire as the benevolent force it is. If he had continued the way he was, he would have done more harm than good in the end."

"Is that why you killed him?" Seraphina asked. Davorin jerked and his horse snorted, pulling forwards and almost kicking a bystander. Davorin yanked the reins back and managed to get his horse under control. Barely.

"Why would you think I did it?" Davorin ground out, jaw stiff. He glared at the coffin a hundred steps before him, the distance meant to impress some sort of message on the people. That the dead Dagan was still so much more than Davorin or Seraphina could ever be. Davorin had been careful to maintain that distance for seven months. This was the last time, he promised himself. Soon, everyone would see his worth. His father would see his worth.

"Of course it was you, brother," Seraphina let out a glinting laugh to match her finery, earning another set of shocked looks from the people standing on either side of the street, their expressions of grief carefully schooled. Seraphina glanced sideways at her stiff-backed brother riding beside her. "His death was brutal and unsubtle. Who else would it be—that girl Dagan was found with? Ha!"

Davorin did not answer. He clenched his jaw tighter and kicked his heel into the flanks of his horse. Seraphina's cruel smile followed him as he made his way through the distance that separated him from the coffin until he was riding directly behind it. A statement that Davorin had not intended to make until later. He was not worried about that. He was more worried about what Seraphina might say or do. She would wait, though. She would wait until it suited her to whisper a word into the right ear. Until then, she would hold the knowledge over his head.

Davorin needed more than his father's army now. He needed his father's complete and utter approval, or his life would come to a premature end. Just like Dagan.

* * *

THE WINE and ale were indeed flowing. Those who had been

fortunate enough to receive an invitation to the palace for celebrations were eagerly feasting on the food provided by the Empire. Meat, potatoes, vegetables, even fruit stewed in brandy and sugar, were all being consumed voraciously. People talked and laughed and only glanced up occasionally to see if the Emperor was taking offence. The mourning period was over, after all.

Davorin watched all of this from his table in the corner of the great hall. He did his best to control the sneer on his face. The nobility were trying to curry favour with his father, either stepping up to the throne for a few whispered words or speaking loudly from the tables in the hopes that he would hear. They wore their best finery and looked down their noses at anyone they deemed lesser.

Seraphina had abandoned Davorin in favour of her husband. The Southrons were all sitting at a table together, easily distinguishable by their ostentatious display of wealth and, in the case of Baldur and his warriors, the conspicuous number of weapons they wore. Seraphina's hand was resting on the darker hand of her husband, watching him and those around him with a calculating eye. Personally, Davorin thought that Baldur was a fool for not seeing the way his wife manipulated and prodded people to do her bidding. He was a big brute of a man, muscles bulging in obtuse lines, his jaw square and hard, eyes flashing in anger more than intelligence. He was an effective Lord of Southron.

He was also the public face of Davorin's current competition.

Finally, *finally*, the Emperor was alone. He was an old man, stooped with age, and bitter with power. Davorin did not know how much longer the man would live, but he needed the Emperor alive. Davorin needed his approval. Needed to be publicly named heir, given control of the armies and the Empire's resources or he would not make it far beyond Seraphina's vengeful blade.

Davorin stood and walked over to the Emperor's throne, pulling the sword out of the sheath on his hip as he did so. The entire great hall fell silent, tense. The Emperor straightened his narrow shoulders. His bony fingers tightened on the arms of the stone throne carved into the shape of creatures from a bygone age. The slight shift in the Emperor's gaze gave Davorin pause. Did the old man really think that Davorin would be so stupid as to kill him?

Swallowing the unspoken insult, Davorin knelt on one knee before the throne, the point of his sword resting in the cracks between the stones. He touched his head to the gold-worked handle, the edges pressing into his skin. "Father, I come to you beseeching."

The Emperor wrinkled his nose at the traditional words. But he raised an imperious hand and held it over the head of his kneeling son. Davorin stifled his grin. "Ask," the Emperor said, voice hoarse with age.

Davorin lifted his head but otherwise did not move. He looked straight into his father's eyes and spoke the words he had rehearsed long before killing Dagan. "I wish to convey my horror at the sorrow that has befallen the Empire. I wish to swear that it be righted. I cannot bring my brother," Davorin allowed his voice to crack at the word before continuing, "back from the dead. But I can do my best to take his place. With your leave, I will take charge of the armies and resources that Dagan commanded, and I will fight to continue the glory of the Empire. I will rebuild our economy. I will make the Salusian Empire a name never to be forgotten. I will do everything in my power to bring honour to your name and to be worthy as a Prince of the Empire."

Davorin's words echoed on the stone of the great hall. Hushed murmurs followed. Davorin imagined Seraphina watching him with her usual calculating expression. He hoped that she was grinding her jaw in frustration. But he dared not look away from the Emperor's steel gaze.

The Emperor made no immediate movement. When the silence had become unbearably tense, he finally curled his lip.

Davorin's heart stopped. *No. No, his father would not be so heartless.* Davorin had never been favoured as a child, being the second born, but he was far from incapable. Dagan was gone! It should not matter!

The Emperor broke Davorin's gaze and the floor fell from beneath his feet. The old man smacked his lips twice before frowning and glaring at his son. "No one can replace Dagan."

Desperate, Davorin insisted, "Father, I only ask for what is rightfully mine—"

"No!" the Emperor slammed his fist on the throne, a tiny chip from the delicate carvings falling to the ground. "You were never as capable as Dagan! You will never be Dagan! And you will not have control of the armies of the Empire. You will never be heir. Go back to your scheming, Davorin. You have your estates and your money. Let that be enough."

If he had not practised self-control for so many years, Davorin would have run his father through right there. Instead, he swallowed back the anger and bruised pride. He ignored the prick of tears at the corner of his eyes. And he rose, sheathing his sword at his side. Davorin bowed to his father, a hollow having opened up deep in the pit of his stomach. The one thing he needed was to be confirmed as heir and his father had refused.

"As it pleases you, Father," Davorin said, loud enough for the rest of the great hall to hear. "I can only hope to make you proud."

Davorin straightened and strode down the steps, back to his table and his goblet of wine. He refused to let his emotions show. Had Dagan been so publicly humiliated, he would have railed against the world and shouted at anyone who dared to look at him askance. Dagan would have drawn his blade and sliced off the head of the person closest to him. Dagan would have killed the Emperor and demanded the throne. Davorin was not Dagan.

Davorin wanted nothing more than to stride out of the room and run his sword through something. He wanted to plot revenge against a family that had never understood him or his needs. How dare his father insinuate that he wasn't capable! *Davorin had killed the golden son, hadn't he?* He had killed the greatest warrior in the land and only Seraphina was the wiser.

Davorin flicked his eyes to where his sister sat, perfectly serene and calm with her metal-tipped fingers drawing mindless patterns on her husband's arm. She returned Davorin's gaze with a gentle smile and a dipping of her head. He resisted the urge to throw his goblet at her, instead draining it. She had not even had to do anything to make Davorin look the fool in front of everybody. She might not be able to inherit the throne of the Empire, but she was hardly lacking in power now that Davorin had made himself the laughing stock of Mardego. Let the other nobles talk. Let them whisper behind his back as he refused to be cowed by the fool of an Emperor.

He would prove them wrong. He would prove them all wrong. He would find his armies and conquer in the name of the Empire, without his father's help. He would make his name synonymous with power and strength. None would dare stand in his way. And when the time was right? Well, Davorin would whisper his truth in his father's ear and then slip a knife into him. Just like Dagan.

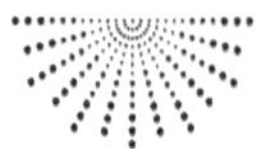

CHAPTER FOUR

*R*avenna huddled in the bottom of the boat, her wings wrapped around her. She couldn't stop trembling. It was not from cold, either, though the spray of the ocean was much colder than she could have ever imagined. Her mind just kept replaying the last few hours, unable to process what had happened. It was worse than anything she had ever considered.

Ravenna had imagined her sister would be the one to sic Crispin on her, having her vanish in an "accident" because of her faulty wings. Ravenna also thought that perhaps one day the other sylphs would grow tired of acknowledging her burdens and beat her, leaving her for dead. Or banish her, even from the Tower and the Intellecti. Worse, even, they could ignore her completely, pretending she did not exist. Only Tacitus had ever stood in the way of that, acting as her champion and surrogate for the motherless sylph she was. But he was only a heart-father. It could never be the same thing. Ravenna never would have imagined that her doom would come in the form of these wing-less…humans.

She cowered lower as the dark-skinned one holding her

rope sneered. Ravenna had struggled at first, thinking that maybe she was stronger, that she could fight them off. They had no wings. They had not been trained to run around the island and leap from trees. They had never been pushed off a cliff. Wingless though they were, these humans were far stronger than Ravenna could ever have anticipated. Her ribs still smarted from their blows. Her screams had yielded no help, either. She wondered if anyone had even heard her.

The leader, a short-haired man with a long knife ("sword" they had called it—though no such thing existed in modern sylph society), said something curious to his companions. She'd only caught a few words. "Price…? An angel!" he crowed.

"Angel?" Ravenna muttered to herself, testing out the word. The one holding her ropes gave them a tug.

"Angel," he repeated, pointing to her.

Ravenna shook her head, biting back tears.

"I'm not an angel," she said. She had not heard that term before, but if ever sylphs had been these "angels," she would have known. She was not what these humans thought. She just wanted to be let go.

"… talks! Listen, it talks!" the lightest one grinned. The language they spoke seemed to suddenly be clearer, though Ravenna knew she was just grasping the translation better. Whatever language they spoke, it was a variant of her own. They had probably only diverged a few generations ago. That, too, made the pang in Ravenna's stomach grow larger. The male prodded her with a foot. "Talk!"

Ravenna said nothing more. She doubted that pleading her case would work. No story or history she had ever read indicated that humans were merciful. She turned her head away and wrapped her wings tighter; the feathers kept her dry from the ocean spray and hid her trembling. The humans grumbled and talked amongst themselves. Ravenna could pick up the familiar words, the lilt to their tongue that was almost like the one she spoke. But she did not want to hear. She did not want to know what sort of things they had planned for her.

At least the other sylphs would never need know her suffering. At least they would not be bothered with her anymore. Maybe Desarra would stop worrying about Ravenna's presence dragging her down. Maybe Tacitus would finally be able to devote all his time to his studies. She hoped he was not too inconvenienced by her loss.

Tears continued to prick the corners of Ravenna's eyes and she blinked them away. She took a breath through her nose and held it. "I am not weak," Ravenna murmured to herself, quietly enough that the humans couldn't hear. "I will not be weak. If not being able to fly did not break me, then these humans cannot break me. I will not cry. I will not beg. I will be strong."

She blinked away the last of the moisture and straightened as much as she could with her hands and feet hobbled. She lifted her head to peer over the side of the boat and, though she fought it, could not stop the knot of dread forming in her stomach at the sight that met her. They had reached the mainland. Surely, they could not have travelled so far that fast. But there it was, rising out of the water, like a terrible mockery of the cliffs of the Aerial City. Her home was far behind her.

This place was nothing like Shinalea. There were pine trees, yes, but they were few and sparse. The ones that stood taller than a human or a sylph were scraggly and twisted. The ground, too, was not lush and green as it should have been. Instead, it was dry, dusty, rocky, pitted with pebbles and sharp points. Ravenna knew, as the boat scraped along the bottom of the shore, that she was headed into a land unlike anything she had ever experienced. This was a land of humans. This was a land of death.

"Up," her captor ordered, tugging on the ropes. Ravenna

schooled her expression into a mask of calm and rose, unfurling her wings as she did so. There was barely ten feet of wingspan on her, but it was enough to make the humans gaze upon her with a mixture of awe and fear. Her back muscles ached from her earlier injuries, the rope chafed against the cut on her arm, and her ribs screamed in protest as Ravenna tried to take in a full breath. But she fought to hide the pain from her face. And she succeeded.

"Come on, Angel," the leader of the group said, stepping out of the boat, his leather boot splashing gracelessly in the water. Ravenna considered struggling again. But the sword at the human's hip and the ropes around her limbs kept her from fighting. They did not stop her from standing straight and stepping out of the boat with as much dignity as she could muster, though.

Her own leather slippers were not thick enough to keep the sharp rocks from biting into her feet. Ravenna stumbled up the beach, the wet sand turning quickly to dust that clung to everything it touched. She followed the others as they climbed up the beach and led her behind an outcropping of rock. And then she saw it.

Face to face with a creature that looked like something out of a nightmare, it peered down at her from atop a long neck and face, four legs ending in shaped stones powerful enough to kill. Standing taller than Ravenna by a good seven inches, its long tail whipped through the air. Ravenna backed up, running into the human holding her ropes. He growled and shoved her forwards, towards the beast.

"No, no," Ravenna shook her head.

The creature let out a high-pitched sound that echoed off the rocks, stamping its foot against the ground with a definitive click.

Ravenna shied back again.

Her captor laughed, the sound full and dangerous. He said something to the others, speaking so quickly that Ravenna could not understand anything. But he pointed to the beast and Ravenna, and the others laughed, too. Ravenna flared her wings, causing the beast to let out another terrible cry. Her captor let out a snarl and grabbed her wounded arm, brushing past her feathers roughly as he did so. Ravenna drew in a sharp breath.

He pulled her to a wagon hitched to the back of the beast and shoved Ravenna inside. She fell forwards, barely managing to keep herself upright. Then the human slammed shut a door made of bars and Ravenna realised, too late, it was not a wagon. It was a cage. Bars rose up from the sides of the wooden platform, arching high overhead lashed together with thick rope. It looked crude, like tree branches strung together with twine, but Ravenna was not foolish enough to believe that. These humans would not have had a cage waiting if they hadn't expected to put something in it. And they would not have done that if they didn't expect it to hold.

A word danced through Ravenna's mind, one that she had read years ago in a tome falling apart with age. Slave. The buying and selling of sentient beings for the purpose of work. Owning another person. Owning their life.

Ravenna's resolve almost broke. She was not going to be strung up as some sort of entertainment, a freak of nature for having wings in a world were wings were impossible. She was not going to be delivered to the religious temples of a people who did not understand what she was. She was going to be sold. She was going to be a slave.

The word sank into her mind, echoing like a cruel jibe from Crispin. It did not actually change her circumstances, the knowledge, but it began to hurt more than Ravenna could possibly imagine. She sank to her knees in the cage cart and allowed her wings to hang limp. Her eyes followed her captors, riding those terrible beasts like it was nothing. Beyond them, the land became even more desolate; the trees changed to scrub grass and the stone sculptures and boulders turned to flat, dusty rock. There was little to break up the monotony except her thoughts. And even those gave way to exhaustion.

Despite her fear, her pain, Ravenna fell asleep, grasping at the only escape she could find.

* * *

RAVENNA WOKE to shouting and the undeniable reality that they had stopped moving. She sat up, stretching her stiff wings as much as she could. Sometime while she slept, the ropes around her hands and feet had been loosened. Ravenna tossed them off and shoved them away before crawling to the edge of the cage.

The sun had set and now the only light came from three large bonfires. Ravenna spotted other wagon-cages, each full of people who were probably going to be slaves as well. There were a few humans picketed in lines with rusty steel chains. Her captors and a few new ones, including a short-haired female who looked like she would happily kill someone who got in her way, walked between the slaves, putting down buckets of water or tossing scraps of bread. The chained and caged humans lunged at the scraps.

The female stopped in front of Ravenna's cage. Ravenna instinctively shrank backward from the emptiness in her eyes. Twin scars ran across the female's pink cheeks and there were at least three weapons attached to a worn leather belt. The female said nothing, and Ravenna did not break that silence. Silence was safer than interacting with this empty female. After a few moments, the female threw a large loaf of bread into the wagon. She also put a full water skin within Ravenna's reach.

Without another word, the female turned and strode away.

"You shouldn't be here."

Ravenna jumped, clutching the water skin closer to her chest, her wings flaring out. She peered out of the bars of her cage and saw a line of picketed slaves not too far from her. The closest, an old female with leathery skin and hair whiter than the clouds, gnawed on a stale crust of bread, considerably smaller than Ravenna's full loaf.

"I never wanted to be," Ravenna said slowly in what she thought was the proper human dialect, hoping the female understood. Her eyes widened, and Ravenna caught a glimpse of the brown colour in the light of the fire. Ravenna bit back a twinge of pain; they were close to the amber fire of the other sylphs in that light. But they were also nowhere near.

"You can talk. Oh, Angel, you can talk!" the female crawled as close to Ravenna's cage as the chains would allow, her hands reaching out reverently. Only the chain attached to a raw, chafed ankle stopped her from coming close enough to touch.

"I..not know what…angel is," Ravenna said, too over- whelmed to wonder why the old female was so much easier to understand than the captors.

The female sketched her hand through the air, tracing the shape of Ravenna's wings as they fluttered quietly at her side. "Angel," she said again, full of awe. "A divine creature. A winged human with the power of the gods. An omen of prosperity and good fortune. A saviour.

Ravenna tossed her head back, her dark curls jerking through the air. "I am not those. There's…no such thing as gods."

"And what of The One Who Watches? The Old Ones who wander unseen under the stars? Are you not theirs?"

Ravenna scowled. Sylphs had long ago done away with such nonsense. There was no such thing as gods, or divine beings who could influence the course of things with a thought. Reli- gion was pointless and foolish, like trusting everything that you could control to someone else. Sylphs, especially Intellecti, followed fact. Knowledge. Logic. Sense.

The old female shook her head, a disbelieving smile on her face. She gnawed on the remaining crust.

Ravenna's stomach growled and she took a bite of her own bread, chasing it down with water. She did not realise the female was watching her until Ravenna was almost halfway done with her loaf.

"They feed you more than us," the female said frankly. "You are so much more than the rest of us."

"I do not understand what is happening," Ravenna replied, looking down at the remaining bread. The female human's words made no sense. She was not *more*. She had never been more. She was just Ravenna. Unable to help herself escape from this living nightmare. A worthless sylph. She clutched at the bread, crumbs breaking off to fall against the wooden platform. Part of her wanted to finish it off; she hadn't eaten since the day before. The other part wanted to give it to the female in the hopes she would explain what was happening. Maybe she could help Ravenna. "I do not know humans."

The female's brows raised in surprise. "You don't know humans? How?"

Ravenna shook her head. "You were…myths? Stories?"

This brought a laugh from the old female and she threw her head back, drawing the attention of other slaves and the captors who had chained them there. The female with the empty eyes took a step towards Ravenna's cage from the bonfire where she was eating something. The leader of the group that had captured Ravenna shook his head and put an arm out to stop the female, gesturing lazily at the slaves all around. He was saying something, but he was too far away to hear. Whatever he said, though, worked. The female sneered and turned back to the fire, paying Ravenna no more mind.

The old human female frowned, nodding her head at the

captors. "Be careful or they'll hurt you. People don't pay as much for a slave that's been beaten."

"I need to get out of here," Ravenna breathed, understanding only half of the female's words. The ones she did understand were the ones that set her feathers on edge.

The female's frown deepened.

"You can't," she said. "Even if you managed to get free, you would have to fight her, by the fire. She used to be the Captain of an army that would stretch as far as the eye could see. Some say she's Death incarnate."

Ravenna frowned. "Army? Captain?" They were somewhat familiar, maybe a word that she'd read in one of the ancient stories in a crumbling tome. But they had no such things on Shinalea.

"A, ah, group of soldiers. Warriors. Fighters. They train together and follow the orders of their leaders, like the Captain. They go to battle against other armies and peoples. Sometimes for protection. Sometimes not," the female explained.

"We have no such things," Ravenna said. No warriors. No fighters. There was no need for such things on Shinalea. The sylphs only carried daggers for hunting, and even then, the main hunters were the Lords of the Wind. The Intellecti knew of such things from the history books, but for many it was nothing more than a forgotten story.

"Then I'm sorry you had to leave," the female said. Ravenna opened her mouth to agree and closed it again. The sylphs might not have had armies or warriors, but they knew how to cause pain. Ravenna had been on the receiving end of that far too many times. Was she upset that she had been captured by slavers and taken to be sold? Yes. Was she sad she had to leave Shinalea? A twinge in the pit of Ravenna's stomach said yes. So she listened.

"Me, too," Ravenna said. She looked down at the remainder

of the bread in her lap before holding it out through the bars for the old human. To her surprise, the female shook her head.

"No, my dear, you eat that. Your trials ahead will be much harder than mine," the old female said, a slight smile touching the lines around her mouth.

"I don't understand," Ravenna said.

"No, you wouldn't. But you must, I fear. The slave markets are a harsh and terrible place, where flesh is judged by people who don't understand humanity. The strong are taken as labourers or fighters for the Pits. Some say they are the lucky ones. The old ones, like me, or the ones who are weaker and not so pretty, they are household slaves. Cooks. Housekeepers. Nurses. I will probably be taken on to clean for some minor household and be beaten when the days become too long for my old bones. But the pretty ones…the exotic ones. They are the most valuable. They are bought as bed warmers. Concubines. Decorations. It is a cruel life, one where you have no say over your body. Invasion. Humiliation. Childbearing, only to lose your child to slavery…" the female trailed off, a lone tear sliding down her weather-beaten face. She looked up at Ravenna, no smile able to hide the pity and pain the old female felt.

Ravenna shrank, her breath catching, bringing spots to her eyes. She had not understood everything the female was saying, but what she had understood was clear enough. "I…I am to be one of those?"

"If you were human, I would say yes. You are a beautiful specimen, my dear. But your wings…your being an angel, that may change things," she said honestly.

Ravenna pulled her wings closer, the feathers wilting while pressing together as tightly as they could. "You may be deemed too valuable to be a casual bed warmer. You may be sold to a wealthy family who wants children begot by an angel. You may even be too valuable for that. Hope, my dear, that you are too valuable for that."

Ravenna nodded. She looked down at the bread once more. There was no way she could stomach the thought of eating it. What she had already consumed was sitting like a stone in her belly. But she looked at the old female, bent and broken, who held such awe at the sight of her wings. Ravenna steeled herself and ate the bread, finishing off the water as well. She would need all her strength to escape.

"Would you like me to tell you a story about angels?" the female asked gently as Ravenna leaned back against the bars of her cage. "About why you are so precious to us, even if you don't say you are an angel."

Ravenna bit her lip and nodded. The woman smiled. And then her half-understood stories of benevolent beings who fought on the side of good with fiery swords and dragons at their behest lulled Ravenna to sleep.

THEY TRAVELLED through the desert for three days. Ravenna was the only one of the slaves who had a wagon to herself. She figured it was because of her wings making her a "precious commodity." The old human female occasionally managed to get close enough to Ravenna to whisper more stories about angels and dragons and wars long past. Ravenna's knowledge of their language improved enough for her to try and catalogue the stories with what she knew from her own studies, but everything was different. The humans' history was so separate from her own that she couldn't distinguish any familiar parts. Except the Fire Wars. Everyone remembered the Fire Wars. At least that much was familiar in this horrid dead place.

The third day brought the slave wagons to a crawl, the sun beating down on them so harshly that Ravenna had to shield herself with her wings. They ached from being held up so much, but at least her skin did not burn and blister like some of the other prisoners. The slavers rode around the caravan on their horses—Ravenna had learned the name of the beasts, as well as the fact that they were harmless and didn't eat flesh. The female, the former Captain, bristled more often as the day wore on, her anger sharpening so that she took to beating the slaves who annoyed her.

By midday, it became obvious what had her so tense.

A town appeared on the horizon. At first, Ravenna thought she was hallucinating. It looked like the Aerial City, carved in stone, but on the ground and far less beautiful. After they grew closer, she saw that the town was, indeed, made of stone, but stone that rose up from the desert, not cliffs. The buildings were all sand coloured and ranged in size from small and squat to large, elaborate pieces with columns and wide balconies that would have been the ugliest of buildings in the Aerial City, but here, were likely the grandest buildings.

The other thing that surprised Ravenna was the abundant presence of life. Not human life, for she had determined those parasites could live anywhere, but plant life. The scrub bush that had been the only sign of life for days was giving way to trees with long thin leaves and gnarly branches. A short, green grass grew in a few places beneath the trees.

As they drew closer to town, Ravenna spotted more strange trees and lush plants sprouting from the ground and flowers growing in jewel tones that she had never seen. The air was no longer as dry or as terrible as it had been. There was moisture here, and it was almost beautiful. Almost.

The caravan stopped at a collection of tents and squat buildings some hundreds of feet from the edge of the town. Ravenna covered her nose; the smell of putridness was over-whelming. This was more than just human filth. This was rotting flesh and the smell that came from suffering. From blood.

"Welcome to the Slave Markets," the old female said, shuffling her chains closer to Ravenna. "It's not Hell, but it's mighty close."

Ravenna did not know what Hell was, but she had no doubt it was not good. The old woman and her chain of slaves was yanked away to a very large pen. Ravenna reached her hand out, hoping to touch the female once, expressing her gratitude. But the female continued on without a backwards glance, her back bent to her fate.

It was Ravenna's turn next. The Captain opened the door to the cage so quickly Ravenna barely had time to flinch before the human was climbing inside and putting a manacle on Ravenna's wrist.

"Don't fight, Angel," the female hissed, her eyes burning. "It will only be worse for you if I have to tear your wings off."

Ravenna pulled her wings close and said nothing. The female got the message, though, because she nodded and pulled on the chains. Ravenna followed her out of the cage. When the bars fell away, Ravenna could almost taste freedom. She stretched her wings out to their full span for the first time in days. They ached and her muscles groaned in protest, but she was too relieved to be out of the enclosure to care.

"None of that!" the Captain snarled, yanking on Ravenna's chain and pointing a dagger at her throat. Ravenna furled her wings slowly. She cast her eyes anywhere but the Captain and noted that she was already getting a good deal of attention. From other slaves, from other slavers, from people with clothes of greater finery than the linen, leather, and wool that most wore.

"How much for the Angel?" One human sidled up to the Captain, an eager gleam in his eyes. He licked his lips, jowls wobbling as he took in Ravenna. The Captain did not even answer, she just jabbed the human in his side with an elbow and pulled Ravenna forwards.

They entered a low building, most of which had been built

into the ground. Inside, the air was cool and crisp and much cleaner than outside. Ravenna spotted a bubbling spring in the corner, the water gurgling quietly. This whole place was built on a system of springs, Ravenna decided. An oasis where human parasites could thrive. This particular spring was small enough that it would not have meant more than a few mouthfuls of water at a time. But it was obviously enough to be a sign of wealth and power to control it. And it was definitely controlled.

A female, enormous and clothed in loose, sheer clothing, the likes of which Ravenna had never seen, sat on a low couch near the spring. Her skin was a dark tan, though her hair was a bright yellow—a poor imitation of Desarra's copper-gold. Her eyes were brown and sharp, though they were hidden in the roundness of her face. She wore jewellery of gold and gems around her neck, her wrists, her ankles, even rings on her fingers.

This obscene human was obviously powerful. And in a place like the Slave Markets, that could not be a good thing.

"What are you doing here? No one comes here without my express permission!" the female creeled.

The Captain curled her lip. She jerked on Ravenna's chains, bringing the sylph fully into the room so that the reclining female could see Ravenna. "I thought you'd want first pick of this one, before I took her through the normal channels, Jazer."

The female sat upright. It took her a moment, her flesh rippling as she did so. Ravenna swallowed, hoping the bread the Captain had given her wouldn't decide to repeat on her. Jazer looked wide-eyed at Ravenna and her wings.

"An angel," she breathed. "Where did you even…?"

"That's not what I'm selling," the Captain sneered. "I bring you the only angel in the world, and you want to know what backwater she was found in?"

Ravenna wanted to protest she was not the only angel, that she was not an angel at all, but she kept her mouth shut. They did not know about the others. They thought she was alone. An oddity. Her captors must have thought that the general emptiness of the island meant Ravenna was alone. Perhaps because she could not fly. Ravenna was used to being an oddity. It was enough to keep Tacitus and the others safe. So she would be the only angel.

"She is magnificent!" Jazer breathed. The female rose from her couch and staggered over to Ravenna. Her hands reached out, eager and greedy. The moment her fingers brushed Ravenna's wings, she jerked back, flaring them out.

"Don't touch them," Ravenna hissed. Jazer's eyes widened even more and a grin split her face.

"She can talk!"

"You can figure out all the tricks she can do later," the Captain said. "If I take her through the markets the normal way, there'll be riots for people trying to get their hands on her. Priests. Wealthy bastards. All of them."

"So you came to me, the owner of the Pits. Yes, yes, you are no fool," Jazer flapped her hand, still staring at Ravenna. "How much do you want for her?"

"Enough gold to get me back into the good graces of the Salusian Empire," the Captain growled. Ravenna pulled her brows together. The Salusian Empire?

Jazer laughed. "Not even twenty angels could buy you that, but I will pay you five-hundred weight of gold."

"Seven."

"Five and a half." Jazer rubbed her hands together, the rings clicking.

"Six." The Captain lay her hand on her sword.

"You have a deal!" Jazer crowed, snatching Ravenna's chains from the Captain. The Captain nodded, a smile touching her harsh features. She signed some papers that Jazer had on a small table, and the larger female handed over a slip of paper for the payment officers. Then, just like that, Ravenna's captor turned from the room and was gone.

"So beautiful," Jazer crooned, reaching out once more to touch Ravenna's wings.

Ravenna jerked them back, pinning them tight to her back and snarled, "No."

Jazer's face twisted into something cruel and horrible. It was much worse than the disdain that Desarra would display, or the leering looks that the slavers had given her. This was a promise of pain and torture. Bloodletting without mercy. Jazer jerked the chains enough that Ravenna was forced to step closer to the human, breathing in her cloying scent.

"Listen to me, Angel," Jazer snarled. "I don't know what sort of place you came from, but I will tell you something about where you are now. Here, *I* am Master. I control every ounce of food and water you get. I control what you do. I am the Slave Master. I run the Pits. If I want to throw you to the desert lions to be eaten alive, I will. If I want to auction you off to the highest bidder to bear half-angel children, I will. And if I want to touch your beautiful wings, I WILL."

Jazer reached out and spread her hand over Ravenna's wings, the rough skin catching on some of the smooth barbs.

Ravenna shuddered at the violation. No sylph would ever presume to touch another's wings, not unless they had a true reason. It was the most intimate of acts, to allow another to touch your wings, to preen you. And this human thought it was just a matter of possession. Ravenna bit the inside of her cheek to keep from crying, from yelling curses at the Slave Master.

Jazer smiled, showing crooked bleached teeth with uneven streaks. "I can do what I please with you. You are mine, now. Do you understand? Or do I have to beat you into submission?"

Ravenna swallowed, her mouth dry. She closed her eyes, the feeling of someone, especially someone so vile, touching her wings replayed relentlessly in her mind. She could fight her way out, maybe. This female was large, but she would not be strong or fast. But once outside? Ravenna would be torn to pieces by the guards and buyers. Even if she did manage to get away, where would she go? She would not survive in the desert long enough to get back to the beach that would take her to Shinalea. She would die.

She was not going to give up just yet, though. Not when Tacitus had told her otherwise, all those years ago. *Find a different way.* Ravenna swallowed again, trying to drum up moisture in her mouth. She raised her icy eyes to Jazer's cruel brown ones. "I understand," Ravenna rasped.

"Good." Jazer sashayed over to her low couch and sank into it, Ravenna's chains still wrapped around her hand. She picked up a tiny silver bell and rang it, the sound tinkling and sweet in the air. What followed was not.

Two males with desert tan skin striped white and pink with old and recently acquired scars, wearing leather baldrics and loose linen trousers, a knife and sword at either hip, walked in and bowed to Jazer. "Master," the larger one said, his voice twisted. Ravenna caught a glimpse of a split tongue and winced. Had it been self-inflicted? She doubted it.

"Take the Angel to be branded," Jazer jerked her hand towards the male and handed over Ravenna's chains. "Do it on her hip. I don't want anything visible to be ruined. And when you're done, feed her something. Those slaver's rations wouldn't fill a child's belly, let alone keep her figure."

"Yes, Master," the taller said. The other bobbled his head in agreement. Mute, probably, Ravenna realised. Had his tongue been cut out where the other's had been split? Ravenna kept her own mouth shut. "And where should we put her?"

Jazer narrowed her eyes, taking Ravenna in. Ravenna tried to keep the trembling from her feathers, but it was a battle. One she was losing. "She's too valuable for the harem. Put her with the household slaves in the palace by the Pits. She will become my shadow."

Ravenna did not get the chance to ask or even consider what that was. The unfamiliar words slid over her wings like grime and then her chains were jerked, forcing her to stumble forwards. She was dragged along, pulled back into the harsh daylight. Murmurs broke out at her appearance and a few shouts sounded, growing closer. Ravenna flared her wings defensively and tried to get her bearings. Had she come in that way? No, it was different. Maybe. This human nest looked so foreign, so wrong.

The soldiers, guards, slaves, whatever they were, pulled Ravenna over to a structure that was little more than a scrap of fabric stretched over top of a few wooden poles to shelter the inhabitants from the sun. The air under the shelter was even more stifling and hotter than the desert air. It did not take Ravenna long to figure out why.

A tiny scrap of a male stood before a fire made up of fiercely glowing coals. A variety of long metal shafts were being heated to a throbbing red. Ravenna pulled back, jerking on her chains as she flapped her wings desperately. The two humans were too strong for her, considering her weakened state.

The mute slammed a hand into the back of her neck and Ravenna fell to her knees. The other jerked her tunic up and her breeches down, revealing a patch of white skin on her left hip. This was worse than having her wings touched by Jazer. Ravenna beat her wings violently, throwing the human off for a moment. The other grabbed her wings and held them out of the way, bending a few feathers. Ravenna let out a low moan, tears already welling in her eyes.

"Jazer's personal brand," the larger male panted, holding Ravenna still. The small male nodded and pulled a brand out of the fire, a circle cut through with a jagged line. Ravenna didn't have time to fight any further or to plead her case before the metal was pressed to her hip.

The scream that escaped her throat echoed throughout the slave markets. Some people knew it was nothing more than a branding. Some people, less used to the realities of the market, covered their ears. But an old female standing on the auction block, the bids for her pitifully small, knew that sound was an angel crying out in pain. She shivered.

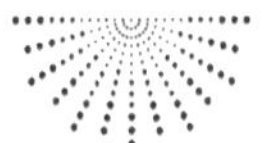

CHAPTER FIVE

*R*avenna had two days to acclimate to her new surroundings and recover from being branded before she was put to work. The first day was spent in a room with windows no bigger than her hand and hardly enough space to stretch her wings. Not that she would have noticed. That first day was little more than a feverish haze. Sweat shone on her brow and her skin looked wan and even more pale than usual. Her hip burned and throbbed where the brand had been pressed into the skin.

A figure appeared in the doorway, looking down on Ravenna with no expression. Yet somehow, this tiny female seemed to convey pity. She had the same dark skin as the slaver that had caught Ravenna, and her hair was long and wild. She held something in her hands, a pot that gave off a sour smell. Ravenna licked her lips, too exhausted to do much more than twitch her wings as they trembled at her side. She had vomited up any food and water into a small bucket, and even if her life or dignity was in danger, she was not certain she could fight it. Was not certain she wanted to.

"You hold still, now," the female said, her voice melodious.

Ravenna watched blankly as the female came closer, her bare feet brushing softly against the stone floor. The female crouched before Ravenna. She reached out to lift Ravenna's worn tunic. The sylph flinched, her breath starting to come in shallow gasps.

"No, relax," the female said. She put a cool hand on Ravenna's arm then pulled back. "You're burnin' up. Not good. Jazer be angry at that."

Ravenna thought she understood the words, but she was not certain. Had she been in the forests of Shinalea, she could have easily found the herbs she needed to treat her fever. She could have gone to Kratos for a poultice for her brand. She could have rested in bed, letting Tacitus bring her soothing, cool, water…

"*What are you doing?*" Tacitus asked, standing before Ravenna in a wavering image. Though his wings were spread, they did not block the harsh light that streamed through the window. Vaguely, Ravenna felt the human female prodding at her hip, making the brand burn sharper. The sharp stench of infection filled the air.

"I want to go home," Ravenna told Tacitus. He frowned, wings lifting.

"*And what home would that be? You are not yet a full Intellecti. You are not like the rest of the sylphs. And you managed to get captured by humans to be treated as an animal.*"

"Not my fault," Ravenna said. She flinched at the touch of the female but tried to keep her eyes focused on Tacitus. "I'll find a way out of here. There has to be a way."

Tacitus shook his head, disappointment etching itself into his features. Ravenna whimpered, though she did not know whether it was from the pain or the sight of her heart-father's disapproval. "*I told you not to be weak. I told you not to give up on yourself. To fight. To fly. And look at you now. Passively submitting to the touch of a human who intends to harm you. A slave to a monster.*"

You submitted without question. You are no sylph. You are no daughter of mine..."

Somewhere in Ravenna's mind, she knew that the fever from her infected wound was talking. Tacitus was not really there in the room with her. He would never say such things. But the words were truth. Ravenna had not fought the humans, except on Shinalea. One simple cut on her arm and she had submitted to their control. That had been her role in life for so long. And look where it had brought her. Ravenna allowed her eyes to flutter close as the black abyss of unconsciousness rose up to meet her. She did not know how to be any different.

The next day, Ravenna's fever broke, though the brand was still flushed and raw. The female, Ravenna learned, had spread ash in the wound to make certain that it would heal with Jazer's personal mark plain for all to see. Someone in the massive stone house had decided, though, that Ravenna had rested enough. She was bathed roughly, dressed in a quickly modified tunic that went to her knees and hung open on her back for her wings, then introduced to the other slaves that made up Jazer's household. Then, Ravenna was shown her new life.

She learned that the Pits was the local name for a natural sinkhole that had opened up some generations before. Jazer's palace, as she called it, overlooked the yawning hole. It was big enough to host fights in and the sides had been carved into stadium seating so the fights could be made into a spectacle for all to see. Jazer was the owner of the Pits, and she had a good number of fighters in her service. Occasionally, they would fight against creatures that the slavers captured—enormous lions native to the desert; the occasional giant lizard that looked like a wingless dragon; wolves and the like—but more often than not, they would fight against the fighters owned by other slavers.

It was a cruel blood-sport that supplied the entertainment and money for the sparsely-populated regions beyond the Pits.

There was little else for days. Coming to the Pits to bet and fight was both lucrative and provided a much-needed distraction for the outcasts of the Salusian Empire.

Ravenna kept hearing the name, Salusian Empire, but no one would talk about it more than to give her a disdainful look and shake their heads at her ignorance. After a while, Ravenna stopped asking and just listened to what the others had to say about the house beside the arena. She learned to hold a tray and to duck her head at the sharp sound of rebuke. No one raised a hand against her, but a young slave had been beaten before her eyes for accidentally dropping a goblet of wine. The message was clear.

All the while, that nagging doubt lingered in the back of her mind. Ravenna was unused to such open cruelty, but submission was not new. No matter how she fought it, Tacitus' words from her fever-dream rang true. She had submitted without a fight. She had submitted to almost everything in her life without a fight, excepting learning to run through and amongst the forest. And she did not know how to change that.

The third day dawned hot and clear. The two humans that had branded Ravenna stomped into her prison and dragged her to a bathing spring where she was scrubbed, her hair oiled and pinned away from her eyes, and dressed in a ridiculous costume. The trousers were like the billowing trousers in fashion at the Aerial City. They cinched at Ravenna's waist, flowed down her legs and collected at the ankles. If she expected a pinch of homesickness, she was disappointed. All Ravenna felt was an abiding disgust for the person who thought these black sheer things were all the clothes a person needed.

Only, they weren't all the clothes. Ravenna was provided with a beaded top that strategically covered her chest and left everything else bare. Including her back and wings. A beaded headdress was placed on her hair and a shining silver chain was attached to her ankle. Ravenna did not have to look at her reflection in the spring to know what these people wanted her to be.

Angel of Darkness. A concubine. A glimpse of the dark night or a white star.

To these humans, Ravenna was beautiful. Their gasps, leering gazes, admiration, and awe made it perfectly clear that, even disregarding the wings, Ravenna was special to them. It was so strange, given that the sylphs had never thought her as such. Sure, her limbs were lithe and her muscles powerful. Her figure trim and her features aristocratic. But everything else had been treated with such frowning disdain that even her attributes had been ignored. And then there were her flightless wings. Ravenna was now supposed to be portraying a beauty she had never felt, but all she could feel was disgusted.

"Yes," Jazer hissed in pleasure as Ravenna was brought out to the enormous balcony where the Slave Master sat and oversaw the games in the Pit. There were other chairs and couches, surrounded by tanned children waving fans. Ravenna's chain was attached to a stake in the centre of the balcony and she knew that this was to be her world. "You will do quite nicely. Do you know your tasks?"

Ravenna bit back the desire to snap and fight against her fate. It could have been worse, she thought. Much worse. "I am to serve drinks and food to your guests."

"Very good," Jazer ran a possessive hand over Ravenna's night-black feathers. The sylph shuddered and drew away. "No flapping those wings of yours and trying to fly away, now, hear?"

Ravenna nodded, not wanting to reveal her greatest shame to this parasite.

Jazer raised a hand, rings glinting in the sun. "Say it!"

"I could not escape if I tried," Ravenna spat out.

Jazer lowered her hand and quirked a painted-on eyebrow.

Ravenna swallowed, fear of pain overriding her sense of shame. "I cannot fly."

Jazer was silent for a moment. Then, she tossed her head back, the jewellery on every inch of her body clinking and taunting. Jazer's laugh, though, was the worst of all. It scraped along Ravenna's back, making her wish for a weapon. Any weapon. She could do nothing with it, though. In that moment, Ravenna knew that she had been broken. And she had not fought that, either.

She lowered her head.

"You cannot fly," Jazer sneered. "Why not? One of those slavers break your precious wings?"

"No," Ravenna said. "I was born unable to fly."

"Well, well. This does change things. I no longer have to worry about clipping your wings to keep you by my side," Jazer fingered the blade at her round hip. She grinned wolfishly at Ravenna. "And you are still as beautiful as ever. The world will never know that you cannot fly. You will still be my Angel. My sign of good fortune and divine blessing."

Ravenna winced back from the caressing touch of Jazer, a sob building in her chest. Who was she kidding? She had told herself she was strong. Tacitus had told her she was strong. Ravenna had vowed she would not break, that she would not give in to the horrors of the human world. That she would be everything Tacitus had told her she could be. The truth was, though, that Ravenna had been submissive and quiet for so long that she had never been strong. She had only ever tried not to be a burden to others. Running through the trees? That was as close to freedom as she had ever been.

And now look at her.

"Oh, tsk," Jazer drew a finger over Ravenna's black hair, playing with the beaded headdress. "Don't cry, Angel. My guests are arriving. You must be prepared to serve them and then to stand at my side and watch the games."

Ravenna took a single breath for herself. Then she straightened and bowed her head to Jazer. Her expression remained cool and calm. She would not let the others see what turmoil lay beneath. At least she had that.

Whatever it was that Jazer wanted from Ravenna, she at least knew how to keep the sylph safe from any wandering hands and eyes, from the guests that were more likely to take than to ask. Ravenna served drinks and food to the hungry-eyed males and their females, clothes finely crafted and, Ravenna thought, absurd. The whispers about her followed with their gazes. But the shame and disgust that Ravenna had felt eventually faded away into numbness.

Now that Jazer had an "angel" in her possession, it seemed like the games were more about showcasing Ravenna than the fighters. Jazer quickly increased the number of fights from once a week to twice a week then three times. Every fight, Ravenna stood behind Jazer's couch, shielding her from the sun with her wings. And every time, the audience would watch Ravenna with wide, startled eyes that such a being existed out of legends of dragons and elves and magic when their world contained none. As the weeks, then a moon, passed by, Ravenna sank deeper into the numbness, telling herself over and over again that things could be far worse.

Then, things changed.

Jazer had a particularly rowdy group of guests that day. They were supposedly some wandering tribe's shaman and leader, enjoying the respite from the desert in the springs that surrounded the Pits. They were already wine-drunk and kept asking Ravenna for more.

"Please, Angel, another drink to make the sun beat less harshly," the shaman slurred, leaning forwards and holding out his goblet. Ravenna heard Jazer's huff of annoyance behind her but went to do her job anyway. Saying nothing, she poured another goblet-full of wine and tried to ignore the roar of the audience as they cheered the bloodshed behind her. The fights were the only things that Ravenna actively ignored. After having become a slave, she didn't think she could stand anymore blood and violence, proof of human cruelty.

"Mmmmm, yes," the shaman licked his lips and raked his dark eyes across Ravenna's exposed skin. It was nothing new, but this time she took a step back, the delicate chain around her ankle dragging as she did so. After Jazer discovered that Ravenna was unable to fly and lacked the will to run, the chain had become more for show than anything. Possession.

"Angel, why don't you sit with me and my tribe fellows for a while?" the shaman waved a light-brown hand to the leering humans beside him. Ravenna shook her head. "No? What do you mean, no?"

"I cannot," Ravenna said, backing up another step as the shaman rose. His bejewelled scabbard was empty, but the threat of violence was present all the same.

"I say you can," he snarled. "After all, you are nothing more than a slave."

"I cannot," Ravenna repeated, her voice firmer. She took another two steps backward, hoping to run into Jazer's couch, so the Slave Master would stop her guests. Jazer was a cruel woman, but the alternative was much, much worse. It was the darkest of Ravenna's fears about her new life. The shaman let out a wordless hiss and advanced, following Ravenna. She retreated again, the backs of her legs hitting the stone railing that surrounded the balcony. Ravenna glanced desperately to her side and saw Jazer's couch was a good distance away. She had not been retreating to Jazer. She had been retreating to the edge of the sinkhole.

Her momentum was too much. Ravenna stumbled over the edge, the chain on her ankle snapped with the slightest pressure. And then, she was in open air, falling.

This was too much like falling into the gully as a child. Like falling from a tree. For two heartbeats, Ravenna felt as she were suspended midair. Her eyes took in the startled looks of the spectators, the open-mouthed horror on Jazer's face. Ravenna reached out to grab at something, anything. All she managed to do was twist her wings and beat them against the air.

Then suddenly, Ravenna remembered her training. She remembered running through the forest, leaping through trees and surviving in that moment between jumping and landing. She remembered what it was like to feel the wind cupping beneath her feathers. Her wings might not have been strong enough to carry her in flight, but they could help her twist right-ways-up and slow her fall.

Ravenna landed on the floor of the Pits with a resounding *slap*, her bare feet bracing against the dirt; her knees absorbed the shock along with her wings. A dust cloud enveloped her, making her cough. She straightened and blinked rapidly, clearing her eyes. She was alive. Not only that, but she was uninjured.

A cry rose from the audience and suddenly, they were cheering. Ravenna winced at the noise and looked around to see if there was a way out of the Pit. She spotted the fallen form of a human, staring up at her in shock. He was about ten feet away from her and lying on his back, an enormous gash in his left leg. The rest of him was so covered in dust and gore that Ravenna couldn't tell anything about him except that he was powerful and had green eyes. They were not staring at her, Ravenna realised, but behind her.

She whirled around and saw a desert lion stalking towards her, eyes bright with bloodlust. The lion's shoulders were massive slabs of muscle, its haunches made for springing. Its sides heaved with breath, ribs showing easily. It snarled, showing Ravenna its fangs already dripping with the fallen soldier's blood. Its paws were easily the size of Ravenna's face, claws digging into the dirt with ease.

"Ah," she muttered.

"Here!" the soldier cried. Ravenna turned and lunged for him, just as the lion did. She reached him first, grabbing the leaf-shaped bronze blade lying at the soldier's side. The lion roared and barrelled into Ravenna, throwing her through the air. Once again, she used her wings to land upright. The lion paced and roared again, eyes glancing between the soldier and Ravenna. It was fairly obvious which was the easier target.

"Oh, no you don't," Ravenna hissed. She did not think about the fact that the fallen soldier was human, that he likely deserved whatever punishment this starved-in-captivity lion deemed worthy. Ravenna only knew that the lion was advancing and that she should do something about it. So she did.

She let out a cry and ran for the lion, her wings twisting in the Dalketh motion for Eagle Lifting Prey. When Ravenna crouched and sprang, the air caught beneath her wings just as they should have. Instead of flying, though, she came down on top of the lion. It roared as her blade sank into the space between its shoulders.

Ravenna fell off the lion's back and rolled in the dust, her left wing trapped beneath her. She groaned and forced herself to stand, to face her opponent. The lion, though, was uninterested in attacking Ravenna or the human it had already injured. It was staggering away, moving towards a boulder. Collapsing before it could reach the meagre shelter, the lion was dead.

Ravenna almost did not hear the shouting of the spectators. She was too busy dealing with the roiling of her stomach and the horror at what she had done. Turning, Ravenna bent over and emptied her stomach. Her muscles trembled and her wings ached at being used in ways they had not been for weeks. Tears fell unbidden from her eyes, though she quickly brushed them away.

"Hey," the human had managed to stagger to his feet and was

limping towards Ravenna, hands raised in concern. "Are you alright?"

Ravenna nodded. Shook her head. "What have I done?"

"You saved me, is what," the human held out his hand. Ravenna looked at it, a furrow in her brows. "You shake it," the human said, his own legs trembling almost as much as Ravenna's. "It's a sort of sign of trust and friendship. Sort of."

Ravenna took the man's hand and he shook it. "Thank you, Angel."

"Ravenna," she said softly, the words barely heard over the ecstatic cries of those watching. "My name is Ravenna."

"Well, Ravenna, I'm Radim."

"You see!" Jazer's voice rang out over the roaring of the audience. Ravenna and Radim looked up to see the Slave Master standing at the front of the balcony, her arms spread wide in victory, jewellery glinting in the sun. "The Angel shows her true nature! She is a warrior!"

The audience cheered all the louder and Radim patted Ravenna's shoulder, seemingly ignorant of the wound on his leg. "Welcome to the Pits, Ravenna. You've just become the star attraction."

CHAPTER SIX

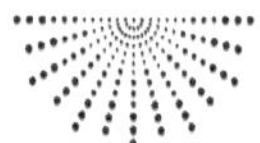

*R*avenna's life, once again, changed dramatically in a blink and a misstep. No more living with the household slaves, she was sent to bunk with the other warriors of the Pits, deep in the caverns that surrounded the arena. Her days of following Jazer around had also ended, leaving Ravenna to train with the humans.

She was terrified.

"Have you ever held a sword before?" Radim asked, raising his eyebrows. He stood next to a giant of a human, whose hands were probably large enough to wrap around Ravenna's skull and crush it in an instant. This was the most experienced of the slave warriors, a human Ravenna had learned was named Tekko. He had a shaved head and more pink, scarred flesh than unmarked leather-tan skin. He was frowning at Ravenna like she was the scum beneath his shoe.

Well, she was not too pleased, either, being trained to fight with yet another group of horrible human parasites. Ravenna was not interested in fighting. She had never even wanted to kill anything in her hunts, though she had done so out of necessity. Killing that lion had been self-defence, but it did not mean she liked it. It was starving and desperate for food, probably tortured until it was mean enough to go after the first thing that got in its way. It was a horrible fate. Yet now, Jazer was convinced that Ravenna was going to be a great warrior. And Radim seemed to think that they were friends since she had saved his life. She silently cursed both impressions with every breath.

Ravenna flared her wings slightly and shifted the grip of the leaf-shaped blade in her hand. It felt clumsy and awkward and she hated it. "No. I've only ever used daggers for hunting."

"This isn't a dagger," Tekko growled. "And if you don't lift that point in the air, you will be dead before your next match even begins."

Ravenna curled her lip in a snarl but did as Tekko demanded. If learning how to fight meant surviving one more day, then she would learn how to fight. And she would do it well, to keep these humans from coming anywhere near her.

"Good. Now attack the dummy." Tekko waved his giant hand towards the straw dummy that had been set up across the arena. Skeptical, Ravenna raised her brow, but did as she was told. She edged forwards, trying to keep the sword up whilst looking around to see if anyone else was going to sneak up on her. She would not put anything past these humans. After a minute or so, she reached the dummy, raised her sword and brought it down in a swipe that should have, to her estimation, hacked off one of its arms. Instead, the sword got stuck in the straw.

"Not enough power," Radim said.

She whirled, letting go of the sword and jumping back in a motion that had been trained into her from an early age.

Radim whistled, impressed. "Well, well, looks like you have some fight in you after all."

"That wasn't fighting," Ravenna snapped. "That was Dalketh."

Radim and Tekko exchanged a confused look. Radim shifted

his weight off of his still-healing leg, "Dalketh? Some sort of angel thing?"

"I'm *not* an angel," Ravenna said for what felt like the hundredth time. At this point, it seemed like Radim was saying it just to get a rise out of her. She took a deep, calming breath and plastered calmness over her face, just like she would when dealing with Crispinus and Desarra. Ravenna released the breath. "Dalketh is a series of exercises designed to help balance a sylph's energies and manoeuvre in flight. They stretch and use all the muscles in the body and wings and teach balance, control, grace."

She did not mention that it was also what had helped her run through her beloved forest and jump through the trees like a bird or flying snake. She did not tell them that the uneven walls of the Pits were enough for her to use her experience to climb and jump out of there. The soldiers pacing the perimeter of the fall into the Pits were enough to deter Ravenna from that.

Tekko nodded brusquely. "Show me."

"Show you what? Dalketh? It's not a fighting style," Ravenna pointed out.

Tekko just nodded again and waved an impatient hand.

Ravenna swallowed the urge to roll her eyes. She kept her expression the same icy-calm and took a few steps back, stretching her wings out to their full length. Radim and Tekko's eyes gleamed at the sight, but they said nothing.

Ravenna spread her legs to shoulder width, sank down a touch, and began the routine that she had learned all those years ago. Her wings twisted in conjunction with her hips, her arms flowing through the air to move the energy in her body. Her legs sank and rose, stretching the muscles, allowing her to fall into a lunge or a crouch. She flowed, her eyes closing as the familiar feel of the exercise took over. This was home. This was control over her body, making it do everything she asked of it… except fly. This had been her safe space for so long, a place where no one would interrupt her with errands to run for the Intellecti or demands to go climb the Stair and spend the day in the Aerial City. There were no taunts about her flightlessness and lowly status. In Dalketh, Ravenna was grace and control and power.

She was not a slave.

Ravenna opened her eyes as she slid out of the last pose.

Tekko nodded, arms crossed and expression unnervingly thoughtful.

Radim just gave her a cunning grin.

"Again. Faster," Tekko said.

"This isn't a fighting exercise. And no matter how many times you put me through this, I won't know how to hold a sword or fight a warrior," Ravenna said again.

Tekko ignored her.

"Again. Faster."

Sighing, Ravenna sank back into the starting position. She moved through the exercises at twice the speed, her body gladly doing as she asked. Not even a quarter of the way through, Tekko stepped closer, "Faster."

Ravenna bit back the urge to move away from the giant human, though she did increase the speed of her movements. Her heart was beating faster, and she had to think about her breathing, something she rarely had to do. This was getting closer to her forest runs, though she was not jumping through the canopy.

Tekko took another step forwards, "Faster."

Ravenna clenched her jaw and complied. The calm that Dalketh usually brought was quickly dissipated with the human's proximity and her increasing heart rate. Tekko took a third step forwards, this time getting too close to do the exercises properly. Ravenna started to take a step back, but Radim had come up behind her, making it impossible for her to move that direction. Ravenna bent her arm in a sweep across her face and halted in shock when Tekko's own arm was there, connecting with her arm in a hit that reverberated through her entire body.

He leaned his head in, still pushing down on her arm. She felt the strain of the movement, her muscles pushing back. But she was still in Dalketh and this was her element. This was where she had the power.

Tekko bared his teeth in a feral smile. "Now fight back."

He started to attack with his hands. No blades.

Ravenna staggered sideways, out of the way of Radim and the larger warrior. She slid into her Dalketh stance that had kept her steady against Tekko's initial attack. And then she countered his movements with the ones that were instinctive, natural. Where Tekko punched and kicked his way into Ravenna's defences, she blocked and stepped out of the way, countering with the next movement in Dalketh.

It was not the natural exercise that she had come to know. This was more like the improvisation that her runs had forced her to learn—what seemed like a lifetime ago. Standing around and following Jazer around like a pet hadn't kept Ravenna's muscles quick and ready. Tekko got a few hits in past her defences and Ravenna was beginning to lose control of her breathing. But this was still Dalketh.

Finally, Tekko stepped around her back, trying to get past the barrier she had created in her defensive stance. Ravenna snapped her wings open, using the powerful muscles to beat across Tekko's chest and knock the giant backward into the sand. She whirled and let out a snarl of frustration. Tekko stared at her, the dust settling on his scarred skin.

Ravenna struggled to catch her breath, chest heaving and fury running through her veins. She *hated* these humans. They were beating her, giving her bruises and wounds that would take ages to heal, making her betray her belief that violence was not an answer, that knowledge and facts and reason could solve every argument. But she had knocked Tekko down with a single snap of her wings and that feeling of strength was heady. Finally, Ravenna felt anything but weak. She might never be at the mercy of humans again.

Tekko climbed to his feet. Seeing the pleasure that had flashed across Ravenna's features, he nodded. "Dalketh is meant for fighting," he said with a gleam in his eyes. He brushed some of the sand off his clothes. "Again. Until you cannot lift your wings from the ground. And tomorrow, we add a sword."

Ravenna spread her wings with a *snap*. She held her hands up in the second motion of Dalketh and dared Tekko to advance with her eyes. The thought flitted through her mind that maybe this was what Dalketh was truly meant for. Maybe Ravenna was meant for this, too.

* * *

"Ravenna!" Radim waved an arm at Ravenna as she carried her plate of food to the table farthest away from the other people. She froze, looking over at him suspiciously. Radim slid off the bench and jogged over to Ravenna. "Why don't you come eat with us?"

"I'm tired," Ravenna said flatly. It was the truth. She was almost three weeks into her training and not only was it becoming more intense, but she was having a hard time keeping her wings from dragging on the ground. Her body adapted to the new method of Dalketh well enough, and she had even learned how to use a sword reasonably well. But she was wing-weary. Tired of the world. Of life.

"Well, just come sit and eat. You don't have to do any talking. And we promise not to say anything if you fall asleep in your food," Radim said, eyes begging. Ravenna wanted nothing more than to slink away to her corner spot and eat as quickly as possible. Alone. She did not want to spend any more time with these humans than she had to. Training was survival. Eating? Socialising? That was another thing entirely.

"Very well." Ravenna followed Radim back to the table where the other slaves quickly made room for Ravenna and her wings. Even Tekko graced her with a nod.

"I hear the witch is planning a whole week of celebrations and tournaments for the end the month," Radim said.

"…Witch?" She couldn't help her curiosity. She had never been able to quell that.

"The magnanimous Jazer," Tekko grumbled, scowling into his potatoes.

"No, that I understood. What is a witch?" She already knew about the tournament. Jazer had come down to talk with Ravenna earlier that week, making it quite clear that the tournament was to showcase the "Angel" and that if Ravenna lost any of the matches, it would be bad for her.

As bad as things got, Ravenna knew that it could easily be worse. So she trained harder.

Radim stared at her. "You don't know what a witch is? A person who uses magic. Known to mumble curses, conjure storm clouds, and consort with demons?"

Ravenna shook her head. "There were no such things where I came from. Sorcerers are the only human "magic" users I know of."

"Well, I wouldn't necessarily call them *human*. Not when they come straight from the depths of Hell," Radim grinned.

Ravenna frowned.

"I heard a female talk about Hell before, but I don't know what that is. She said this place was Hell." Ravenna took a gaping bite of her meat, probably some sort of lizard. It did not matter; it tasted terrible and had all the protein she needed for building her muscles.

Now everyone in her vicinity was staring at her. Tekko rubbed a hand over his bald head, sucking in a breath. "You don't know what Hell is? Don't you know of the Creation? The divine beings and the Will of the Heavens?"

"The beliefs amongst sylphs are…different," Ravenna replied. "We believe in facts, in history, in things that stand before the eye or that can be proven. We believe in what you feel in your heart and mind to be truth."

"I've never heard of beings that don't have a religion," Tekko murmured, looking to Radim for confirmation. The other warrior shook his head.

"I once heard about a wanderer who claimed to have met an elf, back when I was a lad. Even elves have religion. It's different than ours, but still religion."

Tekko snorted, stabbing his lizard with his knife. "There's no such things as elves. You were being fooled."

Radim narrowed his eyes.

"Religion…" Ravenna tested the word out, rolling it around her mouth. She gave a wing-shrug, her feathers rustling. "Tell me about your religion."

So passed the rest of the meal, with Radim and Tekko and the other slaves talking about the creation of the world by their One Who Watches and the various races, about the lesser divine beings who served a purpose greater than even they could completely comprehend, about the history of the religion, the holy people who served their gods, the sect who believed in a singular force behind all of the other beings and gods. Ravenna mostly listened, trying to understand what it would be like to believe in something greater than yourself. To believe that you mattered to a being that existed outside of time and pain. That you were never alone and were never given something greater than you could bear.

It was comforting and somewhat beautiful. And Ravenna realised something just then. These humans, these fellow slaves and warriors, they were as trapped in this life as she was. The other humans, the ones who cheered when they shed blood or paid more for the beautiful ones, the powerful ones, they were the enemy. The parasites.

For the first time in what felt like a lifetime, Ravenna allowed herself to smile. The wing-weariness lifted a little.

Then Radim pushed away his empty plate and looked seriously at Ravenna, a slight frown marring the corners of his mouth. "Ravenna, what are you doing here?"

She drew her brows together. "I don't understand."

"Well, I know we get treated better than other slaves, that we get full meals and decent lives except for the constant fighting, but you don't have to be here," Radim said. Ravenna's confusion deepened. "At first, we thought that your wings were maybe weak, healing from being captured and in cages for so long. But then you started training and…well, they're not weak at all. So why are you here? Were you exiled by your people? Do you think this is fun?"

Ravenna surged up from the table, fury pulsing through her veins. No amount of icy control could keep her from showing her anger and Radim flinched. "You think I *want* to be here?" Ravenna hissed. "That I want to be away from my home, my life? I was *captured and enslaved!*"

"So were we all," Tekko said, rising as well. He loomed over Ravenna, but she refused to back down. She lifted her wings above her head, spreading the feathers. Tekko blinked, but was not intimidated.

"Why don't you just fly away?" Radim asked pointedly.

Immediately, Ravenna's wings fell, slamming into her side, pressing close to her body. Jazer had not told them. They had not figured it out. They thought she chose to be there, learning to fight and revel in the bloodshed that was to come.

Ravenna took a few steps back, wrapping her arms around herself. "Before I was captured, I had never caused bloodshed except when hunting. And even then, I tried to do that as cleanly as possible. Cause no pain. Now? I'm being turned into a trained killer. For what? Entertainment."

Tekko stepped forwards, stretching out a hand. Ravenna hissed and shook her head, fixing the giant in her ice-blue stare brimming with every scrap of humiliation and anger she could muster. Tekko didn't take another step.

"I cannot fly," Ravenna spat out.

Radim sucked in a breath, eyes widening.

Ravenna spread her wings out to their full span, showing the worthless pieces of flesh and feathers to the fellow slaves. "These wings? They're *nothing*! They're not big enough to carry someone in flight—not when sylphs don't have hollow bones like birds. So what are they good for? Hmm?"

She turned and showed off the wings, hating them more than she ever had. So what if they helped her jump through trees? There were no trees to be found. "Are they nothing more than tools for fighting? Or something for you *humans* to gawk at, thinking I'm some fallen divine being here to save you all?"

"Ravenna, we—" Radim started, pushing up off the bench. Ravenna surged forwards, pushing past Tekko with a twist of her body. She jammed her finger into Radim's chest, eyes blazing, and teeth bared.

"I would *never* have stayed here if I could get away, if I could fly to freedom. But it looks like I'm just as stuck as the rest of you. Or do *you* want to be here? Slaves with access to weapons and the ability to use them. Why don't you fight your way free, then?"

"The bronze would never stand up to their steel," Tekko murmured.

Ravenna did not require an explanation. She knew the answer. She knew that they—as well as she—would be slaughtered with ease if they ever tried to fight back against their masters. And yet they had the audacity to accuse her of wanting to be amongst these hateful creatures.

She let Radim stand, let him move closer to her with concern in his eyes and an apology on his face. Ravenna even let him extend his arms as though they were going to wrap around her, offering a modicum of comfort. But when he actually tried to brush his hand against her arm, she said in a voice with an icy tone, "Don't. Touch. Me."

"I didn't mean—"

Ravenna turned on her heel and stalked from the dining cavern, the stone above her head nothing more than an illusion of being caged in. Her whole life, the sky had been a cage. Why should stone matter more than that? Ravenna went to the bathing springs, where one of the few other female warriors was emerging; her dark brown skin glistened with water and yet was so unlike the charcoal-ash or golden skin of the sylphs that Ravenna had known. That longing for familiarity was just one more pain to brush off and never acknowledge again.

Ravenna stepped into the water, letting the warm spring take away the soreness from the day. She splashed about for a bit, washing the dust and dirt and a few smears of blood from her skin. Her wings fanned her dry, their natural oils shedding water easily. Ravenna looked at her reflection in the water. She still saw that pale-as-the-moon sylph who had been sneered at her entire life. Tacitus had never sneered, but his pity had stung just as much. Yet she longed for him, for his wings wrapped around her. She longed for the peace of the Tower. Instead, she stood here, beaten, broken, and wing-weary.

There were a few bruises shadowing her shoulders and chest where Tekko had gotten in an impressive kick. The brand on her hip shimmered an angry pink under the water. She was more muscular than she had been before, trading thinness for power. Her black hair was now pulled back from her face and hung down her back in a thick braid with spikes woven through it, for safety during a fight. Her face had always been expressionless or calm, the aristocratic features Queen Mariala had assured Ravenna came from her mother lending an air of aloofness. Now, she just looked hard. Dangerous.

A drop of water fell from Ravenna's chin, rippling her reflection. She frowned and waited for the water to clear so she could have something to direct her loathing towards, but the water just rippled again as another droplet fell. Tears. Ravenna brought her hand up and wiped the moisture away from her face. More just replaced them.

Letting out a strangled cry, Ravenna sank completely into the water, not caring that her wings would get fully wet and take hours to dry, not caring that the spring water stung a little as it touched the open cuts on her back where Radim had struck with the edge of his blunted sword. She just sank into the water and let the salt of her tears mix with the water.

Before then, Ravenna would have said that she understood what it was to be wing-weary. Constant disapproval from Desarra, the pitying silence from the other Intellecti, the inability to participate in many aspects of sylph life, it was enough to make her feel that bone-deep sadness. Now, she would have given anything to feel that way again. Now, she was certain that this abject misery bordering on apathy was going to kill her.

At least with the tournament in two-days, someone else might get there first.

CHAPTER SEVEN

The feeling of wrongness that ran up Davorin's spine had been growing for days. He had never been beyond the borders of the Salusian Empire before and now he had been nearly two weeks beyond the reach of his father. It was a freeing feeling, not being bound by the Emperor. It was also wrong.

Davorin belonged to the Empire and it belonged to him. He had not killed Dagan out of jealousy, after all, but the knowledge that Dagan would have ruined the Empire. Yet his father had not seen it. Had not granted Davorin the control of the Empire's armies that Dagan had been almost carelessly given. Go back to your money and your estate, Davorin, you're not wanted here.

Well, it was time to put that carefully hoarded money to use.

Davorin looked behind him and saw the few hundred soldiers-for-hire that he had scrounged up in the borderlands. They were mercenaries, plain and simple, but they had agreed to the monthly salary Davorin had offered and were as close to an army as he was going to get anytime soon. Their leader, a gruff man called Warrith with more snow in his hair than the

Emperor, was not one to be trifled with. He had lost three fingers and was still just as dangerous with a blade as any able-bodied youth—as Davorin had discovered when they sparred.

"You don't seem sure about this course of action," Warrith commented as he drew his horse up next to Davorin's. The desert stretched around them almost as far as the eye could see, the first time Davorin had experienced such emptiness. But the mounds rising up on the horizons—the slight tinge of moisture in the air that spoke of an oasis in this wretched place…That was where he was going to find his prize.

"If you have a better idea as to how to raise an army quickly, you are welcome to suggest it," Davorin grumbled. Warrith raised a bushy eyebrow and scratched his short beard.

"You know as well as I do that this is the fastest way," Warrith answered. "But you don't seem convinced."

Davorin growled and spurred his horse forwards. The irascible mercenary kept pace with ease, as did the troops behind them. "The Slave Markets are our destination for today. I hear they're putting on a tournament in their famous Pits," Davorin said, silently snarling at Warrith. He didn't want to talk about his plan, or acknowledge his doubts.

"Do you think you can find something to please her?" Warrith pressed on, ignoring the way Davorin's hand went to the hilt of one of his swords and gripped it, knuckles turning white. "Hers is the largest army outside of the Empire and Southron. Don't know why, though. All that the desert holds is sand and lions. Not much to fight."

"Her lands abut the Iron Mountains. And the coast," Davorin said, not for the first time. Though there were other threats out there to defend against than mountain mysteries and raiders. Dagan had been one of them.

"Well, be sure you pick the right gift," Warrith said.

Davorin nodded, the prickling feeling on the back of his neck growing. Was it wariness, uneasiness at being so far from all that he knew, or something else? As the mercenary troops entered the edge of the Slave Market town, tropical greenery greeting them, the feeling only increased.

Davorin led his troops into the centre of the town, where the largest mud-brick buildings were located and people were hawking wares from booths. The infamous Slave Markets were nowhere to be seen, but the faint stench was hard to mistake. He dismounted and handed a pouch of money to Warrith. "Find a place near some water where our people can set up camp. Buy food and supplies as necessary."

Warrith's eyes gleamed the colour of the plants around them. Davorin hissed and snaked his hand, grabbing the older man by the front of his tunic. "And don't think about wasting my money," he snarled. Warrith smiled, revealing crooked teeth.

"I wouldn't dream of it," the mercenary said. Davorin released him and let the older man take the reins of his horse. Money was a limited resource and he hated wasting it on that man and mercenaries, but he had work to do. Davorin turned to examine the wares offered by these people, though he doubted anything would be quite good enough, and found himself facing an enormous woman with cunning eyes and a bejewelled dagger in her hands. She lifted it and started picking her teeth with the knife. Davorin curled his lip.

"We don't normally get someone of your…position in town," she grinned.

Surely, they could not know him by looks this far out of the Empire?

"My position?" Davorin shifted his stance so he could easily block whatever attack the woman had coming his way, or whatever bodyguards she had at her disposal.

"Someone leading an army is never going to be a man of small stature," the woman answered, pointing at him with the tip of her dagger. Davorin wanted to snatch it from her hands, but something told him to wait and let her talk. Years of playing nice to the courts of the Emperor had trained Davorin to be patient, even in distaste. "Not to mention you have a certain… presence about you. A foreign dignitary, perhaps?"

"Something like that," Davorin said. The Slave Markets had no love for the Empire, nor anyone else but themselves. They were a nation unto themselves. And more than human flesh was sold there; information could be bought just as easily. Caution would serve him well. Though Davorin doubted his mercenary army would keep silent, no matter how well he paid them.

The woman raised her painted-on eyebrows and her smile became more genuine. "Indeed?" she said. "I do like someone who knows what they're about. I am Jazer. I own the Pits and run the Market."

Davorin frowned. The Pits were almost as infamous as the Slave Markets. What could the owner of the Pits want with him?

"I take it you're not here to purchase, ah, the more delicate pleasures the Markets can offer?" Jazer said, eyeing him. Davorin ground his teeth but shook his head.

"I am looking for a gift," he said, deciding that it might be useful to throw this Jazer some sort of bone. Perhaps she could help, if she was as connected as he assumed. His distaste was nothing compared to her usefulness. "Meanwhile, my troops are gathering supplies before we head east."

"Well, then," Jazer nodded approval. "In that case, I would invite you to accompany me to my private box and observe the tournament in my arena. Afterward, I will personally assist you in searching out this…gift."

Davorin hesitated, not wanting to trust that things could be this easy. This woman Jazer wanted something from him, he just was not sure what. He did not like her, and he certainly did not want to waste time watching some idiotic slave fights. Weak warriors up against starved beasts or angry veterans of the arena? Not his idea of sport. But Jazer owned the Pits and ran the Slave Market. She would know what gift would get Davorin his prize.

He lowered his hand from the hilt of his sword and offered his arm to Jazer. She took it with a girlish giggle and led Davorin through the market, the eyes of every person watching, some with horror, some with interest, some with cunning. He ignored them all and accompanied the Slave Master to the Pits, ready to be bored for an afternoon.

Eventually, the arena appeared before them, a giant hole in the ground that was ringed by elaborately carved stone structures. Jazer grinned wolfishly at Davorin as he took in the admittedly impressive sight. The stands could hold nearly a thousand people at least. And the balcony and stone box that Jazer led him to reminded Davorin of the palace back in the Empire, though he was loath to admit the connection.

Perhaps his coming to this desolate desert collection of people was worth more than he had thought. Certainly, it suited Jazer quite well, if the jewels that adorned most of her body were any indication. He had not really bothered to notice them before, but with her glinting in the sunlight now, it was hard to ignore.

Who would have known that a purveyor of slaves could have come so far?

Jazer settled into a stone-carved chair that looked more like a throne than a place to sit and watch the arena before them. She gestured for Davorin to sit next to her in one of the slightly lower chairs. As soon as he did, young slaves bearing shades or fans surrounded them.

"I don't normally allow others in my box on the opening day of a tournament, but I have a feeling that you won't want to miss this," Jazer sneered, plucking a fruit from a bowl offered up by a bronzed boy. Davorin took a piece of fruit as well and tried not to grimace as he felt its overripe juices beneath his fingers.

"You certainly seem well connected," Davorin replied

politely, his many years spent learning court etiquette with Seraphina finally giving him some useful skill. "I am certain that this chance meeting will be fortuitous for the both of us."

"You *are* a charmer," Jazer laughed, tossing back her head. The stands circling the arena started to fill with people from all walks of life. Sounds of distant conversations and the movement of people began to rise. "Tell me more about this gift you came all this way to find."

Davorin debated licking his fingers of the too-sweet juices the fruit had left behind. Before he could do so, a child of no more than five approached with a bowl of water. Davorin swallowed at the brand on her shoulder but dutifully cleaned his fingers. Though slavery was illegal in the Empire, it was not strictly enforced. Davorin knew that slaves were not uncommon, but knowledge was something much different from experience.

Jazer watched him closely, her eyes glinting some sort of approval as he flicked the water off his fingers.

He slid his eyes to her, hesitating. Finally, he spoke, "Have you heard of the Red Palace?"

Jazer's eyebrows flew up her forehead and she nearly fumbled the fruit in her pudgy fingers. "You are the one who has been making noises about courting herself? The Queen of the Desert? You are either more daring than I thought, or you are completely insane."

Davorin allowed himself a wry grin, though he was tempted to just stab the woman and be done. "Why ever would you say that? Queen Lenore has greeted me well and with kindness."

"She treats everyone well and with kindness," Jazer said. She waved a hand in front of her, indicating the growing crowds of people in the arenas. "I once invited her to partake in viewing the arena and she refused to come. She told me that if I hunted for slaves from her lands then she would send her army to raze this place. Even the smallest part of her army would tear this place to pieces in a day. But I know she's dealt with slavers in the past, though I can't get any details. Everything with her is just covered with that veneer of polite kindness!"

"And yet, I have no reason to believe that my advances would be unwelcome," Davorin said. Indeed, he was fairly confident that she would hear his case and allow him to court her, if only he could prove his devotion. He had been devoted to the Empire for years. How hard could it be to prove to be devoted to a woman? He had entertained women before, even gone so far as to win their hearts. Surely, courting this one would be no different, even if she were a queen.

Jazer watched him silently for a moment, her teeth working the corner of her mouth into a twist. Eventually, she nodded. "If anyone could do such a thing, I would believe it of you. You have the blind determination necessary, I'll give you that."

Davorin inclined his head.

Jazer looked as though she was going to say something more about Davorin, or make suggestions for his gift, when a burly slave with scars on both cheeks came up behind Jazer and whispered in her ear. The Slave Master grinned, clapping like a child. She waved the enormous slave off and turned to Davorin.

"Now I am going to show you something that I can guarantee you have never seen before," Jazer purred. "What would you say if I told you I had acquired a dragon?"

Davorin snorted, "I would say you were lying. Dragons have been gone from this world so long that they are nothing more than myths. I, for one, have never even seen any evidence that they existed at all."

He paused and turned to Jazer. "*Do* you have a dragon?"

Her eager expression turned just a touch dark. It was the same expression Dagan used to wear before drawing blood. Davorin hated that expression. "No. But I have something even more rare."

Davorin shook his head. He took the goblet of pure spring

water another slave brought and sipped it while Jazer stood and sauntered to the edge of the balcony.

"Welcome to my tournament!" she cried, spreading her arms wide to the arena. "It has been too long since I called for a tournament. And now, we have warriors from all over the continent, come to fight and prove who amongst them is the best. There will be no killing, for what would be the point in senseless death of valuable commodities? But I can guarantee you bloodshed! And I can guarantee you something that you will never, ever, see again!"

Jazer pointed to the gate where the warrior slaves were filtering into the arena. The last to appear had Davorin sucking in a desperate breath, his heart pounding in his ears.

"I give you, my warriors and their Angel!"

"Impossible," Davorin breathed. He rose from his chair for a closer look at the woman wearing leather armour, her skin pale, unblemished, her black hair and wings like night. She could not possibly be real. *Had Jazer had a slave slip something into his drink?* Davorin cast his eyes at Jazer, desperately seeking for truth.

The Slave Master bared her teeth in a semblance of a smile, her eyes blazing with pride.

"It is true," Jazer said. "No trickery. And the best part? She is a fallen angel. She cannot fly."

Davorin did not care about that, did not care about what her existence meant to the religions of the various peoples. He only knew that she was an impossibility. This world was without magic. All thoughts of it being real were lost to the mists of time. Yet standing before him stood this precious commodity. He turned to the leering Jazer and managed, somehow, to hide the desperation in his voice. "I will have her."

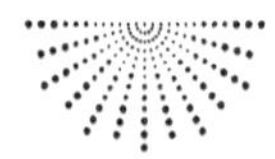

CHAPTER EIGHT

The morning of the tournament dawned as red and as bright as any other day. The light turned white and the heat rose quickly as the sun reached its zenith, but Ravenna did not see it. She was in the slave quarters in the Pits, drinking a dark, hot beverage the slaves seemed fond of. It was too bitter for her tastes and nothing like the calming tea she had enjoyed back in Shinalea, but it woke her up.

"Here," Radim dropped a pile of leathers on the table in front of Ravenna. She looked up in surprise. He gave her a slight smile, likely all the apology Ravenna would ever receive from him. Or that she would allow. "They're fighting leathers. I had the armour masters modify them to fit your wings."

Ravenna frowned. That was something she had not considered. Until then, all she had worn when training were her linen tunics and breeches, the backs cut out of the tunics to accommodate her wings. It had not been terribly secure, but it was all these humans seemed to be able to manage. Tentatively, Ravenna held up the leathers.

The torso was stiffened and probably made for a male rather than a female, but it would provide a decent amount of protection from her opponents' blades. The back had two large slits on either side of a panel that laced together, which would provide protection for the spot of bare skin between her wings and along her spine. Ravenna tested it and noted that it had been stiffened with a piece of metal. Obviously Radim had thought a good deal about this.

"Thank you," she said. Ravenna unfastened the back panel and slipped the leather over her tunic, folding her wings through the slits in the back. Radim cinched up the laces on the panel and stepped away.

"Does it fit? I had to guess about your measurements," he said.

Ravenna stretched and twisted, extending and retracting her wings.

"It fits," she said. It was stiff and would take a bit more use to move comfortably in, but it would work.

Radim nodded and handed over the leather pads for her thighs and shins, which strapped directly over her breeches and reached the tops of her boots. When Ravenna was done, she felt more than ever like a human warrior. She did not belong in this world.

"Ravenna," Tekko said, stepping up behind Radim and examining the leather armour. Both slaves also wore the leathers, though theirs were worn with scratches and cuts from many battles. "Here."

Tekko handed her a shining blade, bronze and shaped like a leaf. It was finer than the practise swords they had used and felt lighter in her hands. The edge was razor sharp and would split one of Ravenna's feathers easily. She tightened her grip on the hilt, nodding her head in thanks.

"Be aware, Ravenna," Tekko said, his voice more serious than she had ever heard it. "You have natural talent and a good deal of ability, given your experience with your Dalketh. But you have only just begun using it for fighting. You know enough to be dangerous, but those you will be facing know enough to be deadly."

Ravenna said nothing, keeping her expression as emotionless as she could manage.

Tekko exchanged a look with Radim.

"Keep that ice in your eyes and your opponents won't know what to do with you." Radim tried to joke, even tried to smile. Ravenna just kept silent. Radim sighed. "Look, I know that you hate us. But we really are on your side. Us slaves have to stick together. We have no one else but ourselves and each other."

Ravenna let out a slow breath, nodding. "I know," she murmured. Her fingers gripped the leather-wrapped handle of her blade. That and the leather armour she wore were all the comfort she had.

One of the message runner slaves dashed into the nearly-empty eating hall. "It's time," he panted before dashing off to go find any stragglers.

Radim's shoulders stiffened as he led the way out of the cave with a grim expression. Then they met up with the other slaves fighting in the tournament as well. Apparently, they were all to parade around the arena before the fights began. At least they would be able to see their opponents, the slaves that other Masters had brought to fight against Jazer's warriors.

Ravenna turned to face the grating that led into the arena of the Pits. There was a grid of light and shadow on the dusty floor where the sun shone into the passageway. It made Ravenna's stomach curl.

Tekko placed a gentle hand on Ravenna's shoulder, speaking in hushed tones. "Jazer won't let them kill you. You're too valuable. But that doesn't mean you won't get hurt. Please, Ravenna, be careful."

She fought back the bile that rose in her throat and nodded. "You be careful, too," she breathed. Ravenna thought she hated Radim and Tekko, the only slaves who had bothered to spend time with her, to talk with her. They were just another horrible example of the human species. But now they seemed to actually care about her. To actually be concerned with her decisions and well-being. And that was even before they knew she was not there by choice. Ravenna swallowed her doubt and took the first of three calming breaths.

The grate began to rumble upward on old chains and the cheering of the people in the stands grew louder. Jazer's voice sounded over the yelling, but Ravenna hardly noticed it. Her nerves were finally taking over, telling her to run. She took the second of three breaths, trying to remember the powerful feeling that came from using her Dalketh to fight and win against Radim or at least hold her own against Tekko. She might not be all that capable with a blade, but she was not weak. She had abilities that these humans would never have seen. She had wings.

The slaves stepped out of the passage and into the sunlight, slight puffs of dust coming up with each of their footsteps. The roaring of the crowd grew impossibly louder. Ravenna fell in line behind Radim and even returned his hesitant smile. She took her last calming breath and settled an icy expression on her face.

It was time to fight.

THE WARRIOR RAVENNA faced had reportedly come many days' journey just to fight the supposed Angel. She was tall, towering at almost the same height as Tekko and was almost as wide. Her body, though, did not have the same muscle tone that Tekko had.

Ravenna had not ever heard of a tournament before a few weeks ago. She had thought it to be a pitched battle with the slaves that Jazer owned fighting together against the slaves of her competitors. Instead, they paired individuals to fight against one another, or pairs to fight against beasts that had been starved and beaten. Ravenna's fight was the final fight of the first day and the crowd was as hungry as ever for blood.

The warrior female swung her weapon in her hand and leered at Ravenna. She carried a stick with spikes at the end, something Tekko said was called a mace. All Ravenna knew was that the spikes were dangerous and the female carrying them swung wildly to try and put enough power into the blow to do serious damage.

"Why don't you give up now, eh, Angel?" the warrior taunted, showing cracked teeth.

Ravenna kept silent, holding her sword up, her wings halfway unfurled for balance.

"You're too pretty to ruin in the arena."

Was Ravenna supposed to answer? Was that part of human fighting? Tekko had not ever said anything to her beyond mentioning the things she needed to fix. Radim had been more interested in actually beating her than talking. Ravenna kept silent and watched the warrior advance.

"Or is it that you don't want to draw blood?" This came with a snort and another swing of the mace. Ravenna waited. "A pretty little bird like you, too innocent to hurt someone? Is that it?"

The warrior came close enough to do some damage with the mace. It swung through the air, aiming for the space where Ravenna stood. Ravenna lunged to the side, folding her right wing in front of her and spreading it open, knocking the female off balance and shattering the grip on her weapon. The mace clattered to the ground.

The crowd of humans let out an audible gasp and cheered. Ravenna drew her brows together, trying to ignore the sound. It was just so *distracting*. In the moments that Ravenna had tried to gather her concentration, the warrior had picked up her mace and was charging forwards. She swung the weapon too fast for Ravenna to see. Ravenna winced and jumped away as the spiked head ran through the feathers on her left wing.

One of the primaries bent out of shape, sending a slight twinge of pain through Ravenna. But that was hardly important. What was important was that this warrior had come too close to injuring Ravenna's wing beyond repair. In that moment, she understood that her wings were not just weapons and tools. They were vulnerable. All her years running through the forests and practicing her falling, Ravenna had not even *considered* that her wings would be anything but powerful. They had never been anything more than bruised before. And Kratos was well-versed in healing wing injuries the sylphs acquired. But here? amongst these blood-mongering vicious beings? Her wings could be torn to shreds.

Ravenna had been stupid in allowing this female to get that close. All the desperation she had felt the night before, all the pain and agony at the mockery that was her life, that all faded and was replaced by something Ravenna had only tasted in small doses. Anger. Not the terrified hatred that she felt when thinking about humans like Jazer and the slavers that had taken her from Shinalea. Not the heady feeling of power when she fought back against Radim and Tekko. No, this was vein-burning, wing-flaring, fire-making anger.

Ravenna let out a snarl and pushed her wings downward in a motion known as Falcon Goes to Dive. The dusty air in the bottom of the arena surged around her, filling the space where she had been. Ravenna got close enough to see the ring of light brown around the female's pupils before she began striking.

Her sword lay forgotten in the sand behind her. The warrior dropped her mace to defend against Ravenna's hands, legs, and wings. Ravenna fought with every ounce of fire burning through her. She was furious that this woman had gotten close enough to do damage. She was furious that she had even been put in this position. She wanted to curl her fingers into a fist and pound something. So she did.

The woman did not suffer long from shock. She might not have had her mace any longer, but as Tekko had said, she was part of a breed of slave that had been trained enough to be deadly. She blocked some of Ravenna's strikes and hit back with her own. One fist to Ravenna's stomach pushed her back enough, allowing the female time to reach for her mace. Ravenna sucked in a desperate breath and surged forwards once more, not letting the female pick up the weapon.

It went like that for what felt like an eternity. Ravenna would punch the female across the jaw and then receive a strike to the centre of her chest. She would fall back only to lunge forwards again or buffet the warrior with her wings. They moved farther and farther away from the forgotten weapons and closer and closer to the walls of the arena. The female's mouth was set in a permanent snarl.

She caught Ravenna across the cheek with a powerful blow, snapping Ravenna's head back. This time, when Ravenna stumbled back, she stayed back for a few moments. Her carefully controlled breathing that Dalketh demanded was long forgotten in favour of sucking in desperate mouthfuls of air. To her satisfaction, though, her opponent was doing the same.

The massive female snarled at Ravenna and cast her eyes about for her weapon. "So you're not completely worthless, then," she taunted, trying to get around Ravenna and find something useful to fight with. Even Ravenna could see that this fight was not going to be won by hands alone. Ravenna was smaller, but she was faster, and she was not weak. This female was bigger, but her muscle was not nearly as impressive as Tekko. And she did not have the fury that Ravenna had. "Which begs the question, then, *Angel*. Why are you here fighting in the dirt with scum like us?"

It was the same question that Radim had asked but without

the air of concern behind it. This was a taunt, so much like the ones that Ravenna had endured her entire life. Why are you walking, flightless worm? Why do you run up to the Aerial City? Why don't you just use your wings? Pale. Flightless. Worthless. A burden.

Now it was slave. Angel. Some sort of divine being that was kept around to gawk at or to take pride in owning.

Ravenna had borne enough.

Her icy-blue eyes sharpened, and her guarded expression cracked. Her brows lowered, her lip curled, and she glared at the female with venom. The warrior faltered, taking a step back towards the arena wall.

Ravenna flared her wings as wide as they would go, took a step, and leapt into the air. She would not be able to fly, but the downstroke of her wings had her surging upward, towards the wall of the arena. She twisted midair, one wing parallel to the wall, the other to the ground. Her feet slammed onto the rock, and then she was turning, falling through the air. Only, Ravenna had fallen before and knew exactly what she was doing.

Her feet slammed into the stunned female's chest with enough force to drive her backward and into the ground. The warrior let out a gasp and fell to the dust and rock. Her head slammed once, bounced, and lay still against the ground. Ravenna did not wait for her opponent to recover. She put her boot on the female's throat and hissed into the dazed eyes that looked back at her.

"I fight for *me*," Ravenna said.

The female blinked acknowledgement and lay her head back on the ground. Defeated.

"ANGEL! ANGEL! ANGEL!" The cry sounded over and over again, startling Ravenna out of her anger. She pulled her wings in tight and twisted, turning to look at the humans staring down at her with eager, desperate expressions, yelling at the top of their lungs. The sound was suddenly deafening.

Ravenna tried to hold on to the feeling of power and self-assurance that the fight had brought her, but it was slipping away to something else: nerves and a touch of bile in her throat.

No, she thought. Enough was enough. She had not done anything wrong. She had not killed her opponent. She had not done something shameful. She had used her wings and her own power to bring down an opponent who was facing her in a fair fight. They hadn't had any choice in the matter, either. Ravenna was *not* going to be ashamed of something she could not control. She could not control her black feathers or hair. She could not control her skin colour or the ice of her eyes. She could not control her inability to fly. She could control how she behaved. How she fought. And she had fought well.

Ravenna turned to Jazer's balcony, an unfamiliar dignitary beside her. Ravenna twisted her face into a mask of anger and disgust. She flared her wings wide, heard the cheering of the crowd, and pointed at Jazer. Ravenna fought for herself, not Jazer. Not for a human parasite who sucked the life out of everyone around her for her own benefit. Ravenna would not let Jazer or any other human or sylph drain her ever again. She pointed that finger at Jazer in a promise.

And she did not miss the way Jazer's grin faded as she did so, either.

CHAPTER NINE

"You think I would just give up my greatest prize?" Jazer sneered. She lay back on that ridiculous low couch, forcing Davorin to glower down at her or sit on the floor. He chose to stand. "I paid quite a princely sum to acquire her, after all. And I spent more getting her up to fighting weight and taking my greatest warriors away from the arena to help train her for three weeks."

"I will pay more," Davorin snapped. He was going to have that Angel. He did not much care how it came about. Jazer did not quite realise that, yet. If she had, she would be cowering on that couch, not preening like a cat.

"She is my greatest asset! Do you know how many people will come to see the Angel fight? Or priests from a hundred religions on pilgrimages to see this 'divine being' and gain her blessing? She is something that hasn't been seen in these lands for a hundred generations and you just want me to *give her up?*"

Davorin let out a slow breath through his nose. He tightened his grip on the hilt of his sword, wondering how bad it would be if he just drew it and killed Jazer right then. Given the number of loyal people she had surrounding her, he imagined it would be quite bad. Or someone would have killed the old bat years ago. "I will give you seven hundred weight of gold for her," Davorin said at last.

He saw the gleam in Jazer's eyes, the touch of greed that would be her undoing. But Jazer's greed had gotten her this far, so she was obviously smart, too. Well, he would just have to override her greed and outsmart her.

"You think I would take such a small sum for something so valuable? I made nearly two hundred weight on her just today, and it was only the first day of the tournament!"

Davorin let out a rumbling growl and glared openly at the Slave Master. "Nine hundred weight."

Jazer tilted her head back and twisted the rings on her fingers so they caught the light. Coupled with the bubbling of the spring, it was probably supposed to make some kind of statement about opulence or power or whatever. Mostly, it just made Davorin's blood boil.

"I'll think about it," Jazer said with a dramatic sigh. She sat up and faced Davorin, holding her bejewelled hands in her lap like some sort of prim child. He curled his lip. "Why don't you go and enjoy yourself in the pleasure hall? I'm sure I'll have an answer for you by the time the sun sets."

He wanted to stab her with his sword and have done. No one dismissed a Prince of the Salusian Empire so callously! Especially not that he was now Firstborn Son, after Dagan's death. The thought of his father's anger threw cold water over Davorin's own anger. He needed to think of the bigger picture here, not just one upstart woman in the desert who thought she had power. With all his courtly charms, Davorin inclined slightly at the waist. "Then I'll return at sunset."

He turned and strode out of the hardened mud building, grimacing at the light as it pierced his eyes. The town buzzed with conversations about the day's tournament, most of those conversations centring on the Angel. How she had seemed so small against the challenger but had prevailed anyway. How she had abandoned her sword for a more personal defeat. Where Jazer could have possibly found an Angel to fight for her. The awe at such an acquisition. The wonder at her existence. Even a few prayers to her for mercy or hope or love.

Davorin snarled and turned away from the people, stalking towards the pleasure hall Jazer had mentioned. If nothing else, it would be good to drink something other than spring water. Davorin did not acknowledge the fact that the words spoken were exactly the thoughts that had run through his mind. He would have the Angel, no matter the cost. She would be essential to his plans. Already he had started ruminating on how to use her best to his advantage. He didn't care about anything beyond that.

"Wine," Davorin demanded at the carved stone bar. The pleasure hall was sunken into the ground to take advantage of the coolness the earth provided. The dark, almost cavernous space was lit by tiny flames on tapered candles, making it difficult to see anything clearly. It was a place that fairly reeked of debauchery. It reminded Davorin of his brother's war tent.

The barkeep handed Davorin a flagon of sour wine and he drank it eagerly, not even wincing at the acrid taste. He placed another coin down and gestured to his empty flagon. "Another."

The barkeep didn't bat an eye, just filled the flagon and moved along to the next customer. Davorin nursed the second drink, not wanting to lose his senses entirely. He had to think clearly, and while he had craved the relaxation that the alcohol brought, his planning was more important.

At least until, "Well, well, who would have ever thought the new Firstborn Son would be slumming it all the way out here in No Man's Land?"

Davorin turned to the slightly familiar voice. He frowned when he spotted the stocky, sharp woman standing before him, her hair cropped close and her eyes betraying a sort of cunning that he had seen in his own eyes. Twin scars adorned her cheeks. Davorin blinked, then remembered. "Captain Nadezhda. The Ruthless Plague that led my brother's armies at his side. I thought you dead."

Nadezhda showed her teeth like a desert wolf. "I wasn't stupid enough to get caught up in the chaos that Dagan's death brought."

Davorin inclined his flagon of wine in her direction, a salute. Not many of Dagan's close advisors had been as smart. And as a result of their leader's murder—still believed to have perpetrated by the naked woman with her throat slit who was found alongside him in his bed—they had been executed. It had not been a slow death, either.

Nadezhda did not wait to ask for Davorin's permission; she sat on the stool next to him and was immediately poured a tankard of some thick ale. "Frankly, I'm surprised you even remembered my name. Dagan wasn't keen on sharing."

"Dagan wasn't keen on many things," Davorin retorted. He took a slow sip of the wine. "But I made it a point to keep apprised of all my brother's doings. How else was I supposed to smooth his doings over with the nobles of my father's court?"

The Captain snorted a laugh. "No wonder we were able to get away with being gone so much. Dagan was convinced that his conquering for the Empire was the reason. Who wouldn't want a conquering leader, ready to dive into battle at the slightest provocation? It showed power, he said."

She was trying to goad him, Davorin knew. He was no idiot. This was the woman who had served at Dagan's side for nearly ten years. She was as ruthless as his dead brother and no fool, either, to have survived this long. "I recall that you weren't particularly upset with the actions Dagan took."

Nadezhda awarded Davorin with a genuine smile, tilting her head in his direction. The dim light of the pleasure hall flashed on the scars marring her cheeks. "You never were as useless as Dagan made you out to be."

"Not everyone thinks as much," Davorin admitted before he could stop the words from spilling out. He frowned down at the wine, wondering just how potent the drink had to be to get him to admit that to someone who had, for all intents and purposes, rivalled him for so long. He covered his slip with the dashing grin that had gotten him so far in court. "Why else would I be out here, enjoying the things that this desert oasis has to offer?"

The woman next to him set her mouth in a thin line, her eyes probing. She did not say anything for a bit, instead taking a long, desperate drink of her ale. After she swallowed and licked the foam from her lips, she turned to Davorin, her eyes pained. "Do you know what it's like to be an exile from the Empire? Except I'm not even truly exiled, I'm just presumed dead. And if I ever show my face back there again, I'll be killed."

"Slowly," Davorin agreed with a nod.

Nadezhda snarled, "My entire *life* was the Empire. Without that, I have nothing! No money, no home, no reputation. Some reward for loyalty."

"So, what, you're just going to sit here and complain to me?" Davorin asked with a bite in his tone. "After Dagan died, I asked to be given control of his armies and the resources of the Empire. I invoked the ancient words."

"Obviously, that went well," Nadezhda sneered.

Davorin resisted the impulse to throw his wine in her face. She understood his plight; there was no need to be rude. Even if the woman did drive him completely crazy.

"My father told me to go back to my estates and live my life. I have money. I have the title. But am I good enough to be the Firstborn Son? Apparently not." Davorin slammed his flagon down on the stone bar, enough to draw the wary glance of the barkeep. Davorin put a coin out in apology and the wine was mopped up without comment. He took a deep breath, glancing around to check that no one was listening and to gather his senses. He had done well thus far without calling attention to his title, but the anger coiled in his chest could easily ruin that. Shouting about the Empire in this unclaimed land was a dangerous prospect. You did not know whether the people would hate you or bow at your name. If he had to pull rank with Jazer and her cronies, he would. But not until the time was right.

"All I want is to get back into the Empire," Nadezhda admitted, her tone too contrite and sad for Davorin's tastes. This woman was ruthless, not sad. It didn't fit her at all. "I want my life back."

"And I want to win back the Empire and restore it to the glory of its golden days," Davorin said. "I'm doing something about my ambitions. What are you doing?"

"Slavers were the only ones who would take me on without any questions. Even the brothels turned me away," Nadezhda grinned. Davorin allowed himself a chuckle at the weak joke. The former Captain turned her attention to the bottom of her drink. "I caught me an Angel, you know. Best thing to happen to me, and I threw it away to that idiot Jazer for some money. Not even hardly enough to buy my way back in. Maybe I'll get work as a merc or guard or something."

"You would give up your rank just to get back into the Empire?" Davorin was surprised. She had not struck him as the sort to be willing to give up anything to do with power. She had climbed the ranks eagerly, perhaps too eagerly. After all, Dagan had trusted her for a reason.

Nadezhda shrugged. "Time was I thought leading the armies at Dagan's side was the only thing I would ever want. Then, I lost everything. I'd settle for going back home."

"Why settle?" Again, the words were out of his mouth before he could stop them. This time, though he had a feeling he would not regret them. The idea was in his head and, just like he knew that he would have that Angel, he knew this would work in his favour. She was familiar with his needs, the needs of leading an army. She had fought at Dagan's side and was one of the pieces that kept that massive army together. She was also desperate.

"Things aren't that easy," Nadezhda scowled. "Do you honestly think that I would be here in this slavers den if I had somewhere else to go? I've tried everything. For months after Dagan died, I tried to get some semblance of my life back. I even went to Southron, thinking maybe I could join the warbands there. I got turned away without a second thought."

"Then they're fools," Davorin said decidedly. He turned in his chair to face Nadezhda fully, taking her in. She would never be beautiful. She was too tall and powerfully built for that. She had further exacerbated the issue by cropping her hair close to her skull and revealing her scars proudly. She had the look of a brute, but the mind of a loyal leader. "Come lead my armies."

"What?" Nadezhda spit out her ale. The barkeep glared at her, but she glared back and won the battle. She turned to Davorin, wary. "You said it yourself, you don't lead the armies of the Empire. Your father refused."

"I never said anything about the Empire," Davorin said. "I'm out here for a reason."

"And what, exactly, would that reason be?"

"I'm going to prove my father wrong. I'm going to prove them all wrong," Davorin said with relish. The thought of his father supplicating him, apologising to him, it was a heady feeling. It filled his every thought and sent surges of desire through his veins. Davorin shook his head of the thought, pushing it to the side. Right now, he had to deal with Nadezhda. Then Jazer. "I'm going to continue Dagan's work, but I will succeed where my brother failed."

"He expanded the Empire's boundaries to cover nearly the whole centre of the continent, excluding the desert and the mountains," Nadezhda scoffed. "I always knew you thought highly of yourself, but this is ridiculous."

"I am not the brute that Dagan was. I do not need to win territory by bloodshed alone. Being part of the Empire means something. It will be worthless if the people rise up once they decide that there have been enough of them killed. Not to mention Dagan nearly emptied our coffers, despite raising taxes to support his efforts. He was a wastrel and a brute."

"So, what, you're going to take the desert? The Red Queen stands in your way. And the mountains? They have chewed up and spit out anyone who has tried to even get close. People don't go to the mountains and survive," Nadezhda pointed out. "Why bother conquering them at all?"

"Because no one has done it," Davorin replied. "My reasoning shouldn't matter to you at all. I am offering you a chance to have everything you had before and more. You could go back to the Empire. Not as an exile. As a hero."

Nadezhda took a deep breath then let it out slowly. She finished off the last of her ale and turned to look at Davorin, obviously still wary. "Okay," she said.

Davorin nodded but held back his victorious smile.

"Good," Davorin said, finishing his wine. "Now you can come help me convince Jazer to part with that Angel. I think the threat of arming her slaves ought to persuade her nicely."

CHAPTER TEN

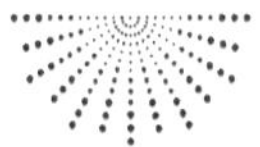

Ravenna did not get to join in the celebratory feast that the warrior slaves were granted after the first day of the tournament. She had barely had her cuts seen by the healer assigned to the Pits when Jazer marched towards her, fire in her eyes.

"You," Jazer snarled, jabbing a finger at Ravenna's chest. Ravenna kept still, though her expression hardened. She considered toppling the Slave Master back, buffeting her with her wings like she had done in the arena. Jazer would look very amusing flailing on the ground. But the consequences would be dire. Ravenna kept perfectly still.

"You're coming with me." Jazer spun on her heel and strode out of the healer's chambers. Ravenna followed, keeping her wings relaxed in case of quick action. She passed by the dining hall where the other slaves were gathering to their feast, spirits higher than normal. Ravenna spotted Tekko and Radim talking together. Radim lifted his eyes just as Jazer passed with Ravenna behind her. She waved, offering a weak smile. He flattened his mouth into a thin line and looked away. Tekko held her stare, nodding his head firmly at her.

Ravenna did not understand.

What could she have possibly done that was so bad Jazer had come to fetch Ravenna herself? Surely, the Slave Master was pleased with how the fight in the arena went, despite Ravenna's silent promise. Ravenna had won. The Angel had won. That must have counted for something.

Jazer was panting with exertion from climbing the stairs out of the Pits. Ravenna doubted that Jazer ever actually came down to the Pits if she could help it. She seemed the type instead to lord over the slaves from above. So why was the Slave Master fetching Ravenna personally?

Ravenna followed the woman into the desert air, the sun gone but the heat remaining. The activity of the oasis had dwindled, though there were still noises from the pleasure hall. All those people come all this way for the tournament. Their escapades would make Jazer a small fortune, Ravenna imagined.

"Here. I brought her," Jazer hissed, stopping in her tracks. Two figures stepped closer, emerging from the shadows cast by the desert at night. Ravenna took a step back at the sight of the smaller figure—the female who had brought her to this horrid place. The Captain. She had not captured Ravenna from Shinalea, but she had led the group of slavers that brought her to Jazer.

Run. The voice whispered inside Ravenna's head. She was tempted to follow it. There were no chains around her feet or hands. She could easily be out of this place with a few swift steps of her feet and the training she had given herself and been given from Radim and Tekko. Then what? Ravenna would hit open desert and, while she could navigate, she would likely be dead before she even reached the sea.

Ravenna braced herself, spreading her wings aggressively, but she did not run. The female grinned toothily at Jazer. The other person, male, taller and more fit than the Captain, watched Ravenna with open interest. His expression was stone silent, except for the cunning in his eyes. He wore leather armour, obviously of better make than what Ravenna had been provided in the arena. And at his hips were two swords. His right hand rested on the hilt of one, caressing it like a pet.

"So you have," he finally spoke in reply to Jazer's declaration. His voice sent shivers down Ravenna's back, and not in a good way. There was power in that musical voice. Power and ambition. He took a step towards Ravenna and she lowered her stance, ready to fight. Was this some sort of private fight that Jazer had organized? Why wasn't she in the arena?

"Don't be ridiculous," Jazer snapped at Ravenna. The large woman looked like she wanted to cuff Ravenna about the ears, but the sylph was too far away and had her wings to defend herself. "This is your new master, Angel."

Ravenna flicked her eyes to the male. The world seemed to close in around her, making it difficult to breathe. She had just gotten used to being here, in this place that the other slaves called Hell. She had just decided that she would fight for herself rather than for someone else. She had, dare she say it, friends. And now, in the blink of an eye, that was all gone. Ravenna understood in that moment what slavery really was. It was not merely working until your bones were raw or doing tasks that you would never want for yourself. It was not just being nothing more than dirt beneath people's feet. It was being nothing more than a thing to pass between people. A voiceless possession. It was a loss of self, until nothing more than a monetary value remained. Her sense of herself would be slowly stripped away. Then what would be left?

With a flick of her head, Jazer stalked off, leaving Ravenna to her fate. She had not wanted the Slave Master to care, but any acknowledgement would be better than none. Ravenna had not even been able to say goodbye to Radim and Tekko. Was her life going to become a mockery of the travesty it was now?

"I am Davorin." The male sketched a bow, which looked

decidedly less grand when there were no wings to fold and flare. "Firstborn Son of the Salusian Empire."

Ravenna said nothing.

The Captain barked out a laugh, "That won't mean anything to her!"

Davorin straightened, frowning at the Captain. He sighed through his nose and looked back towards Ravenna, who had not moved from her fighting crouch. "I have no intention of fighting you, Angel. If you would please come with Captain Nadezhda and myself, I can offer you a bath and warm food."

Ravenna did not move.

Davorin took another step forwards, holding his hands up, palms facing her. "I give you my word that you won't be fighting in the arena ever again."

"So, what," Ravenna spat, "I'm to be some bedwarmer?"

The words came unbidden, the memory of a kind old female following them. Ravenna wanted to kill all the slavers for what they had done and the lives they had destroyed, including hers. And these humans, for buying and selling her like some trinket.

Davorin shook his head, chuckling. "You are far too magnificent for such things. I have other plans for you, ones which you will find far more pleasant, I can assure you."

Ravenna wanted to flee far from the way his words tensed her muscles. He might be assured, but she was not. Whatever this parasite, this horrible creature, had in store for her, Ravenna doubted that she would much like it. But the time to run had passed. She would never make it, now, not with the Captain's eyes following her and this self-assured male and his plans for her. Ravenna closed her eyes for a moment, forcing herself to accept this new life, pushing the bile down once more. She felt like a child again, being forced to accept the things the other sylphs threw her way. Words. Shoves. Buffets from wings.

"What is your name?" Davorin asked as Ravenna slid out of her fighting crouch. Her wings pressed close to her sides, the feathers compressing. She looked at Davorin with as much anger as she could muster, which flowed cold as ice through her veins. "I cannot surely keep calling you Angel, though you may be one."

"I am not an angel," Ravenna spat. The Captain and her keeper exchanged a confused look. "I am a sylph."

"Ah," Davorin said, drawing his brows together. "I apologise. Your kind has been absent from this land for so long that the proper term for you has been forgotten. But that does not answer my question. What is your name?"

Ravenna shuffled her wings. "I am Ravenna."

Davorin bowed again, this time with less drama and more satisfaction in his expression. "It is a pleasure to meet you, Ravenna. Now, if you do not mind, it is a bit of a walk to where my people are camped. I imagine you are hungry and wanting to bathe after the trials of your day."

Physical discomfort was nothing compared to her desire to be as far from Davorin and the Captain as possible. But Ravenna just gave a defeated nod and walked between the two as they left the centre of the oasis behind. Hell it may have been, but Ravenna felt a pang leaving it behind. She hoped Radim and Tekko would be alright. That was all she had to offer: her wishes. She hoped it would be enough.

The encampment looked like a city of tents to Ravenna. She almost thought that she had come to a place like the Aerial City, except the people lived on the ground and took their belongings with them. For the first time in ages, Ravenna felt pure curiosity. She had not ever seen a human city, considering that the oasis was built around a Slave Market and the Pits. Maybe these people would be different from those in the Pits. Maybe they wouldn't make Ravenna want to drag a blade she did not have through their skin.

Her stomach dropped as they walked into the encampment. The people sitting around the cooking fires or outside their tents were males and females, as one would expect. But they all had a hard, eager look about them. And the ones without weapons looked the most dangerous.

This wasn't a moving city of people, Ravenna realised. This was an army. A word that hadn't been whispered amongst the sylphs for generations. She only knew what she was looking at because she had studied the tomes that even Tacitus did not want to bother with and because of her time with the humans. Ravenna had read about the Fire Wars and the military strategies of an ancient time. She remembered the word. It meant death followed in its wake.

"You will sleep here." Davorin halted beside a small tent situated next to a much larger one. The sides of the smaller tent were almost opaque while the larger had heavy sides and guards around it. Davorin held open the flap to the small tent, barely large enough for the bedroll and basin that were already there. "Nadezhda will escort you to the warm pools where you can bathe. She will bring you food in your tent afterward."

Davorin turned on his heel and strode away, leaving Ravenna with the slaver.

"Come on," the Captain said, her eyes gleaming just a little too much for Ravenna's taste. "Let's get you cleaned up."

The female, Nadezhda, grabbed Ravenna's wrist and practically dragged her to the edge of the encampment where a pool steamed quietly, a remnant of the springs that ran underneath the oasis. The Captain demanded that Ravenna strip and bathe, which she did because the alternative was worse. Ravenna had seen how the Captain treated other slaves on that long journey through the desert. They were beaten or whipped or starved if they did not do as Nadezhda asked. Never too badly, because they were to be sold after all, but badly enough to break their spirits. Like the old female who had told Ravenna stories she could barely understand.

Ravenna stepped into the pool and shivered as the water

worked its way through the dust on her skin. The few cuts and bruises she had earned in the Pits that day stung, the pain waking Ravenna further. She scrubbed with the pitiful handful of soap that Nadezhda gave and then started out.

"Oh, no. You have to clean those pretty wings of yours," the Captain sneered at Ravenna from the edge of the spring. "Soap them up."

"You don't soap your wings," Ravenna snapped in return, perhaps too far into her anger to care about the result. There was also the matter that Davorin was her master, not this horrible female.

"Then how could they possibly get clean?" Nadezhda did not wait for an answer. She jumped into the water up to her hips and lunged at Ravenna. With a strong, callous hand, Nadezhda snatched one of Ravenna's wings. She squeezed hard enough to twist feathers out of place and send darts of pain shooting up Ravenna's back. Ravenna screamed in fury, pulling the appendage back. Nadezhda held on too tight, keeping Ravenna from escape.

"Stop fighting!" the female snarled, tightening her grip on Ravenna's wings. The feathers were getting twisted and Ravenna feared that they would be pulled from her wing, tearing the thin ligaments that kept them in place. Just like in the arena, Ravenna was struck with the fact that her wings were as vulnerable as they were powerful. And she hated feeling vulnerable.

Ravenna let out another angry scream and wrenched her wing free of the slaver's grasp. She did not waste any time, pushing through the water to climb out into the desert.

Nadezhda was close behind, unsettling madness twisting her features. The larger female surged towards Ravenna.

She skipped back and crouched, ready to fight.

Nadezhda obliged.

The Captain had obviously trained a good deal more than

the woman Ravenna had fought earlier in the Pits. The strikes were more precise, less worried about sheer strength as she was with being exact. And she was much faster. Ravenna, though, was using Dalketh, a style that had not been seen by humans for who knows how long, if ever. She also had her wings. And, perhaps more important than all of them, Ravenna's fury burned louder and deeper than Nadezhda's.

Nadezhda managed to get a kick to Ravenna's thigh, but that forced her to get close enough for Ravenna to beat her over the head with her wings. The sylph surged forwards as Nadezhda recovered from the distraction. Ravenna pushed her hands out, palms open, with a concentrated hiss. They struck Nadezhda in the chest, hitting the breastbone. The human female gasped for breath and staggered back. She was not down, by any means, but she was unable to fight back for a few precious heartbeats. Ravenna folded her wings in front of her naked body and then popped them open with all the strength in her body.

Nadezhda caught the full force of the blow and fell backwards, landing in the dirt. She sucked in a deep breath and scrambled upward, ready to attack again.

"That is enough," Davorin's voice cut through the air like a whip.

Ravenna spun, spreading her wings in defence, not even caring that her body was on display for Davorin and what looked like a good number of people in the camp. Ravenna lifted her chin.

Nadezhda climbed to her feet and tried to brush off the desert dust and sand. It clung to her wet clothes and shoes, turning to mud. "That bit—"

"I said that is enough!" Davorin said, voice sharper than before. He stared down Nadezhda until she lowered her gaze and bowed her head. Davorin took a step towards Ravenna. "I see that Jazer allowed you to be taught more than you should."

"I was trained by other slaves for the arena," Ravenna said, keeping her chin up, her expression haughty. "Obviously, they knew more than your Captain."

Nadezhda growled, stepping towards Ravenna's outstretched wings. Davorin held up a hand and Nadezhda stopped. "Will someone tell me how this began?"

"The stupid chit wouldn't wash her wings," Nadezhda spat.

Ravenna's spine straightened.

"You don't wash wings with soap," she hissed. As soon as she said the words, something changed in Davorin's calm expression. His jaw hardened and his eyes flashed.

Davorin took in a slow breath and let it out before speaking, as though he were chiding a child. "Just because I have indulged you this far does not mean that you can disregard my wishes, Ravenna."

Ravenna swallowed, her mouth suddenly dry. She had made an error, thinking that Davorin's reluctance to fight her or make her a bedwarmer stemmed from a dislike of violence where she was concerned. The assured power in his stance and his voice should have told her that, but Ravenna had slipped. She was not arguing with Crispinus or Desarra. She was facing far worse than being tripped down the stairs. Jazer had been openly cruel and power-hungry. Davorin was much, much more subtle.

"Captain," Davorin said, waving casually to Nadezhda. The female strode forwards, leering at Ravenna. "Bring Ravenna to my tent. And have Warrith send two of his most discreet soldiers to me as well."

"Yes, my liege," Nadezhda purred, bowing at the waist in a mockery of the respectful sign it should have been. The Captain straightened and grabbed Ravenna's arm, her fingers curling into claws that bruised. Ravenna folded her wings flat against her back, a flush rising in her pale skin. She felt shame at her nakedness, in the way that the soldiers looked at her, in the feel of Nadezhda's fingers wrapped around her arm. Mostly, though, Ravenna felt shame for being so foolish as to think that her weeks training in the Pits made her strong enough to take on the world.

Davorin's tent was the large one that stood next to Ravenna's. It had furs on the ground to keep the sand out. There were pieces of furniture that were far more solid than the bedroll Ravenna would have to live with. There was a strong desk and the lamps that lit the tent were crafted from the finest wrought iron. It was opulent and a foolish set of things to have to carry from encampment to encampment. Unless, Ravenna realised with a sinking stomach, it was to prove a point. Whoever Davorin was in this world of humans, he was not one to be trifled with.

Firstborn Son of the Salusian Empire, he had called himself.

She did not know what the other words signified, but she knew what Empire was. And none of the tomes had claimed it to be a good thing.

Davorin strode into the tent just as Nadezhda threw Ravenna on the ground. The sylph did not try to stand again. She just wrapped her wings around her and tried to hide the fear in her eyes. Two soldiers, both male and both looking like they had been bred for violence, stepped into the tent a few moments after Nadezhda left. Davorin walked to his desk, seemingly ignoring Ravenna.

He drew the sword that hung on his right hip, leaving its twin in its sheath. Davorin ran a tanned finger across the edge and shook his head slowly. "Hold her wings open," he ordered.

Ravenna bucked and scrambled backward, but she was no match for the soldiers. They pounced on her in an instant, pressing her flat to the furs on the ground. Ravenna struggled, trying to keep her wings flat against her back. For a moment, she succeeded, but even that, too, was for nothing. They spread her wings open as wide as they would go and to keep her from struggling, lay their torsos across them. Ravenna blinked away tears from her icy eyes.

"Just because I do not see fit to turn you into my concubine, nor do I want to put you into the arena like a mindless brute, does not mean that I do not demand perfect obedience. You may not be the divine being our religions tell us you are, but your existence alone means something. And you are mine to control," Davorin said. His voice snaked to Ravenna from behind her. She whimpered, unable to see him and know what torture he was going to inflict. Would he tear out her feathers? Cripple her wings?

"Tell me you understand," Davorin said. The tip of his blade touched Ravenna's back and she stilled. He was pressing the sword to the sliver of skin between her wings. It ran along every sylph's spine and was where some of the more delicate muscles connected to the spine. A deep cut there would take months to heal properly. Out here in the desert with no sylph healer to help the wings, it would probably not heal properly at all.

"I understand," Ravenna breathed.

"Good," Davorin said. "Then this will not be a difficult lesson."

Before Ravenna could react, he had drawn his sword down that line on her back, splitting the skin. Pain sang through her back and Ravenna barely managed to hold a scream in her throat. This was not like the brand that Jazer had put on her hip. This was sharper, more precise. Ravenna could tell by the way her wings were trembling that Davorin had not severed any muscles, but the amount of blood that flowed into her feathers and onto the furs told Ravenna that it would scar.

She whimpered again.

Davorin's mouth was next to her ear, his words dripping like oil, "One wound for your disobedience. Do not forget again, Ravenna, or I will have to take more drastic measures."

"I understand," Ravenna whispered once more. Hoping it would be enough.

"Release her," Davorin snapped. The soldiers let her wings

go and Ravenna jumped to her feet. She wrapped her wings around herself, keeping the feathers away from the blood that ran down her back. "Take her to her tent and fetch a healer. Oh, and for goodness sakes, get her some clothes."

"But her wings won't—"

Davorin turned to face the male, loathing was sharp across his features.

"Figure. It. Out."

RAVENNA FELL ASLEEP that night to the throbbing of her back and the tears on her cheeks. She wanted to go home. She would happily endure Desarra's taunts and Tacitus' disappointed sighs when she didn't concentrate hard enough. Ravenna would smile and bow through every horrible memory if only she could be home again and feel safe once more. She missed Tacitus and the kind touches that he would give when she had a bad day. And her grandmother, who brooked no nonsense and demanded Ravenna's best, all while smiling and making her feel valued.

Ravenna wanted these things more than anything. Rubbing her eyes with a tear-soaked hand, Ravenna knew that it was unlikely to ever happen. She knew that the punishment for sylphs to venture to the mainland, this den of death, was exile. She had to adapt to this new life, horrible as it was. It did not stop her from missing home.

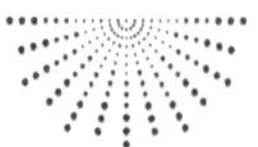

CHAPTER ELEVEN

The next day, the camp was packed up and the army set out across the desert. Ravenna was put on one of those strange beasts they called horses. She supposed she should be afraid of the animal, given how alien it was to her and how they had scared her during her first trip through the desert despite reassurances, but she could not bring herself to care.

Davorin had instructed Ravenna briefly on how to ride, and then she was hoisted into the saddle and on her way. Her wings lay behind her on the horse's rump, both to keep them out of the way of the pounding hooves and to keep the strain off her back. The cut had been seen to by a healer, but it still stung. And Davorin's satisfied expression that morning did not help.

"When we get to the Red Palace," Davorin instructed, his horse close to hers, "I expect you to be on your best behaviour. I assume you know how to behave in the presence of royalty."

Ravenna nodded.

Davorin curled his lip.

"You will speak only when spoken to. Your eyes must never meet those who are not slaves unless they ask you to look up." Davorin turned to study her again. "At least your eyes aren't black. I would have a hard time describing you as anything but an Angel of Death if that were the case."

Ironic, Ravenna thought. Her ice-blue eyes had always been a source of shame on Shinalea.

"You will be respectful. You will not talk about your time with that fool Jazer and the Pits. If you are asked how you came to be a slave, you will spout some story about how you were weak and struggling after becoming unable to fly—you are flightless, correct?—and how I offered to take you on as an indentured servant until such time as you were able to fly again. And you will not do or say anything to ruin my plans."

Ravenna nodded, tightening her grip on the reins in her hands. Hands now calloused from sword fighting. "And what are your plans?" Ravenna asked softly so none of the other soldiers could hear. She didn't know where the Captain was and hoped that Nadezhda wouldn't appear to cuff her on the head for her words.

Davorin remained silent for a few moments, the sun making it difficult for Ravenna to see his expression. "I should give you another wound for your insolence," Davorin began. Ravenna tensed, feeling the long line on her back stretch at the motion. "But you are right to ask. How can you know not to interfere if you have no idea what you're interfering with?"

Should she nod? Agree? Kick her heels into her horse's side and run headlong into the desert? The last one appealed most, but Ravenna was barely keeping herself on the horse's back as it was.

Davorin continued speaking and Ravenna did nothing. She knew the consequences, but a shiver of regret still slid down her wounded spine. Ravenna shoved the thought away. In its place, a black emptiness grew, swallowing all of her fear and shame and regret until there was only the emptiness and her anger.

"I am in the process of courting the Red Queen. Do you know of her?"

Ravenna shook her head, her mouth pressed together in a thin line.

"I thought not. She rules the desert lands from the No Man's Land where the Slave Markets are located to the base of the Iron Mountains, claiming all the oases and the riches that are buried beneath the cliffs and sand. Despite the scrubland that you see around you, these lands are extremely rich. Queen Lenore rules over the desert lands from her stronghold in the Red Palace. I intend to wed her, and in so doing, marry her lands to the Empire. You are going to help make certain that happens."

"I do not know anything of your Empire or of the Red Queen or any of your human lands," Ravenna said, her voice flat and emotionless. *Nor do I care*, she thought.

"You will learn," Davorin said. It was a command, made by one who expected his orders obeyed. Ravenna ducked her chin in acknowledgement. Davorin hummed, frowning. He was about to speak again when another horse came up to him on the other side of Ravenna. She turned and caught sight of Nadezhda. The Captain scowled. Her right eye was swollen shut and a shade of purple that Ravenna had only seen in the deadliest blooms. Apparently, hers was not the only wound received last night.

"Have you prepared your 'gift'?" Nadezhda sneered at Ravenna.

Davorin straightened in his saddle, his left hand twitching towards his sword.

"Is there something you needed, Captain?" Davorin asked cooly. Nadezhda winced and frowned at the colourless desert beneath the horse's hooves.

"Warrith says we can reach the Red Palace by midnight if we don't stop, but someone is going to have to pass out provisions for the soldiers to eat in the saddle."

"Is there a question in that statement? We continue on."

Davorin nodded firmly and the Captain sighed in response, turning her horse back to the trail of people following their leader.

"Am I your gift?" Ravenna asked after a few moments' silence.

Davorin quirked an eyebrow.

"You are far more intelligent than I would have expected, given where I found you."

Ravenna wanted to bristle at the quiet insult. Her feathers went so far as to rustle together before they stilled. Why bother? This male...no, what did he call it? This human, this *man*, he owned her blood and her wings. He controlled her life and could demand exacting obedience. He could insult Ravenna as much as he liked, and she could do nothing. There was no point in fighting it, in bristling and readying her words to defend herself. Ravenna closed her eyes for a heartbeat. Two. Three.

When she opened them, the part of her that wanted to prove Tacitus right and show the world that she was strong and capable and worth more than anyone might ever know, that part fell behind her. Left in the desert sun to wither and die.

Good riddance, Ravenna thought. She let the emptiness stretch its bounds a little more.

* * *

THE RED PALACE appeared suddenly on the horizon. One minute, the sky was as dark as Ravenna's wings, only broken by the points of endless stars. The next, a monolith the likes of which Ravenna had never seen winked into existence, lit by countless torches. Beside her, Davorin straightened in his saddle, eyes glinting in the dark.

"We ride on!" Davorin called out to the soldiers. They let out murmurs and spurred the horses into a faster pace. Ravenna's mount followed Davorin's. The increased pace exacerbated the stiffness that Ravenna felt, along with the sores on the insides of her legs. Even the most convenient things about these humans seemed to cause her pain, she thought dully.

As a distraction, Ravenna focused on the Red Palace. It was exactly as its name would suggest, a massive palace carved out of red desert stone. The palace rose up with towering domes and spires that grew more detailed the closer they drew. Stretching out before the palace was a series of gardens, cultivated and tame—nothing like the wild oasis of the Slave Markets or the forests of Shinalea. There must be a series of springs under the palace, just like the Slave Markets, Ravenna realised as the air grew moist and the desert seemed to disappear.

The gardens were not filled with plants that had no business in a desert, but the palms and the scrub bushes were stronger, greener, than their counterparts in the dry. There were exotically coloured flowers, large trees with leaves that were broad enough to provide shade for a sylph. There were vines and ferns, stretching towards the sky. It was like a forest, Ravenna decided, if forests grew in places where heat was predominant and moisture never a problem for desert plants.

"We stop here," Davorin announced as his horse's hooves touched the line where the gardens began. He swung out of the saddle just as Nadezhda came up next to him, already leading her horse by the reins. "Have everyone unpack their bedrolls. We don't want to be setting up camp on Queen Lenore's doorstep. Tomorrow, we'll get more settled."

"Are you going up there tonight?" Nadezhda asked. She sounded angrier than usual, perhaps even bitter.

Davorin shook his head. "I wouldn't want to spring my presence on our host so late at night. Especially not with such a gift as I have to offer."

Gift, Ravenna mused. That was the second time she had

been referred to as a gift. Like a necklace or a pretty bauble. Did that mean Davorin would not be her master for much longer?

She turned her head to find him watching her, eyes narrowed slightly. He stepped up to the horse and held out his hand, a silent offering and command Ravenna was loathe to obey. But she placed her hand in Davorin's and ignored the way her skin crawled at the contact. Then, she swung her leg over the back of the horse, as she had seen done, and dropped to the ground.

Davorin's hand was the only thing that kept Ravenna from staggering to the ground. Her legs felt like water and her wings were stiff. Her back felt like the wound had split open again from the exertion. Ravenna wanted to do nothing more than fall to her knees and rest until her sense of the world returned. But it never would. Instead, Davorin held her upright, waiting until she was standing strong, her wings stretched partly out before he gently released her. She loathed him for that.

"Nadezhda, find a roll for Ravenna," Davorin ordered. "I must talk with Warrith before everyone gets too settled in."

Nadezhda, to Ravenna's surprise, did as she was told without more than an annoyed look in Ravenna's direction. Perhaps her blackened eye was paining her more than before. Ravenna followed the Captain through the throngs of soldiers caring for their horses and setting out rolls to sleep. None of them spared her more than a glance and the occasional whispered prayer. Ravenna ignored them all.

"You will sleep here," Nadezhda toed a particularly tattered roll that was set beside a weathered and worn soldier. He peered at Ravenna through leathery eyes and a taut frown before shrugging and returning to setting out his own place to sleep for the night. Ravenna was too tired to argue with the Captain, even if it was completely futile. She just lay on her stomach, folding her wings atop her back and resting her head on her arms.

Nadezhda trudged off without another word. Ravenna let out a shuddering breath, squeezing her eyes shut. Her body hurt. Her spirit hurt worse. But the emptiness soothed those hurts, taking the pain and desperation and turning it into quiet, cool nothingness. Ravenna let out another breath, calmer this time.

"Goodnight, Angel," the soldier breathed next to her. "And may the gods have mercy on us all."

—

"Get up."

Ravenna woke suddenly with the hardened leather boot of Nadezhda digging into her side. She rolled to her feet instinctively; a mistake. Her wounded back split open on the rocky ground, forcing Ravenna to arch up in pain. She stretched her wings, trying to decrease the strain on her back, but it was worthless. This was a pain she would just have to shove to the back of her mind, like her anger and her sadness. After a few moments of desperately gasping at the air, Ravenna managed to relax.

"Everyone else sees some sort of divine, magical being when they look at you," Nadezhda spat, lip curled in disgust. "They think you're some sort of messenger to the gods, or an avenging force. Some even say that you are the long-lost companion of the dragons, the precursor to dragon riders. Those fools still believe in magic and divine beings. They believe in their gods or the One Who Watches."

Ravenna dusted off the tunic and breeches she had been given, the back torn almost completely off to accommodate her wings. It was not anywhere near as nice as the pieces she had worn in the Pits. Maybe if she had stayed, some lucky warrior would have killed her by now, taking the title of Angel-killer. At the very least, Ravenna would not have minded being back in the Pits, away from these cunning humans and their deceptive ways. The people in the Pits did not lie to you like these people would.

"And what do you see when you look at me?" Ravenna asked, her face expressionless.

Nadezhda spat on the ground.

"I see a weak creature who doesn't know a single thing about the real world."

Ravenna looked out over the desert and slowly pivoted on her heel to see where the cultivated gardens began. They were already buzzing with motion from animals and insects as the dawn light broke over the land. Maybe under different circumstances, it would be a beautiful sight. As it was, Ravenna felt nothing. It was just another place where she would be treated as a possession, a thing to gawk at and make do your bidding. There was nothing special about that.

"Two months ago," Ravenna said quietly as she turned back to Nadezhda, "you would not have been wrong. But I'm learning."

The Captain seemed unsure as to whether Ravenna was showing signs of rebellion or just falling into her expected role. She ran a sun-browned hand over her cropped hair. "Davorin wants to see you."

Ravenna nodded and fell into step behind Nadezhda. A stickiness formed on her back the closer they got to the gardens, despite the crispness of the early morning air. Davorin was waiting, his worn leather armour exchanged for oiled pieces with gold designs etched into the material. His sword belt now gleamed, though the two swords in the sheaths were the same worn blades he had used to slice open Ravenna's back. Davorin turned to Ravenna, his brown eyes taking her in without any outward show of what he thought.

"I see you opened up your wound again," Davorin said. Ravenna reached around to touch the space between her wings and found that the stickiness had little to do with the increased moisture in the air. Her fingers came away touched with red. "No matter. It will make the story for Queen Lenore all the more believable."

Even as he spoke the words, a bare-chested servant came running up the path, the billowing trousers and nearly-black skin startling Ravenna into thinking it was Tacitus moving towards her. Of course, it could not be. The sylph was days away, enjoying his time reading through the ancient tomes. This servant was not even that dark, charcoal ash colour, nor did he have the burning amber eyes and golden wings that Tacitus had. Another human. Another pain.

Davorin leaned over to whisper in Ravenna's ear as the servant approached, "Remember, Ravenna. No matter what I tell the Red Queen, you belong to me. My plans are all that matter. If you do not comply, I will tear every feather out of your wings and burn them on a pyre."

Nothing she had not done before. Still, Ravenna nodded and silently vowed to do as she was told. Everything would be better, then.

The servant approached Davorin and inclined at the waist, palms flat on his thighs. He straightened and started at the sight of Ravenna, her wings flared slightly, letting the dawn light pass through her feathers. Davorin allowed the staring for a moment before pointedly clearing his throat.

The servant bowed again. "My lord, Her Majesty has requested that you attend upon her in the Great Hall."

"Very well," Davorin said, sounding bored. This was probably some intricate political dance that the humans performed, Ravenna mused. She just kept silent and did her best to ignore the stares of the soldiers and the servant. "Lead the way."

Another bow and the servant turned, leading Davorin to the steps of the Red Palace. Ravenna walked just behind, taking in the splendour of the gardens. She spotted tiny birds with magnificent feathers, lizards that almost blended into the plants where they rested, even the gleaming eyes of a larger creature that slunk through the shadows so smoothly it was impossible to see. At least her new home would be beautiful.

The Red Palace was more intimidating up close than from a distance. The carvings that were only slightly apparent from afar proved to be so intricate that one detail flowed into the next without hesitation. There were plants, trees, humans, scenes, all carved directly into the red stone. The eyes of the humans seemed to watch the approaching intruders with an accusing stare. Ravenna folded her wings closer to her body, ignoring the pain that brushing her feathers against her back caused.

They were led into the palace, where the air was cool and crisp, and past many stately statues and doors. The servant did not hesitate in throwing open a door thrice as tall as he and striding through. His shoulders seemed to straighten and his steps became almost graceful. The chamber they entered truly deserved the name of Great Hall. It was long and wide, the floor polished until it gleamed red and cream, the pillars stretching impossibly high to touch the ceiling. At the far end was a dais, on top of which was a simple throne. Various attendants, dressed in the loose styles of the desert, stood near the throne.

But the woman who sat on the red stone throne was what drew Ravenna's attention. She had golden skin, not the golden-brown of Davorin or the acquired tan of Nadezhda. This was a tone perhaps three shades lighter than that of the sylphs, of Desarra. The woman's hair was a red-auburn that shimmered like fire. It was piled on her head in a mass of tiny plaits inter-woven with gold. She wore a flowing orange tunic that reached her ankles. They were called...dresses, Ravenna thought. Her fingers were tipped with shining copper claws and her shoes were woven leather sandals.

She was perhaps only a few years older than Ravenna, but

her presence matched that of the Queen of the sylphs. This, more than Davorin or that pretender, Jazer, was a true ruler. A human who held true power.

"My Queen," Davorin crossed a hand over his chest and bowed at the waist, almost as low as the servant who had led them there.

"Lord Davorin, yes?" the woman asked. "This is the third time you have graced my halls and yet I still do not know what to expect from you. I was woken this morning with the news that an army had all but materialised on my doorstep."

Davorin straightened, looking contrite. Ravenna kept her face impassive, though disgust flowed through her. "You have my most sincere apologies, Queen Lenore. I did not mean to alarm you. I was merely moving my people through your land on my way to the Iron Mountains. They were in desperate need of rest and resupply. I did not mean to trespass on your kindness."

Lenore lifted her chin. "Your words are so smooth one would have thought them rehearsed, if not for that grain of truth."

Davorin bowed his head. "I would never speak falsely to you, my Queen."

Lenore put her hands on the arm rests of the throne and relaxed. A female servant wearing billowing pants that tightened at the ankles and a loose shirt, much like the Aerial City fashions, approached the throne with a bowl of dark fruit. Lenore selected one and ate it slowly before speaking again. "The last two times you came here, you came unattended. Now you bring a servant wearing a cloak of feathers. Certainly impractical for the desert."

Davorin cast his dark brown eyes to Ravenna and she lowered her own. Her role was clear. She stepped forwards, conscious of the fact that she was neither clean nor dressed well enough to appear before such a person. "It is not a cloak, my

Queen," she said softly, barely loud enough for Lenore to hear. Then, Ravenna flared her wings as wide as they would go.

Lenore dropped the fruit in her hand, and the servant nearly fumbled the bowl. Slowly, Lenore rose to her feet and stepped off the dais, walking towards Ravenna with eyes wide. She got close enough for Ravenna to see that even they were almost amber. Not quite sylph-like, but close. Ravenna's heart beat faster in her chest.

Lenore reached out a hand towards Ravenna's left wing, as if to touch. Then, she hesitated and flicked her eyes to meet Ravenna's icy-blue gaze. "It is impossible."

"Yet here I stand," Ravenna murmured. Lenore's eyes filled with tears and she clasped her hands over her mouth.

"I found her festering away in the Slave Pits," Davorin said, stepping past Ravenna's wing. He put a hand on Lenore's shoulder. While the servants all tensed at the act, no one moved. Lenore did not shrug off the touch. "She has been cursed, though I don't know how, when magic is all but forgotten in these lands. Her wings no longer carry her in flight."

Lenore reached out a hand again, her fingers stretching for Ravenna's wing in pure desperation. She looked at Ravenna, eyes begging permission, and the sylph nodded once. Too many humans had put their hands on her wings, one more would make her feel no more dirty than she already did.

The queen's fingers were gentle. The pads of her fingers brushed against Ravenna's feathers as though they were made of silk. The touch lasted only a few seconds. Lenore turned to look up at Davorin. "The Slave Pits? With that monster Jazer?"

Davorin nodded. "I couldn't leave her there, not a true Angel. So I brought her here to you, in the hopes that she could heal. She has pledged to serve however she can in exchange for her freedom."

Lenore looked at Ravenna, her delicate features sharpening. "Is this true?"

"Yes," Ravenna said. "My freedom is worth more to me than anything. I will happily serve in your house so that I might be free."

All true. Ravenna surprised herself with the intensity of truth behind her words. She had already decided to obey Davorin, to do as he asked and coax this queen into his plans. But that was before meeting Queen Lenore, before seeing the power and the peace on her servants' faces. Before seeing her eyes sent a pang through Ravenna's heart. The emptiness had not spread that far, yet. She would keep her head down. She would let Davorin think she was complying with his wishes. But with Lenore lay hope.

"Of course," Lenore breathed, tears filling her eyes again. "Of course, you may stay in my household. But I could not ask you to be anything other than what you are. You may have free reign of my Palace. If you need anything, only ask."

"You are very kind," Ravenna bowed her chin, slowly folding her wings. "Thank you."

Lenore replied only with a smile, the corners of her eyes wrinkling gently and the tears that had gathered in her eyes slipping silently down her cheeks. She took a shaking breath and wiped her tears away. Lenore turned and gestured to one of the male servants. He approached and bowed, first to Lenore, then to Ravenna. He wore the style of the desert, flowing trousers and a sleeveless shirt, his arms bare, revealing lean muscle. He looked much like the other servants, but for the fact that his skin was not dark or golden-brown, but a reddish-brown colour, and that he was of a height with Davorin. His hair was dark brown and his eyes a vibrant green.

"This is Miklos," Lenore said, putting a hand on the servant's shoulder as he smiled at her. "He will take care of you."

Ravenna nodded. She looked at Davorin who graced her with a warm smile she recognized as intended to mask the fire and the cruelty. "It is alright, Ravenna. You are safe now."

She said nothing, only followed an eager Miklos out of the Great Hall and into a passage behind the throne. Safe. Never before had such a blatant lie rung so loudly in her ears. No, Ravenna would never be safe in this world of gaping-mouthed, bloody-handed humans. But at least she was not defenceless.

CHAPTER TWELVE

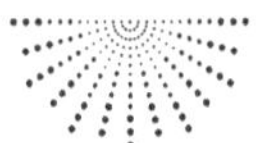

*M*iklos practically raced Ravenna through the halls of the Red Palace, hardly giving her time to gather her bearings. After a while, though, Ravenna realised that they were moving downwards. The hair on the back of her neck stood on end. She stopped, flaring her wings slightly.

"Stop," Ravenna demanded. Maybe if she established her authority with these servants early on, they would be more likely to leave her alone.

Miklos kept walking, not even turning his head to look at her.

Ravenna frowned. "Stop!" she repeated louder.

Still, Miklos kept moving, walking through the halls with almost perfectly silent steps, his body displaying an artless grace that reminded Ravenna of the tawny cougars that roamed Shinalea. They were perhaps the only real threats to the sylphs but were beautiful to watch and usually preferred to hunt smaller prey. Miklos was not a cougar; Ravenna refused to be cowed by him. She remained still, her arms at her side and tensed for Dalketh should he turn and see her inaction as insubordination.

Miklos reached the end of the hallway before realizing that Ravenna was not following. He paused and turned, blinking at Ravenna in confusion. "Why did you stop?" he asked.

Ravenna baulked at the sound, stepping back. His words sounded off, wrong. It was almost like the rough accent that all the humans spoke with, but not quite. The words were a little quieter, the consonants enunciated sharper, the vowels controlled. Combined with his deep, musical voice, it was a little unsettling.

He stepped towards Ravenna, raising his hands to show he meant no harm. "I am taking you to a healer…Angel?"

"I am not an angel," Ravenna muttered, wishing that everyone would *stop* calling her that.

Miklos tilted his head and frowned.

"If you aren't an Angel, then what are you?"

Ravenna flinched a touch, her feathers rustling. He was not meant to hear that. She shook her head and tried to brush dirty strands of hair from her face. "Your name is Miklos, correct?" Distraction. Yes, that would work.

He smiled, the motion gentle and amused. "Miska. Everyone calls me Miska. Do you have a name?"

"Of course I do!" Ravenna snapped. Miklos—Miska—said nothing, just waited. "Ravenna," she mumbled, her mouth barely moving.

Miska drew his brows together, frowning.

"Ravenna," she said, louder.

"Rav…Ravenna?" Miska repeated, testing the sounds on his tongue.

She nodded, not sure whether she should smile or keep aloof. She chose the latter.

Miska tested her name out a few more times before bowing, his eyes lifted to watch her. "It is a pleasure to meet you, Ravenna."

"Where are we going?"

Miska took a step towards Ravenna and she retreated. He shrugged and held up his hands, retreating back a step. "I will not hurt you."

"Where are we going?" Ravenna repeated.

"To see a healer, then to the bathing springs. I will then take you to your quarters," Miska explained. He gestured to the hallway in front of him. "Please, come with me?"

Ravenna hesitated, a motion that was not unnoticed by her escort. His features fell in a flash of disappointment before returning to pleasant and welcoming. It was that disappointment that made Ravenna take a careful step forwards. She wrapped her wings close to her body, ready to strike at a moment's notice if necessary. But she took another step forwards. Then another. Until she was walking beside Miska and he was leading the way once again.

The healer's rooms were located in a series of chambers off a darkened hallway. The chambers were lit with torches and candles, enough to mimic the light of day, but it was impossible to miss the fact that the rooms were far, far underground. Ravenna shivered, and not with the dampness in the air. This felt too much like the Pits. It felt too much like a cage.

"Welcome," a gnarled older woman said, smiling wide enough to introduce numerous wrinkles in her leathery skin. She was hunched over and stood at about half Ravenna's height, her neck always craned to look up. Her hair was a mousey grey-brown and sprang from her head like hay. The woman held her hand out to Ravenna, still smiling. "I was told we had a legend in the Palace. What is your name, dearie?"

Ravenna wanted to pull back and retreat from this wretched creature that hid in the underground. She glanced at Miska, drawing her brows together. The servant ducked his head reassuringly, his green eyes twinkling in the candlelight. He seemed to be studying her, unwilling to look away until he had gathered every bit of information from her facial expressions, body movements, and words. Ravenna did not know why, but the look alone had her extending her hand to the old healer.

"I am Ravenna," she whispered. Her wings shivered, the feathers fluffing out.

"Ravenna," the healer repeated. She nodded firmly. "A strong name. I am Warra. Now, why don't you have a seat on that table there and we'll get you sorted out. Looks like you have a few bumps and bruises. Hmm…someone's been fighting, by the state of your hands. Apart from that, I don't see anything terribly wrong with you. A little lean. Hair a bit dull, probably from lack of nutrients…yes, we'll get you fixed right…"

Warra's rumbling, comforting voice fell off as she circled Ravenna.

The sylph did not move, even as she felt the healer's fingers brushing the feathers on her back. She did not touch the wound itself, but Ravenna still wanted to flinch away.

Miska followed the healer's movements and stepped around Ravenna's back. He let out a low snarl.

"Who hurt you?" Miska demanded, stepping out in front of Ravenna so he could look her in the eye. "Who cut your back?"

"What makes you think it was a person?" Ravenna said.

Warra stepped around Ravenna as well, eyes sad.

"Because, my dear, no animal or accident could do something so precise."

Ravenna turned her head away, shame prickling her eyes. She jerked backwards as Miska reached out to touch her. With a wordless snarl, Ravenna jerked up the hem of her tunic and pulled her breeches down.

Miska recoiled at the sight of the brand, still angry and red, as Jazer's people had rubbed a mixture of charcoal ash and oil into the wound every day to ensure its tattoo-like permanence.

"Animals did this," Ravenna bit out around the tears that clogged her throat. "Why could they not have opened my back?"

Miska blinked furiously and turned his back on Ravenna, a

motion which caused an unexpected pang. Ravenna swallowed her tears and rubbed at her face furiously.

Warra snatched Ravenna's hands.

"You are *safe*," she insisted. Her face no longer smiled and her age lent her gravitas and solemnity rather than kindness. "You will never be so hurt again. I will take care of you. Miska will take care of you. Queen Lenore will take care of you."

"Your Miska can't even look at me." Ravenna snatched her hands back and wished she could just disappear.

"Miska is a good man," Warra snapped. "He has never shown anything but kindness and loyalty, even after he was attacked."

Ravenna studied the trembling shoulders of the servant as he stood before a candle, his hands clenched at his sides. She did not want to ask. She did not want to feel any sympathy for these creatures, especially after Tekko and Radim had been ripped away. "Attacked?"

"Beaten, badly. He was barely more than a lad and had just started his training as a hunter." Warra shook her head. She looked at the man and sighed. "It's how he lost his hearing. But Queen Lenore saved him from that village. Punished them as beat him. And Miska has been the best thing that ever happened to this place, you mark my words."

Ravenna hunched her shoulders, understanding now why Miska did not react to Warra's words, why he had walked along in the hallway and not heeded her demands, why he studied her so intently. He was deaf. He had been beaten so badly that his *hearing* had been taken from him. How could this man possibly still smile? Still promise Ravenna that she would be safe? His injury was yet another example of how horrible this world was.

Warra sighed. She pressed her mouth together and studied the brand on Ravenna's hip again. "Come along, my dear. Let's get you bathed and cleaned up. I'll see what I can do for the scar on your hip, but I fear that whoever allowed it to heal like that mangled your skin permanently. Does it cause any muscle pain? Any discomfort?"

Ravenna shook her head, grateful for the change in topic. "Only when the skin pulls."

Warra clucked her tongue. She turned and placed a hand on Miska's back, barely tall enough to reach that far. The servant turned and hurriedly blinked away the moisture in his eyes. He fixed Ravenna with a watery smile, "I'm sorry."

Ravenna realised his deafness was why his words were so precisely spoken, so perfectly enunciated and perhaps too quiet. He had been able to speak before and could, now, but did not know what his own voice sounded like. How could he hold a conversation? She watched him for a moment and saw that, while his eyes focused on her face, they were not locked with her own. He was looking at her mouth.

He was reading her lips.

"There's no need," Ravenna said with more softness than she thought she had left. "I will recover."

Miska shook his head. "That's not the point."

"It doesn't matter," Ravenna insisted. She started to follow Warra when Miska stopped her, his fingers brushing her hand. Ravenna studied her own moon-pale skin against the reddish-brown of Miska's. Oddly, she didn't feel her skin crawling at his touch.

"It *always* matters." Miska frowned, squeezing Ravenna's fingers as if trying to prove his point. "Always."

Ravenna pulled her hand free. "If you say so."

Before Miska could say anything further, Ravenna turned her back on him, ending the conversation. She followed Warra out into the darkened hallway, leaving Miska behind in the healing chambers.

Warra helped Ravenna bathe, even using her gentle fingers to clean the dried blood out of Ravenna's feathers, without stripping away too much of the natural oils. She tended to

Ravenna's back and put a soothing oil on the brand. Ravenna was given a tray of food, which Miska carried to her quarters, and then she was left in peace.

Surprisingly, the room where Ravenna was quartered was above ground, with wide, open windows that looked out on the magnificent garden and the desert after that. There were gauzy drapes of fabric that shifted in the slight breeze. The room was big enough for Ravenna to spread her wings fully and practise her Dalketh without anyone the wiser. She had a bed thrice the size of the tiny cot in the Pits and a small table and stool that held various pots and potions and even a hairbrush. There were no guards outside the door, no soldiers waiting to pounce on her when she stepped from her room into the garden. Ravenna was, dare she hope, free.

She did not trust it.

* * *

THE SUN HAD NEARLY SET, and no one had called for Ravenna. There was no sign of Davorin or Nadezhda. The few people that had wandered the gardens wore the garb of servants and did not even turn their heads in the direction of Ravenna's window. She had even ventured out into the gardens herself; her feathers twitched at every slight noise, causing her to scurry back to her room before even two full minutes had passed.

No one seemed to care.

Ravenna went through the motions of Dalketh twice, once slow and once fast. She slept, her wings outstretched. Then, feeling exhausted beyond what sleep could cure and hungry, she woke and wondered if she had, indeed, been forgotten.

A quiet knock dragged Ravenna from the last of her sleep. She surged to her feet and flapped her wings once. The gauzy curtains twisted in the violent current of air. The door opened and, to Ravenna's surprise, Lenore, rather than Davorin, poked her head in.

"I didn't mean to bother you, Ravenna," the queen said. "May I come in?"

Ravenna moved towards the open windows. "It's your Palace. You may do as you please."

Lenore slipped in, leaving the door open enough for Miska to appear as well. Ravenna huffed once and turned her back on the both of them. Lenore's sharp intake of breath had Ravenna turning around again. Miska led the queen to Ravenna's bed and she sat, looking shaken. "Miska told me you'd been injured, but I hadn't realised…" Lenore breathed.

"You have lived a sheltered life if you grow weak at the sight of a simple scratch," Ravenna said. Though half-a-season ago, she would have been the one who was shocked. She folded her arms and glanced between the queen and the loyal servant. Miska stood where he could watch both Ravenna and Lenore, while also keeping the door in his line of sight. Was Ravenna mistaken? Was he to be her guard?

"I have not seen war," Lenore murmured, lifting her not-quite-sylph eyes to meet Ravenna's ice. "But I have seen my fair share of injuries. And yours is worse than you let on."

"It will heal," Ravenna replied flatly. She shuffled her wings to lie flat on her back, obscuring the wound. "Was there something you wanted, my Queen?"

"Please don't call me that."

Ravenna raised her eyebrows. "A queen who does not want her title acknowledged?"

"A queen is meant to lead her people, to look out for them and see to their needs. Not revel in the glory and wealth that comes with the power," Lenore replied easily, as though this were a familiar argument.

"Then you would be the first of your kind I've met who actually cares," Ravenna said. Lenore met her hard gaze until it was

Ravenna looking away. Ravenna relaxed her wings and sat on the small stool, suddenly tired of having to second guess everyone and everything. Miska took a step towards her, looking concerned, but halted when Lenore put up a hand.

"How did you come to be here?" Lenore asked.

Ravenna scoffed. "Was Lord Davorin bringing me here not enough? Would you like the full details of my fall into slavery?"

"No, though I am sorry that you had to experience such things. I want to know how you came to be here. In the land of humans. Sylphs haven't been seen here for countless generations."

The word fell from Queen Lenore's tongue with ease, without a second thought. But it was that single word that set Ravenna's heart beating faster and her breath catching in shock. She had told Radim and Tekko. She had told Davorin. But none of them seemed to understand what it meant, only that it was not Angel. Yet Lenore spoke with understanding and she looked at Ravenna with knowledge.

"You know what I am?" Ravenna breathed.

Lenore smiled, her eyes lighting up to be a shade closer to the eyes of Ravenna's kind. It was like looking at Desarra, were she transplanted and transformed.

"I have sylph blood in me," Lenore said. "My...three-times-great grandfather was a sylph. The wings were not inherited, to my disappointment. He was a banished Intellecti, I think. I heard stories. I read his journals and—"

Ravenna stood up from the stool so quickly that it toppled backwards.

Miska stepped in front of Lenore, only ever so slightly, but enough to prove his intention of protecting his queen.

Ravenna ignored him, instead looking at Lenore in desperation. "You have journals? Of a sylph?"

"Of course." Lenore rose and smiled at Ravenna. "I will take you to them."

Lenore led the way out of the rooms, her head held high. She did not look around for guards to escort her, nor did she wait for a servant to precede her. She just strode through the Palace as if she were any other normal human, even going so far as to greet the servants and few guards they passed with a hello and a smile. The devotion in the eyes of the servants was telling.

Miska, on the other hand, walked at Ravenna's side. He still studied her, even as they walked, with such intensity that Ravenna wanted to hide herself with her wings. She did her best to ignore him, thinking instead about the journals. Another sylph stranded here! Yes, it was a couple of hundred cycles ago, but what of it? To read the words of another sylph amongst humans! To read at all.

Lenore pushed against two double great doors of carved wood. They swung open and Ravenna's heart stopped. Tears welled in her eyes. She did not even care when Miska set a hand on her shoulder. She was immediately transported back to the room in the Tower, in her forested home. She was again surrounded by the other sylphs, being shushed when she rustled her wings too loudly.

Tomes. From floor to ceiling and in multiple stacks, multiple sections, tomes filled the room. It was beautiful and heart-wrenching.

"I have not seen so many tomes in one place since..." Ravenna put a hand to her chest to rub out the strength of feeling there. She was not at home. She was not anywhere near home. She was surrounded by humans, a species that had proven their lack of caring for others. It was hard to push her joy aside, though, when surrounded by all the information she could ever want. Here were her friends who never judged, who only told her what she wished to know.

"We call them books," Lenore said.

"Books." It was a harsher word than the one Ravenna knew. It seemed fitting, though, considering the harsh world in which she lived now. The stakes were higher. Her life was not her own. Finally, though, Ravenna was in her element. She could not fly. She could barely fight. But she could read, and knowledge was as dangerous a weapon as blades and spears. Perhaps more so.

"You may come here any time, read whatever you like," Lenore said. Ravenna blinked furiously. Perhaps she had found someone who cared, as Lenore claimed she did. Miska squeezed her shoulder. Ravenna looked up at him and smiled. Smiled at Lenore.

"Thank you."

Soon, she would not need anyone who cared. She would have all the information at her disposal and would be well rid of this wretched place and its humans.

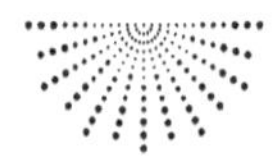

CHAPTER THIRTEEN

*P*erhaps Davorin should have paid better attention to his sister's courting and wedding. Seraphina had been wooed and won in an incredibly short time, given that most engagements of the noble classes could last years. Perhaps if he *had* paid attention, he would not be struggling so with Queen Lenore. She was being quite infuriating.

Oh, Davorin had nothing to complain about regarding how she treated him. She was as pleasant now as she had been when they first met. He was afforded every respect as a guest in her household and his army had been allowed to quarter themselves on the far edge of the garden so as to be close to water. The problem was that Lenore had not moved beyond this formal friendliness. She had not warmed up to Davorin as a suitor, merely treated him as a foreign diplomat. It was exactly how he had treated many dignitaries at the court of the Salusian Empire, so he would know.

Maybe he should have brought her jewellery rather than an angel. An angel could be "freed" and treated as any other being. Jewellery was much harder to dispute as a true gift. The thought was absurd; an angel was a being out of myth. Jewellery was mere possession.

"My lord Davorin." Lenore swept into the garden courtyard, her steps oddly silent given the silver bangles she wore at her wrists and ankles. She was wearing the same ridiculous desert attire that most women here favoured: loose pants that tightened at the ankles, a light shirt that barely covered her midriff, her hair up and off her neck. Only the bangles and a few beads in her multitude of braids bespoke her status as Queen.

Davorin supposed she was attractive, as far as women went. It would not be unpleasant to have her as his wife. It was the power, though, that mattered more.

"Good morning, my queen," Davorin said, bowing at the waist. "What a pleasant surprise. I had not thought to see you until this evening's dinner."

Lenore took his offered arm and rested her hand there so lightly that he could barely feel it through his bracers. "I often take a tour of the gardens in the mornings. Before the sun gets too high for comfort."

"Then please, let me escort you on a ramble. I'm sure you can point out all of the exotic flora and fauna that we never see in the Empire." Davorin put his other hand on hers to trap her there, though he did so with a charming smile. Much to his annoyance, Lenore pulled away with a light laugh.

"Unfortunately, Lord Davorin, I have a particular purpose today and must leave you to your own devices. Though, I'm sure if you called for a servant, they could point out all of the plants and animals far better than I."

"I would rather accompany you, if you do not protest," Davorin said. "The gardens are far less interesting when you're not around."

Lenore tossed her head back and laughed, this time the sound full and slightly mocking. Davorin did his best to keep from grinding his teeth together.

"Where did you learn such honeyed words?" Lenore asked, her grin baring her teeth. "Surely, the women of the great Salusian Empire do not fall for such ridiculous things!"

Davorin had no answer, so he merely bowed. Women usually tripped over their absurd shoes to hear such words from any of the royal household. The words were far from genuine, but they had always seemed to work. Queen Lenore would, apparently, be much more difficult to pin down.

"I have never courted a woman before," Davorin said eventually, trying to look embarrassed rather than annoyed. "At least, not officially. I'm not quite sure how to go about things properly."

Lenore said nothing for a moment. Her light eyes travelled Davorin's features, studying him, testing his truth. Her expression shifted, fell flat and smooth. "There is something you should know, before you ever consider such a thing. I will always put the needs of my people above my own. I would expect my Consort to do the same. Do you understand?"

Consort, not King, Davorin noted. But it would be a start. Once he held the title, it would be a simple matter to gain the other. A glance through the laws, a whisper in the right ear. He inclined his head and gave Lenore a serious look. "I understand completely, my queen. That is, after all, what rulers are meant to do."

Lenore nodded. "As long as you understand."

She turned to leave, putting further distance between Davorin and herself. He refused to allow that, not after he had already put so much time and money into this venture. "Please," Davorin said, taking a step forwards. "Let me walk with you. I promise I won't spout my court-made words…"

The Queen inclined her head. "Very well."

Davorin held out his arm again and this time, Lenore did not pull away when he trapped her hand between his own. "I've been meaning to inquire about Ravenna. How is she recovering?"

Lenore let out a sigh and trailed her free hand along one of the enormous broad leaves that were in the gardens. A bit gaudy for Davorin's tastes, but he would never voice such things. "She has been here three weeks and I still do not know if she's any better than when she first arrived."

"Surely her wounds are healing?" Davorin frowned. Perhaps he should not have sliced open the angel until he knew what her physiology was like. What if she did not heal as humans did, for all her appearances.

"Oh, her physical wounds are healing. The healer, Warra, assures me that Ravenna will make a full recovery, though she will always bear scars. No, it's the emotional wounds that I fear she suffers still. She keeps to her room or she keeps to the library. She doesn't talk unless you ask her a question and even then, it's like trying to pry answers out of stone."

Davorin nodded. Was this supposed to be concerning to him? She sounded like a soldier should. Quiet, obedient, with a tongue that was reluctant to wag even when questioned. "Maybe it is simply her temperament, given that she's not human. I have read stories of other beings, like elves, who were unanimously cryptic and winding with their words."

Lenore shook her head. "I don't think so. She is mistrustful. And she flinches whenever someone touches her. Miska said that she had likely been abused while that *demon* Jazer had her. How could another person be so cruel? Especially to someone like Ravenna?"

Davorin squeezed Lenore's fingers in what he hoped was a comforting gesture. "I don't know, but there is no one else I would have trusted with her care." He stopped and turned to face Lenore head on, cupping her golden face in his well-weathered hands. If he squeezed hard enough, just a few inches lower, her throat would easily yield beneath his hands. But that would be a waste and endear him to nobody.

"You are good and kind, Lenore," Davorin murmured. "That is why I brought Ravenna. That is why I wish to court you. Because you care."

Lenore gave him a weak smile and pulled from his grasp. She nodded and swallowed audibly. Then, she put her hand back on Davorin's arm and continued to lead him through the gardens.

They turned down a gravel path leading around to the back side of the Palace towards the end of the gardens. There was an expanse of open desert that had been cleared of rocks and debris into a flat area with a few mud and sandstone buildings flanking it. A barracks and training yard. Davorin would have recognised one anywhere, though the men and women walking about with weapons and horses were enough of an indication on their own.

"This is where I leave you, my lord," Lenore said when they reached the edge of the training yard. "I must speak with my soldiers about our border with Southron."

"Are they giving you trouble?" Davorin asked, his voice a growl. "Their borders do not extend far along your lands, but they are a crafty people."

"You have not heard, then?" Lenore asked, her eyebrows winging up in surprise. Davorin frowned. "The Lords of Southron have banded together under a single flag. Warlord Baldur's, I believe, though my information may be inaccurate. They haven't made a move against their neighbours, yet, but I imagine it will only be a matter of time."

Davorin struggled to keep his composure. Struggled to keep from drawing *both* his blades and doing considerable damage to something. Or someone. Baldur had moved to unite the other Lords of Southron? They were normally a divided people, happy to come together and bicker amongst each other for a few weeks a year before returning to their own people. Southron was a loose coalition at the best of times. For them to band together under one flag? That was dangerous. And it was probably all Seraphina's doing.

"If you like, I have experience with the people of Southron," Davorin said, trying not to think of how close his connection was. His sister was married to the current leader. A development he would have to deal with, and carefully. "I can tell your soldiers what to look out for."

Lenore's eyes widened ever so slightly as she considered his offer. Not for the first time, Davorin was struck with how useful it was to be Firstborn Son of the Salusian Empire. Lenore might have had the army and resources that Davorin needed, but when it came to true power and influence, he was the richer.

"That would be very helpful, thank you," Lenore said. She inclined her head in thanks before disentangling her hand from Davorin's arm and striding forwards, her back straight, her head high. A Queen addressing her people. One day, hopefully soon, Davorin would be walking forwards at her side, claimed unabashedly as Consort. Though, at the rate Lenore was warming up, it would be the end of summer before she even allowed him to take her hand in public.

* * *

"Get me your fastest carrier bird," Davorin barked as he stalked into his mercenaries' camp. Warrith lifted his head from a slate where he was working out supply requirements. Davorin spun to face the leader of the mercenaries. "Now!"

Warrith jerked his head at one of the younger soldiers sharpening her knife. She rose without comment and jogged off to go find a bird. Warrith lowered his slate. "I take it things aren't going well with your Red Queen."

Davorin curled his lip. "She is more contrary than I had expected, but I will win her."

"Best be careful. Women warriors are one thing. They're decent fighters. Not as strong, perhaps, but speed and endurance matter more. More ruthless than the men, most times. Women in *power*," Warrith snarled the last word and shook his head, disgusted. "They're cursed hard to pin down. Too used to thinking and getting their way. Can be dangerous for a body."

"Queen Lenore is under control," Davorin said through clenched teeth. "I have another matter to deal with."

The younger soldier jogged back up with a heavy leather glove and a fierce-eyed falcon resting on her arm. "This here's Storm Seeker. Fastest bird in the company. Knows places just by name."

"Good," Davorin held out his arm for the falcon and the soldier carefully passed the bird over. The falcon was a mix of stormy greys and blacks, rather than the more tawny colour one would expect. It hissed a little at Davorin as it adjusted its talons on his leather bracer. Davorin placed his note in the tiny band attached to the bird's foot. "Southron. Lady Seraphina," he instructed the bird. Then, he threw it into the air, earning an angry screech before the falcon was gone.

"Southron?" Warrith asked. "We're too far from Southron to be any worry. The Red Desert only abuts the Southron border for a couple of leagues… Ah, wait. The Lady Seraphina. Only daughter of the Salusian Emperor."

Davorin growled acknowledgement.

"I hear she's got herself a power-hungry lord to control. Or maybe that she's the power-hungry one," Warrith chuckled. "I told you! Women with power be difficult creatures."

"Curb your tongue," Davorin spat. "She may be a difficult creature, but the Lady Seraphina *is* my sister, as well as the Firstborn Daughter. You would do well to remember that."

"Or what? You'll have your pet Captain take a whip to me?" Warrith sneered. Nadezhda and the leader of the mercenaries had butted heads repeatedly. The mercenaries would follow Davorin as long as he paid them, but Warrith was forever demanding better food, better accommodations, better pay. He was less a fighter than a cutthroat negotiator and he was starting to get on Davorin's last nerve.

"No." Davorin leaned over the seated man. He snatched the slate up and glanced over it before slamming it down on Warrith's knee, cracking both the slate and the man's bone. Davorin curled his fingers around the collar of Warrith's tunic, cutting off his air before he could cry out in pain. Davorin hauled the mercenary to his feet, ignoring the whimpers and tears. "I think I'll take the pleasure of whipping you for myself."

"Please," Warrith mouthed.

Davorin threw the man away from him.

"You're right. You're not worth it. Your knee is broken, already. Why bother humiliating you when you can no longer fight? You're going to be worthless to the mercenaries now. I'll just leave you to their devices."

Warrith pleaded with Davorin, stumbling after him before collapsing in pain as he fell on his wounded knee.

Davorin ignored him and walked away. Only looking back to stare at the young soldier who had delivered the falcon.

"Do you think I was wrong?" Davorin asked, brushing dust off his tunic.

The woman narrowed her eyes at Warrith, the mewling, simpering creature he had become.

"No."

"Then you have just earned yourself a promotion," Davorin said. "Congratulations. You now run my army."

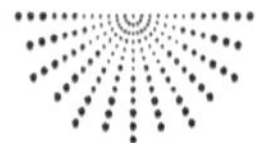

CHAPTER FOURTEEN

"How long did you travel with Lord Davorin before you came here?" Lenore asked. She trailed a finger over the spine of a book on the table Ravenna had claimed, doing her best to look disinterested in the question as well as the answer.

Ravenna leaned back in the chair. She only managed a few inches before the cursed backboard got in the way. Why would you put such a thing on a chair? It restricted movement and aggravated the wings. She shifted in discomfort and pushed down the desire to glare at the interruption. It would not do to annoy her host, no matter how kindhearted she appeared to be. Not to mention, guard dog Miska was lurking nearby, watching the conversation with interest.

"I travelled with him for long enough," Ravenna answered cautiously. "Was there something you wished to know?"

"Only what sort of man he is," Lenore said. The queen sank into a chair opposite Ravenna and propped her head in her hands. She looked, frankly, like Desarra when she was bored. The comparison struck Ravenna; Desarra would never be so quietly crafty as this human queen.

"I only have a few humans against which to compare him," Ravenna answered, turning her attention back to her book. To her utter shock, Miska's hand flashed in her vision and snatched the book away from her. Ravenna gaped at the human for a moment before clamping her mouth shut and putting on her mask of calm. Miska's eyes blazed like green fire and his features were twisted in anger.

"Miska!" Lenore said in shock, but his attention was focused completely on Ravenna. He could not hear the queen.

"You are always like this!" Miska snapped, his anger making some of his words less sharp than they would be otherwise. "Always guarding your words. Always keeping your expression calm. Do you think so little of us? Have we been so terrible?"

"Miska," Lenore repeated, quieter. She reached out to touch Miska's arm, but he wrenched it away, his eyes still fixed on Ravenna. She was shocked by Miska's outburst but remained as outwardly calm as ever. After all, she'd had years of practise with her sister and the other sylphs. She would not give the humans the satisfaction of seeing her own anger.

"Do you think we're going to hurt you?" Miska asked, softer now. He reached out a hand and grabbed Ravenna's. He meant it to be comforting. Ravenna knew that. She knew that he was unlikely to do more than hold her hand. He had not done more than smile gently at her for three weeks. But that didn't change the fact that a human—that anyone—had grabbed her hand without permission. Just another *thing* to hold on to. Something in her snapped.

In a flurry of wings and motion, Ravenna flung the chair away and was on her feet. A twist of her hand had Miska releasing hers, and a single swipe of her wing had him stumbling backwards until he fell onto the floor. The three movements were over before Lenore had a chance to jump from her own chair. Ravenna leaned over Miska, the only emotion the ice in her eyes.

"In my experience," she hissed, "all humans are vile, selfish creatures who revel in the pain of others. Your foolish smiles and desperate words do not prove otherwise."

Ravenna turned on her heel and stalked away from the library, her wings flaring and folding as she walked. She did not turn, did not want to see the expressions on Miska and Lenore's faces. It was better that way.

"It was too soon, Miska," Lenore said. Ravenna wanted to put her hands to her ears, block out their voices, their discussion of her and how they could manipulate her to their whims. She forced herself to keep her arms down, to keep walking towards those great double doors.

"I know," Miska replied, barely loud enough for Ravenna to hear. "But I couldn't stand to see her like this. So sad."

Those words snapped something further in Ravenna. She did not care about appearances anymore. She ran, the loose tunic flowing with her movements. Her feet, clad in soft slippers, barely made a noise on the polished floor, which hurt all the more. She wanted to hear the noise of her feet hitting stone. She wanted to cry out to the skies in anger and desperation. They had forsaken her, yet again.

Maybe it was the human gods and divine beings who were doing this to her. Perhaps they were like the ones who worshipped them: cruel and unbending. Whatever it was that seemed to be playing with her life, it was too much. Sadness, Miska had said. It was not sadness, it was emptiness. And the emptiness was starting to roar louder in Ravenna's ears. She was not sure anything of her would be left if it continued to grow. She was not sure she cared.

"Now, now, where are you going, little bird?"

Strong hands wrapped around Ravenna's arms, wrenching her to a stop. She tried to break from Davorin's grasp, but as he had proven before, his grip was too strong for her. When he squeezed hard enough to draw a yelp from her, Ravenna gave in and stopped struggling. Davorin released one arm and brushed his fingers under her chin, demanding that she look up and meet his gaze.

"What has you running so fast? Trying to escape?" Davorin asked, voice as soothing and warm as a steaming mug of tea. Ravenna hated him for it.

"Where would I go?" Ravenna sneered. "There is desert on all sides of this place."

"True," Davorin acknowledged, dipping his head thoughtfully. "But you are stubborn and perhaps stupid enough to consider it."

Ravenna looked away. "I'm not."

"Good. You still have work to be doing for me," Davorin said, grinning. He reached out and took a strand of her night-black hair, running it through his fingers. "You are going to help me win the Red Queen. Or have you forgotten?"

"I—"

Davorin tensed. Ravenna turned and saw Miska standing in the hallway, a concerned expression on his face. Davorin snarled and pushed Ravenna aside, a hand going to each blade. "How much did you hear?" Davorin demanded.

"He's deaf," Ravenna blurted before Miska could say anything. She hoped desperately that he was reading her lips and understood not to make a move to indicate otherwise. "He can't hear anything."

"Good," Davorin said. He stepped over to Ravenna and put his hands around her shoulders, eyes fixed on Miska. She shuddered ever so slightly. "Don't forget, little bird, who *owns* you. You still have work to do."

Ravenna closed her eyes but nodded. Davorin could not see her expression, but even so, she did her best to let nothing show. "I understand."

Davorin released Ravenna and walked away, passing Miska with a quietly superior smile. Ravenna closed her eyes again, trying to block out the few feelings she had left. Disgust. Hatred. Anger.

She opened them to see Miska standing a few feet in front of her, looking solemn. "I'm sorry," he said simply. "I'm sorry."

Ravenna lowered her head, "Me, too."

* * *

RAVENNA SAT on the stool in a patch of morning sun in her room, the crusted bread she had begged from the kitchens for her breakfast sitting nearly untouched on its tray. Her wings lay spread out, warming in the sun. With her eyes closed and her head tilted back, it was as close to peace as she had come for a long time.

A cough startled Ravenna into her Dalketh stance, wings up and ready, hands poised to protect her face.

Miska stood in the opening to her large window, an apologetic smile on his face. "I didn't mean to startle you," he said carefully.

Ravenna lowered her hands and her wings. "It's fine," she said, not knowing whether she spoke the truth or a platitude.

Miska gestured to the window, an unspoken question. "Please," Ravenna answered, "come in."

He did and, for once, Ravenna did not take a step backwards. She was struck again by how much taller he was than she. And how unlike Davorin he was. His build came from days of quiet work, not fighting and training. His skin was a colour that Ravenna had never seen, even amongst the myriad of humans she had encountered thus far. But his eyes, they were what held the true fascination for her. Most of the humans she had seen had brown eyes. She had not gotten close enough to examine many, but never had she seen such *green* before.

"Sylphs don't have green eyes," Ravenna said before she

could stop herself. Miska blinked and raised his eyebrows. "They're all amber, two shades lighter than your queen's eyes."

"Yours aren't amber," Miska pointed out, lifting a hand as if to brush Ravenna's face beside her eyes.

She flinched slightly.

"I'm…not like other sylphs," Ravenna murmured. "For one, they can fly."

"You have magnificent wings," Miska said. He reached out as if to touch her feathers before pulling away. "Beautiful."

"Flying is not a matter of pure will," Ravenna snapped. "It requires a great deal more than beauty. Mine are too small and I cannot fly. That is the end of it."

She turned away from his penetrating gaze. Instead, she picked at the bread. Her appetite, though, was no more improved now than it had been earlier.

"You need to eat more than bread," Miska said, frowning at her morning meal. "You do not take your meals with the rest of us, but…you are eating, aren't you?"

What was it about this human that had Ravenna wanting to tell him that she had not been truly hungry for ages. That she had not enjoyed a morsel of the food that passed her lips well before being captured by the slavers. Then, as with now, it was more of a means to keep up her strength than something she enjoyed.

"I asked the kitchen people for plain food," Ravenna said. "I just…haven't had much of an appetite."

To her surprise, Miska nodded in understanding. "When the heart feels nothing, it's hard to want to do anything. Even eat."

"Why would you say that?" Ravenna asked, a little more bite in her words than she anticipated. Thankfully, Miska could not hear the tone, only read her lips. Judging by the sad look in his eyes, though, he was reading more than her lips.

"After I lost my hearing, I was the same. The world felt cruel and dangerous and I didn't want to interact with it at all. I didn't see much point. Who would ever bother with a useless boy?" He shrugged but gave off the sense that it had taken many years to be able to do such a thing.

For a heartbeat, Ravenna envied the ability to shrug her worries away as something long past. Her feathers rustled, pressing closer together.

"What changed?" she asked after a moment.

Miska smiled, this one full and stunning.

"Warra wouldn't leave me alone. She helped me discover that I could still understand people, just that I had to do it differently. And then Queen Lenore spent her afternoons reading books aloud to me until I could understand everything," Miska said. He blinked and focused his attention back in the present, back on Ravenna. "We are not all cruel, selfish creatures."

Maybe that was the truth. Maybe Ravenna had been wrong in her assessment. But if that were true, who, then, could she trust to help piece her life together again. Miska? Lenore? They seemed like good enough humans, but the truth was, they could not understand her plight and they were not who she wanted.

"Was there something you wanted?" Ravenna asked desperately, taking a step backwards. Miska ran his fingers through his hair, obviously frustrated by her response. He let out a huff before nodding.

"I think I have something that will help," he said.

"Help? Help what?" she asked.

He shook his head and said nothing, merely held out his hand. If Ravenna wanted to know what this 'help' was, she would have to go with him. Was it something to stop Davorin? Was it something to help with her healing injuries? Perhaps he had found a book that held a map back to Shinalea. Hope bloomed in Ravenna's chest and before she could think it through, she grabbed his hand and followed him through the open window and into the gardens.

"Where are we going?" Ravenna asked as Miska dragged her

along. But of course, he could not hear her. His face was turned forwards, his green eyes glinting in the sun. She just had to trust him. So she did.

Miska led her through the gardens until they reached the edge of the greenery. The desert opened up before them, framed by a few buildings and a large area of sand that had been pounded into place by hundreds of people walking over it day after day. There were humans there, dressed in clothing different from the loose pieces that were found inside the Red Palace. They wore tight breeches with padded tunics or leather armour, long shirts held in place with a belt. Most carried swords at their sides. Some carried long sticks with metal pieces at the end, something Tekko had described as spears. A few led horses or ran through drills with their companions.

Soldiers. An army. This was the Red Palace's collection of fighters. Miska had brought her *here*?

Ravenna tugged on her hand, trying to pry it from Miska's grasp. He released her and turned, frowning. "It's alright. I promise."

She pressed her lips into a thin line but did not say anything. Miska watched her for a few seconds before nodding and turning towards one of the soldiers coming their direction. This man was shorter, broader, and had enough grizzled lines in his tanned face to be of some importance in this arena.

"Miklos! We never see you out here," the man said, clasping arms with Miska. He caught sight of Ravenna and let out a low whistle. "Well, I heard there was a winged being in the Palace, but I thought it was just rumour."

"No," Miska said. "This is Ravenna. Ravenna, this is General Garreth Murdoch. He leads the Desert Army. General, Ravenna needs to hit something. Preferably living."

Ravenna blanched and backed up. This was some sort of joke, surely.

Miska reached out to stop her, but he did not touch her. Just held her in place with a silent plea in his eyes.

General Garreth seemed to notice the interaction but made no comment. He just let out a chuckle and nodded.

"Gods know I get like that sometimes. Things are terrible enough that nothing'll fix it but wailing on a few people," he said. "Ravenna, come with me. I've got some people you can spar with."

General Garreth started walking away without looking over his shoulder.

Ravenna hesitated. She looked up at Miska. "Why?"

"So you can release some of the anger," Miska replied. "And so when you do face your demons, both living and nightmare, you won't do so without experience behind you."

Ravenna sucked in a breath. She nodded. And, just as she was stepping away to follow General Garreth, she reached out and squeezed Miska's hand. "Thank you," she whispered. Miska brushed a strand of her hair away from her eyes.

"I just want to see you well," he murmured.

Ravenna turned and walked across the sand, only looking back at Miska once.

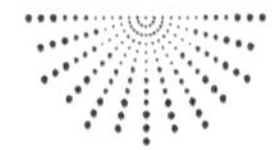

CHAPTER FIFTEEN

The soldiers were more than pleased to have Ravenna there. There were three younger men, a middle-aged woman who looked like she would rather be elsewhere, and General Garreth. He jerked his head at the gangliest of the youths. "Get Ravenna a practise blade."

The youth ran off in a puff of dust, returning a moment later. He presented the light wooden blade to Ravenna with a bow. She took it and tried to ignore the way her body filled with adrenaline and a hint of joy.

"This idiot here is Harrow," Garreth gestured to the gangly youth. He nodded his head to the next, a stocky boy who looked to be barely on the cusp of adulthood. "Canin. And Orion. This she-devil here is our training master, Vareis."

Ravenna nodded as each person greeted her in turn.

Vareis quirked an eyebrow in Ravenna's direction that had her wings bristling. She took a calming breath and forced herself to relax.

"Ravenna is to spar with us today. Vareis, I leave her in your very capable hands."

Garreth did not wait for a response. He just brushed past

Orion and walked off, leaving Ravenna with the open-mouthed youths and the hardened Vareis. The woman jabbed her thumbs through the belt holding her practise blades. She took a long look at Ravenna, eyeing the scratches on the sylph's arms and the ice in her eyes.

Ravenna, for her part, looked back. She saw stern lines and black-and-grey hair that was tied back in an elaborate braid. Vareis had more muscle than the youths she was meant to be training and her leather armour was well worn.

"How old are you, anyways?" Vareis asked. Ravenna considered not answering, but there was no point.

"I was born during the last lunar eclipse over the sea," Ravenna answered. She did not know how these humans measured time, but surely they could remember such an event.

Vareis raised her brow, glancing at the gangly Harrow. He frowned and considered before nodding eagerly and chirping, "Four or five-and-twenty cycles, I would reckon."

Ravenna shrugged. "As you say. Though I don't see what it matters."

"You're awfully young to have that look in your eyes," Vareis replied. "That's all. Now, we'd fit you with a spare set of padded pieces for today, but nothing's going to fit over your wings."

"I will go without," Ravenna said. She was used to it.

Vareis did not question her. She nodded once, then barked at the three gawking humans, "Get to running!"

They scrambled to take off, jogging around the flattened sand area. Ravenna hesitated for only a second before joining them. She recognised that the ground under her feet was not forested ground. She was not jumping over tree stumps or reaching for overhanging branches to clear dips and divots in the ground. This was not Shinalea. But the feeling of running again, of wind moving over and under her wings as she folded them for optimal speed—it was beautiful.

Ravenna ran faster, catching up with the others, before

settling in beside them. Harrow threw her an exhilarated grin. To her surprise, Ravenna returned it.

She ran beside the other humans for five laps of the arena before Vareis ordered them to stop. Ravenna slowed her feet, her wings stretching to catch the wind. Harrow and Canin stared at Ravenna where they stood, their mouths slightly agape. Orion didn't even seem to notice Vareis in his way as he stared. He stumbled into the training master and she barely caught him before they would have fallen to the ground.

"Well, looks like I need to teach these louts how not to get distracted," Vareis grumbled.

Ravenna pulled her wings in, chest heaving. At least the others were breathing just as hard. But perhaps Miska had been right; she had not been keeping up her strength, only focusing on how little appetite she had.

"Alright, so you can run. Now let's see how you get on with a few simple warm up exercises," Vareis said. She slapped Orion on the back hard enough that he stumbled and looked at the training master with a hint of alarm in his eyes.

Harrow snickered.

Ravenna went through the exercises with the other humans for the rest of the morning. She stretched and contorted her body into positions that were completely unfamiliar. She lifted crates and tossed sandbags. And, just before the midday meal, she was taught the proper technique for holding a sword and a few positions in which to wield it and strike her enemy. Nadezhda's face replaced the sandbag in Ravenna's mind a little too easily. She struck. Again and again.

Finally, wings nearly drooping with exhaustion, Ravenna turned to find Miska standing a few feet away from her, an expectant look on his face. Vareis caught sight of the servant as well. She swung her practise blade through the air, scowling.

"You're back," Vareis said. Miska nodded. "You're probably

here to tell me I have to let these weaklings have a break for food or something, aren't you?"

Miska nodded again, a wry smile spreading across his face.

Vareis sniffed. She shoved her blade at Orion, who fumbled it before managing to cradle it in his arms. "Alright, you louts. You get one hour for a break. If you're not back here by then, we're going to have to hunt you down. Now go on, get out of here."

The three youths wasted no time in doing exactly as their training master had ordered. Harrow paused only long enough to turn and wave at Ravenna before he ran off in the direction of the barracks, tiny puffs of dust following in his wake.

Vareis turned back to Ravenna.

"Are you planning on returning this afternoon?" she asked, hands on her hips.

"If you'll allow it," Ravenna said with a dip of her chin. "That is, unless the queen has another task for me?"

Miska shook his head. "No, you are free to do what you wish."

"Good." Vareis nodded firmly. She pointed at Miska, jabbing her finger into his chest. "But you have to get her some proper clothes. And shoes. Those scraps of fabric are going to do nothing to protect her feet. And those idiotic loose clothes that the rest of you insist on wearing are only going to get in the way. Find her a proper tunic, proper breeches, and proper boots. Or you'll have *me* to answer to!"

Miska, to Ravenna's surprise, laughed. The sound was far more musical than she would have expected, almost beautiful. Miska bowed at the waist with a sweeping gesture. "As you say, Lady Vareis."

"Hmph." Vareis turned and jogged away in the direction of the other trainees, leaving Ravenna alone with Miska. He held his arm out and Ravenna did not hesitate before slipping her arm through his. For once, the brush of skin on skin did not bother her. In fact, it felt almost like she was walking with a friend.

"Thank you," Ravenna murmured. Their path crossed into the gardens. Miska led Ravenna down a path that she had not yet seen.

"For what?" Miska asked, looking at her in surprise. "For retrieving you? I thought you would have enjoyed your morning."

"No, I did! I was thanking you for bringing me there," Ravenna said. She brushed a strand of sweat-damp hair from her face. "I haven't felt like that since…"

Miska turned her down another path, leading to a sheltered pavilion surrounded by a small pond. "Since what?" he asked, holding her hand lightly as she stepped across the small bridge and into the pavilion. Ravenna turned to look at him over her shoulder, knowing he deserved an answer even if she did not really wish to give it.

"Since the Pits."

Miska visibly flinched. He released Ravenna's fingers and stumbled into the pavilion, nearly colliding with a table and chairs. She saw that it had been set up for an outdoor luncheon, with dishes of all colours and smells assaulting her senses. She had never seen so many types of food before. She could not even name half of the things that had gone into the dishes. Yet, despite her growling stomach, Ravenna went first to Miska. She waited until he looked at her so he could see her face, see what she said.

"You think this was…like being a slave?" Miska asked, voice breaking.

"The day Lord Davorin bou—found me," Ravenna said, correcting herself before she could make a dangerous slip, "I had just fought in a tournament. I had never been in a fight before being in the Pits. Two slaves, Radim and Tekko, they helped me learn, but it was only a small amount and hardly enough against a slave who had trained for years."

"Please," Miska begged, reaching out to grasp Ravenna's hand. He shook his head. "Please don't—"

"This matters," Ravenna said flatly. She pulled her hand away. "I had been barely trained and had only my sylph exercises and my own abilities to help me. And yet I fought. And I *won*. I was capable and no one was going to hurt me again. That's what it felt like. I was wrong, but in that moment, that feeling saved my life. And that's what it felt like again today."

Miska sucked in a harsh breath. "You will *never* be hurt again!"

Ravenna snorted. "You can't possibly think that. The world is far too cruel, Miska. But I can fight back."

He pressed his lips together in a tight line, his green eyes shone with moisture. He looked like he wanted to promise again that Ravenna was safe, that she would never be hurt. She turned away before he could say something foolish and naïve. She strode to the table and sat in one of the chairs, her wings spread so the back would not crush them.

"Tell me what these foods are," Ravenna said.

Miska hesitated, rocking back on his heels. He let out a slow breath and sat in the chair opposite Ravenna, his expression still stricken.

"This is called Baruti. It's a fried ball of ground bean paste that's been seasoned with our local spices," Miska murmured, pointing to a bowl of brown balls, garnished with a green sprig. Ravenna took it and bit into the morsel.

"It's good," she said around her mouthful, surprised. Miska's brows drew together and his eyes widened.

"What?" he asked. "I would never!"

Ravenna swallowed, realising that he could not understand her when her mouth was full and unable to articulate the words. "It's good," she said again, clearer. Miska blinked and blushed, his reddish complexion darkening greatly. "What did you think I said?" Ravenna asked, tilting her head.

Miska shook his head. "Nothing."

Ravenna raised an eyebrow, disbelieving.

"I'd rather not say," Miska said, the blush deepening.

Ravenna shrugged.

For the rest of the meal, Miska pointed out foods for Ravenna to try. It was as friendly and polite as before, but Miska kept blushing and smiles played upon his features. After a while, Ravenna found herself smiling in return, enjoying each tidbit of food. Her feathers rustled in alarm as she ate something Miska called a "curry" that put a fire in her mouth. He laughed as she downed the thick fruit juice to soothe her tongue. Then there was the slightly sweet pastry with chopped nuts and honey. Ravenna ate two of them, sucking her fingers for any extra sweetness.

By the end of the meal, she felt more relaxed than she had since Shinalea. This was almost better, though, because she was not surrounded by the silent and taciturn Intellecti as they poured over their tomes. She was with someone who truly seemed to enjoy her company. It was a strange feeling. One that had her feathers fluffing slightly and her smiles growing wider.

Finally, there was nothing left to be eaten and Miska stood to escort Ravenna back to the training arena. He assured her that Vareis would allow her to finish her day's training in the clothes she had, and that something would be found for her for tomorrow.

She enjoyed the slow walk back through the gardens as her body adjusted to the comparatively enormous amount of food she had eaten.

"Queen Lenore is holding a ball in two days," Miska said as the greenery became dirt.

"A ball? What is that?"

"It's a party. There is dancing and a banquet and even some entertainment," Miska said.

Ravenna nodded.

"We have similar things. We call them fetes." She used to love fetes, before learning that she would never be able to do the flying dances that all sylphs performed. To dance on the ground was for the nearly-dead and the elderly—even Queen Mariala had refused to dance on the ground. The food was exquisite, but Ravenna could always have good food another time. After she had torn out her feathers, she had never attended a fete again. She had only looked on to the barely-discernible flying figures over the Aerial City from her vantage point in the Tower. Then lied to Tacitus that she had gone to bed early and her tears were non-existent. He had never pressed her.

"Queen Lenore would very much like you to attend," Miska said, jarring Ravenna from her reverie of a stolen past. Miska winced a little. "Actually, she's already had the seamstresses working on something for you."

Ravenna quirked a brow. "Oh?"

"It would mean a lot to her if you would come," Miska said, squeezing her hand where it lay on his arm.

"Are you going?" Ravenna asked. It would be better to attend a fete if she had someone she enjoyed spending time with there, too.

Miska froze. Ravenna turned to him, frowning. His eyes were wide and his expression unreadable. Ravenna's frown deepened. Miska coughed and forced out a smile. "I will be working."

"As a servant." It was not a question. Ravenna knew he had duties and that he wouldn't always be able to come when she asked, despite Lenore's statement otherwise. So why did that make Ravenna's feathers flatten?

"It is my duty," Miska said, inclining his head in a nod. "I will be there to serve drinks and food."

"But you'll be there?" Ravenna asked, that tiny kernel of hope blooming once again. Miska nodded, albeit reluctantly. "Good. I don't like fetes. I don't want to be alone."

The words were spoken before she could stop them. She hoped that Miska had not understood, had not read her lips properly and that the statement could just fall into oblivion. But he squeezed her hand all the harder and whispered words, causing an odd feeling to grow in her wings once again. "You'll never be alone again."

Ravenna replied with a smile that did not quite reach her eyes, hoping to hide the confusion that lay in the icy depths. Miska, though, was far too observant, and seemed to notice everything. He paid too much attention. Ravenna was not sure she liked it. She was not sure she did not, either.

"There you are! Thought we'd have to send out a hunting party," Vareis bellowed as Ravenna and Miska crossed the training yard. The other three trainees were already there, though given Canin's state of breathlessness, he had arrived only a heartbeat before Ravenna. "Miklos! Away with you before you distract every busybody out here."

Miska bowed at Vareis, smiled at Ravenna, then turned and strode back to the Red Palace, power in his steps. Ravenna turned her gaze to Vareis. The woman studied Ravenna for a moment in silence. She nodded.

"Alright. Now. You kept up well enough this morning. Tell me, have you had any fighting experience?"

"Only what I faced in the Pits," Ravenna answered. Harrow choked on a gasp. Orion and Cain exchanged wide-eyed glances. Vareis, though, just snorted and shook her head.

"Slave fighting. Brutes, all of them. Don't know anything about precision. We'll have to teach that out of you, girl."

Ravenna liked the training master. She shifted her wings, revelling in the stretch of her muscles. "There is the Dalketh, too."

Vareis' eyes sharpened. "Dalketh?" she asked, her mouth slowing over the unfamiliar word. "Show me!"

Ravenna bit back a smile and skipped a few steps back from the others. Her wings flared once before settling into the starting position. Peace filled her bones as she went through the fighting dance. This was not the elaborate figures that the other sylphs had carved through the skies during their fetes. This was Ravenna's dance. And she loved every movement.

CHAPTER SIXTEEN

*D*avorin waited two days beyond the date he had expected before a response to his inquiry came. The falcon was brought to him by the new commander of the mercenary armies, Utheria. She had proven to be a far more useful asset than Davorin could have anticipated. In return for her promotion, she did exactly as Davorin asked, kept the mercenaries from rebelling against his rule, and even managed to dispose of Warrith's body before the soldiers the Red Queen had watching him noticed he was gone. From the way her eyes followed him as he strode through the camp, Davorin imagined Utheria would be quite as pleased to serve him in his bed, as well.

For now, he ignored the temptation. Courting Queen Lenore was far more important.

"Storm Seeker is back," Utheria announced, delivering the falcon to Davorin. He seized the message tied to the bird's leg, ignoring its indignant hiss.

Your concern *for my well-being is most appreciated, brother, but not necessary. I assure you, the machinations within my land do not pass by without my knowing. Can the same be said for you? By the way, how is Father? Still denying you Dagan's legacy?*

~ Lady Seraphina, Queen-Consort to the High Warlord of Southron

* * *

DAVORIN LET OUT A LOW CURSE. His sister's words were far from reassuring. He crushed the message in his fist and a haze of red clouded his vision for a moment. Davorin took ten deep breaths, eyes closed. When he opened his eyes, the red was gone and a steady, pulsating anger had replaced the volatile rage.

"My...my lord?" Utheria asked tentatively. Storm Seeker let out a piercing cry. Davorin wanted to snake his hand out and wring the bird's neck, but he refrained. That would be a waste of a useful tool and he was not Dagan. He would never be as foolish as Dagan.

Davorin fixed a charming smile on Utheria, "Would you fetch Captain Nadezhda for me?"

Utheria's tan skin flushed a deep red. "If you'll pardon my impertinence, my lord, I can do just as well as she! She's naught but a former slaver. What use is that?"

Davorin lifted his chin. "You doubt my plans?"

"O-of course not! I just—"

"Utheria, do not think I am unaware of the abilities of the people I command. I know perfectly well what you can do and offer. Just as I know exactly what Nadezhda can do and offer. And at this moment, I need Nadezhda, not you. Now," Davorin lashed a hand out and trapped Utheria's chin in his grip, forcing her to look him in the eye, "do as I ask and fetch Nadezhda."

Utheria squeaked. A very undignified sound for the commander of an army, Davorin thought. But she ran off to do exactly as told. And maybe later, he would take her to his tent and show her what true anger looked like, no matter that Lenore was his real conquest.

A few minutes later Nadezhda appeared, walking as casually as if she had just been invited to a meal between friends. Her eyes were lidded and she looked as though she would rather be napping in her tent and out of the heat. She stopped in front of Davorin and stifled a yawn. "You asked for me?"

Davorin slapped her.

Nadezhda reeled a bit from the blow; he had not been gentle. The Captain put a hand to her cheek, feeling the sting. She studied Davorin with wide eyes. He growled out, "Do not treat me as you would have my brother. I am not Dagan."

Nadezhda lowered her gaze and inclined her head. "No," she murmured contritely. "You are not."

Davorin thrust the crumpled note from his sister into Nadezhda's hands. She read it carefully before looking back up at Davorin. "Well?" he demanded.

"It seems that Lady Seraphina has begun to act on her ambitions."

"Does she mean to challenge me?" Davorin asked. His palms went to the hilts of his twin blades. He took comfort from the familiar feel of the weapons beneath his hands. "She seems to insinuate that my father will never let me have what Dagan had. That I do not even know what goes on within the Salusian Empire!"

"I think she just means to rile you up," Nadezhda said warily. Davorin snarled wordlessly.

"She is infuriating! Baldur was never so capable before Seraphina married him. Now he is the leader of Southron, a land notorious for being impossible to unite. How did she manage that? And now that she has, what will she do? Surely that cannot be enough for her ambitions?"

"I heard reports from some of the Red Queen's scouts that

there were forces gathering on her border. Perhaps you should go see for yourself?" Nadezhda suggested.

"And what of the Empire? Would Seraphina be so idiotic as to march on the Empire and hope that Father doesn't notice before she reaches the capitol?" Davorin ran a hand through his short hair, trying to wrack his brain and come up with some reasonable explanation for his sister's actions, for what she could be planning next.

"I have heard nothing from any of your spies," Nadezhda murmured. "The Empire seems to be running as usual."

The loyal agents that remained in the Salusian Empire and reported the doings of the Court to Davorin were a well-guarded secret. Not one in his mercenary army knew of them, and he would do many things to keep it that way. There would be no telling what the Emperor would do if he discovered his son's scheming. But Davorin would not leave the Empire without them reporting to him.

Davorin growled, "I have to go to the borderlands."

"Your Red Queen is hosting a ball tonight. You would abandon her to the potential competition?" Nadezhda's sneer was back, though slighter than before. Davorin would have to work on his training of her.

"No, it will take time to determine who I'm leaving behind and who I'm taking with me. It wouldn't do to antagonise Seraphina any further. Talk with Utheria and determine which ten soldiers can be missed. Have them packed and ready to go by morning," Davorin said. He started towards the main part of the camp where his tent stood. He paused. "Oh, and Nadezhda, you won't be accompanying me."

"I see," Nadezhda said.

Davorin heard the querulous note in her voice and smiled to himself. It would never do to have anyone understanding his full plan.

"No, you don't. But that's irrelevant. You will keep an eye on

Queen Lenore. Endear yourself to her, if you can. Befriend her servants and learn everything about her that you can. I want to know exactly what must be done to seal this courtship as soon as I get back. The delay is doing no one any good."

Davorin didn't wait for an answer. He went to his tent to prepare for the evening.

Nadezhda did not follow him.

CHAPTER SEVENTEEN

For the first time in her life, Ravenna wore a dress. When the seamstresses brought the garment to her room earlier that day to do a final fitting, Ravenna protested. The two women had ignored her.

Now, though, Ravenna stood before the silver mirror in Lenore's chambers and admitted that perhaps they had been right. The dress was a deep, midnight blue in that same semi-transparent fabric that the desert people favoured. It tied around her neck and plunged deep, leaving her back completely open for her wings. The skirts brushed her feet, which were wrapped in braided leather sandals. The fabric had a few tiny crystals at the hem which held the light skirts down and gave it a whisper when she moved. Lenore herself had put Ravenna's hair up, taking the night-black waves and pinning them into a mass atop her head with more delicate crystals.

Between the blackness of her wings and hair, her pale skin and light eyes, and the deep blue dress, Ravenna felt like a being created from stars and sky. She felt beautiful.

Ravenna reached out to touch her reflection in the mirror. Lenore stepped up behind her and put her hands on Ravenna's shoulders. "You are the most stunning creature I have ever beheld," the queen said, running her fingers over a loose strand of Ravenna's hair.

"You are more beautiful than I," Ravenna murmured.

The human queen looked like she belonged amongst the most graceful of sylphs. She, too, wore a dress that tied at the neck with a plunging back, though her dress was a burnt orange. Her red hair was done up in its customary hundreds of tiny braids, all pinned up as Ravenna's hair was. A circlet of copper and gold sat on Lenore's brow, matching the bangles and jewels that adorned the queen. If Ravenna was starlight, Lenore looked like fire.

"Ravenna," Lenore murmured, her eyes suddenly sad. "Who told you that you were not beautiful?"

Ravenna shrugged and moved away from the mirror. She stood before the great windows, looking out through the colourful fabrics that swayed slightly in the breeze. "Amongst the sylphs, I am an oddity. I was born with black wings, black hair, and white skin. The sylphs are golden winged and have skin of gold or of charcoal shadow. I do not look like them. I cannot fly like them. I am…I always have been different. Lesser."

Lenore spun Ravenna around. Ravenna blinked to see the tears gathering in the human woman's eyes. "You could *never* be—"

"That's the odd part," Ravenna interrupted before Lenore could say something she did not understand. "As soon as I was found by humans and taken for a slave, I was anything but lesser. I was—I *am*—the image of divinity to many of you. If not a divine creature or a god, then a symbol of magic that's been forgotten by the people here. I am praised for my beauty and my figure. My wings are adored, and the fact that they cannot carry me in flight doesn't matter. And when I fought the other slave and won? Then I was an avenging angel. An angel of death. I am attributed with powers that make no sense. But nothing I do seems to convince humans that I am anything other than what I am. At least you understand that I am a sylph, not an angel..."

She took a deep breath, shrugging her shoulders, and wandered over to the mirror once more, her reflection bringing that same feeling as before. Ravenna touched the silver, her fingers meeting their mates. "This is the first time that other people's perception of what I am does not matter."

The human queen, a living fire, appeared in the mirror beside Ravenna, though her black wings concealed all but Lenore's shoulders and face. "Let me tell you a secret, Ravenna. I have ruled the Red Desert for seven years. In the human world, it is unusual for a woman to hold as much power as I do. Fight in armies? Yes. Even serve as a scholar. But true power? It took time for people to accept me and now I rule one of the few kingdoms not conquered by the Salusian Empire or Southron. The Red Desert and the Iron Mountains to the North. Beyond them lies the Wastelands."

"I have seen the maps in your library."

Lenore smiled. "Then you understand what it means for me to be queen here. At first, I was forever worrying about what my people thought, about what other kingdoms and dignitaries thought. I tried to rule my kingdom based on what they thought made a powerful kingdom. I almost ruined my people. One night, I was standing before a wine-drunk dignitary from some backwater fiefdom, long since eaten by the Salusian Empire. He was saying something about slavery and the routes that slavers took through my land, maybe I should tax them. I decided I didn't care what he thought. I would never profit from such a horrible enterprise. So I threw my drink in his face and hunted down every slaver I could find. I never looked back."

"I was wrong about you," Ravenna murmured. "I thought you were like my sister, Desarra. A bit vain, more interested in approval than what makes sense. But you are more like Tacitus."

"Tacitus? Your lover? Brother?"

Ravenna threw her head back and let out a bark of laughter that was the most real sound of joy she had uttered for ages. "No! Tacitus was my heart-father. He raised me amongst the Intellecti after my mother died."

"A wise sylph?" Lenore smiled.

"A dedicated one," Ravenna answered. The queen looked a bit stricken, but the emotion flashed away before Ravenna could blink. Lenore squeezed Ravenna's shoulders before turning away from the mirror.

"Come," she said, bangles jingling like bells. "We have a ball to get to. We wouldn't want to keep everyone waiting!"

* * *

THE BALL WAS HELD in the enormous Great Hall, which had been decorated for the occasion. It was hard to top the already-magnificent carvings and designs in the stone, but the servants of the Red Palace had done their best. Tiny metal cages that held small candles suspended from long ropes high above everyone's heads. If you looked up, it was almost like stars. There were long sashes of white fabric tied around the great pillars, tiny crystals in the fabric reflecting the light. Plants from the gardens adorned the available spaces, adding a sense of exotic life to the scene.

Nothing, though, could compare in Ravenna's mind to the humans wandering around. They were dressed in clothes that should have been absurd but were stunning. The women wore dresses, some similar to the desert-styles that Ravenna was growing accustomed to, some heavier with wider skirts. The men wore breeches and tunics in as many varied colours as the dresses. Some sported the looser fit of the desert, others wore their clothes tight like the warriors. Jewels adorned many people's hands, wrists and necks, with the men wearing nearly as many as the women. They sparkled in the candle-and-torch light, like a flock of birds of paradise.

"Beautiful," Ravenna murmured as she stepped through the enormous doors. Lenore, a heartbeat ahead of Ravenna, looked over her shoulder and smiled. When she turned around again, her spine straightened, her steps became more graceful, and there was a sense of power to her than had not been there before. Now, it was not Lenore the human that Ravenna had gotten to know, but Lenore the Queen.

Ravenna shadowed her, an angel heralding some great mystery to these foolish humans. She knew the truth, knew that it was an idiotic thing, but the humans believed. That gave her power of her own.

People gasped as Ravenna entered the room. Murmurs broke out almost immediately. More than one person seemed to stagger. Ravenna even heard a glass shatter. She ignored it all.

"Queen Lenore." Davorin was suddenly there, bowing over Lenore's hand with almost sincere admiration. He wore leather armour, but this was far grander, etched with scenes of gold. The scabbards that held his twin swords were also grander, more elaborate. The rest was just as before.

"My lord Davorin," Lenore said, her voice quietly polite. "What do you think of my little gathering?"

"I see dignitaries from many lands, some now controlled by the Salusian Empire and Southron. You have nobility from both places, as well as merchants, warlords, generals, even a representative from the Library at Sažem. I would say that your little gathering has quite the collection of people."

Lenore tossed her head and laughed, setting the jewels in her hair flashing. Ravenna frowned. She did not think that Davorin's comment was deserving of such mirth. Her wings fluttered uncomfortably. A portly man wearing all black but for a crimson sash across his chest stumbled backwards.

"Oh!" he said, loud enough to draw the attention of Lenore

and Davorin. The man wiped a nervous hand over his light beard. "I thought they were fake, perhaps some costume," he explained to Lenore. He bowed to Ravenna.

"It is no farce," Davorin said, smiling proudly. He gestured to Ravenna and she obeyed silently, stepping forwards. Davorin ran a possessive hand down her wings, his fingers brushing the feathers roughly. Ravenna swallowed her shudder. "She is a true angel."

"Davorin," Lenore said softly, tugging on the man's hand. He pulled away from Ravenna's wings.

"What is it, my Queen? Should she hide what she is? She is stunning and beautiful and there is no shame in it!" Davorin insisted. He turned an eye to Ravenna, who continued to say nothing. "Show them."

She closed her eyes, wishing to be anywhere else. Maybe standing in front of that mirror, alone. There, she was the only one she had to please. Here…Ravenna flared her wings as wide as they would go, her head high, her eyes still closed. The crowd gasped, murmurs turning to loud conversations. The noise pressed in on Ravenna, too much and far away at the same time.

She pulled her wings close. Her eyes opened and she immediately saw the look of undisguised pleasure on Davorin's face. She was his creature, and he had just proven it to the entire crowded room. Ravenna turned away from him and Lenore. She pressed her way through the crowd, who seemed to part before her. There was one of those great windows that opened onto the gardens. The balcony beyond it was empty. Ravenna ran there, her dress swirling around her ankles and becoming twisted.

She wanted to tear it off, wanted to be wearing breeches. She wanted to be anywhere but there. Away. Far away, actually. She wanted to be home.

"Are you alright?"

Ravenna spun, wings stretching wide. She landed in her

defensive Dalketh posture, only to slide out of it a moment later. Miska stood on the balcony. The concern on his face was the only thing that Ravenna believed to be true at the moment. He wore a pair of black trousers that flowed loosely around his frame. He wore no shirt but had a tunic vest tied at the waist with a piece of silver rope and closed with silver buttons. In his hands, he carried a tray of drinks glasses, reminding Ravenna that he was meant to be in there, working.

"Are you alright?" Miska asked. He set his tray aside and took the steps to bridge the gap between them. Ravenna shook her head once. That was all it took. Miska wrapped his arms around Ravenna's shoulders and pulled her close.

She stiffened at first, unused to the contact. Her wings bristled for a moment, before they smoothed. A moment later and Ravenna was completely relaxed, her arms tight around Miska's form. Miska kept holding her, though. Even when music began to play inside the Red Palace, Miska's grasp remained. Some thirty heartbeats later, Ravenna loosened her arms around Miska and stepped away, more at peace.

"What was that?" she asked.

Miska frowned.

"What was—"

Miska held up a hand. "No, I understood the words. I just don't understand what you mean."

"When you hold someone like that? What is that?"

"A hug?" Miska's mouth dropped open. "You don't know what a hug is? Didn't your family…?"

"No," Ravenna shook her head. "My mother died when I was born. My heart-father, Tacitus, raised me to be an Intellecti. Separate. My differences to the other sylphs kept everyone else, well, apart. But it was a good life." She did not know why she said that last part, as though Miska was questioning it, as though *she* was.

Miska reached out to brush his thumb across her cheek. "I

imagine it was," he murmured, as though he did not quite believe her. Ravenna pulled back. She walked to the edge of the balcony and looked over the garden. Compared to the music and conversation at her back, the garden seemed abundantly peaceful.

"I'm sorry." Miska came up beside Ravenna, leaning his arms on the stone railing. "I don't know anything about sylphs, apart from what you've told me. I didn't mean to insinuate that, well, you knew anything less than what I knew."

Ravenna said nothing. There was a slight breeze over the desert that night, bringing with it a coolness and a hint of moisture that even the spring-fed oasis didn't have. Light flashed on the horizon, though the storm was too far away to hear thunder.

"Don't you want to go in and dance?" Miska asked after a few more moments. Ravenna looked at him, saw the hopeful cast to his expression.

"I don't know how to dance," Ravenna answered with a wing-shrug. "Sylph dancing takes place in the air and I cannot fly, so I do not know how to dance."

"Well humans don't have wings," Miska said. He leaned against the railing and started tugging off his boots, tossing them to the side.

"What are you doing?" Ravenna asked, but he was too engrossed in his task to read her lips. Miska bounced up, his bare toes wriggling on the stone. He grinned widely and held out his hands. Ravenna raised an eyebrow.

"I'll teach you," Miska insisted. "To dance."

"How?" Ravenna folded her arms. "You cannot hear the music."

Miska pointed to his bare feet, "I can feel the beat of the music through the stone. It's not perfect, but it will work. Now, come here and I'll teach you."

Ravenna hesitated. A woman's tinkling laughter reached her

through the open window, drawing her attention. It seemed that her entrance and abrupt exit had been forgotten in favour of dancing. And it *did* look wonderful, with the graceful steps and the precise movements.

"Alright," Ravenna breathed. She stepped into Miska's arms, marvelling at how easy it was to do. His left hand wrapped around her right, his other hand on her waist, just where her wing met flesh. She shivered from the touch.

Miska closed his eyes. "Just follow my lead," he said in Ravenna's ear. Then, after the music started rising, he took a step forwards. Ravenna moved a heartbeat too late and they brushed chests. She tripped backwards a small step. Miska just smiled and kept stepping, the movements slow and steady. Forwards, sideways, a turn. Ravenna felt his hand on her waist gently guiding her where he wanted her to go. She stumbled more than once and looked down at her feet to see where she was going more than she looked up at Miska. But after several minutes, Ravenna's shoulders relaxed, and she found the rhythm that Miska was setting.

Then, they danced.

Ravenna did not know how long they danced, only that her movements became more fluid the more they moved. Soon, the whole balcony was subject to their movements. Miska's hand on her waist, their other hands intertwined. The music rose and fell and Miska never seemed to lose the movement. Eventually, the music became so strong that Miska broke away from Ravenna, leaving only their hands touching, and spun her in a swift circle. Her wings flared slightly to counter-balance the movement. Everything fell apart.

Ravenna's wings pushed Miska backwards, so he stumbled over the long-abandoned tray of drinks and fell to the ground with a clattering of glasses. Ravenna moved backwards with her own momentum, running into the railing of the balcony. Her chest heaved and her heart beat loudly in her ears as she stared at the still-grinning Miska.

The commotion brought other party-goers to the window. Amongst them was Davorin, his arm wrapped possessively around Lenore's waist. The Queen looked at Ravenna and Miska, her mouth pressed in a straight line, her eyes confused.

"Oh," Ravenna said, so softly. How could she have been so stupid as to let her guard down? *Dancing?* With a human? She had forgotten everything that had happened to her and been so wrapped up in Miska that nothing else seemed to matter.

"Ravenna?" Davorin asked, his voice breaking through the suddenly-silent night like one of his blades. "What's going on?"

"Nothing," Ravenna lied, lowering her gaze to the polished stone floor. "I was just…" she cast her eyes around for an excuse.

"I was teaching her to dance," Miska said. His eyes were on Ravenna, desperate and so alien to everything she had ever known.

"An angel doesn't need dance lessons," Davorin scoffed.

Miska was out of line to read Davorin's lips, so he did not respond. He just kept watching Ravenna, apology and concern plain to see.

"If you'll excuse me," Ravenna said, lifting her chin so that she was staring down all who came to see her spectacle. "I am going to take a walk."

She did not wait for an answer, for permission. Ravenna just spun on her heel, placed her hands on the stone railing, and vaulted over the edge of the balcony and into the gardens below. It was not a far fall, but the sensation was so familiar to her. This was like home, like running through the forests of Shinalea. This was what she knew. Not dancing. Not those humans.

Ravenna didn't wait to see if anyone was following her, she just ran off into the night, letting her mind take her back to a time where things made sense.

CHAPTER EIGHTEEN

After a few minutes of running, Ravenna slowed to a stop. The hem of her dress had snagged on at least three trees and she was fairly certain that it was ruined. Mostly, though, she decided that she was tired of running. The nostalgia it brought on was too strong. She wouldn't pretend that she was home because she was most definitely not. These trees were not the ones she knew. These plants were foreign to her. The place she had left behind was made of the wrong kind of stone. And she was not running on an errand that Tacitus had set.

Ravenna fell to her knees and let out a low groan. "I want to go home," she whispered. Tears filled her eyes, unbidden and unwanted. She rubbed at her eyes with the back of her hand and forced the tears back. The emptiness was so much easier than the despair.

Something stepped on a twig to one side of Ravenna. She sniffled and rubbed the last tears from her eyes. "Go away, Miska. I'm not in the mood," she said, realising belatedly that Miska would not be able to hear her. Ravenna sighed and stood, turning to face him.

She froze.

Instead of Miska's green eyes, she was looking into two cat-slitted pools of yellow, glowing faintly in the moonlight and oncoming storm. This creature was much larger than the mountain cougars that lived near the cliffs of Shinalea. And the growl rumbling deep in its chest was far deeper. This was a desert lion, like the one she had killed in the arena with Radim's borrowed blade. But there was no blade here.

"Ravenna!" Miska's voice carried through the jungle garden. The lion facing Ravenna started. Instead of running, as most creatures do when faced with multiple possible predators, it let out a snarl and took a few steps in the direction of Miska's voice. Something was wrong.

"No!" Ravenna shouted, stretching her wings as wide as they would go. The creature let out a rumbling growl and turned its attention back towards Ravenna. It took another step forwards, enough for Ravenna to see more than its eyes, gleaming teeth, and foam-flecked muzzle.

It was definitely a large cat, built along the same lines of the cougars, but much larger. Tawny fur covered its massive shoulders, made for pinning and holding onto prey. Its paws sported long, sharp claws. A long tail with a tuft of brown fur twitched eagerly behind the cat. This beast was larger than the starved creature she had faced before. And there was something in its eyes that spoke of a crazed fervour. Ravenna let out a furious cry and beat her wings once. The lion, instead of turning tail as it should have done, panted eagerly, more foam dripping from its maw. It crouched, showing Ravenna that most of its muscle was gone and that its bones were showing.

Great, she thought. Starving creatures were desperate creatures. *Mad* starving ones were the most dangerous.

"Ravenna, there you are!" Miska's voice was laced with relief as he stepped into the clearing with Ravenna and the lion. His eyes were fixed on Ravenna and he did not even see the predator waiting to pounce. The cat did not hesitate, leaping towards Miska as soon as his back was presented. Ravenna did not hesitate either.

She lunged forwards, reaching for Miska. He smiled widely, reaching back. Ravenna pushed him out of the way, throwing him violently to the ground. She stood where he had been and when the cat reached out to swipe its claws across its prey, Ravenna took the blow. She felt a bloom of pain from her left shoulder and across her chest, but she ignored it.

Dalketh against an animal was nothing like Dalketh against a human. You could predict what a human could do. If you struck their head, they would bend and protect that asset. If you struck at the head of a wild animal, it might lunge and wrap its fangs around your wrist. Ravenna screamed into the cat's ear, the sound, more than the blow she aimed at its ribs with her foot, causing it to break away.

The two circled each other for a breath before lunging forwards again. The gardens fell away, as did thoughts of Miska and her own injuries. All there was for Ravenna was the fight. It was more than it had been when fighting the slave woman. It was more than the pleasure she took in her skill training with Vareis. This was survival and desperation. This was about protecting Miska. And Ravenna was not as helpless as she had been.

Ravenna swung her elbow into the lion's eye in a sweep called Turns Mid-flight. The cat screamed and latched its claws into her gown, the fabric catching and ripping. Ravenna kept in close, pushing herself off the ground with her wings. She surged up and over the cat, landing on its back, wrapping her arms around its throat, her legs around its ribs. The cat snarled and bucked, trying to throw Ravenna off. She held on, her wings beating and buffeting the cat's face as it fought. The cat kept fighting, and Ravenna kept squeezing. After a time too long to count and too short to note, the lion ran out of air and collapsed to the ground.

Ravenna did not wait for the creature to regain consciousness. She braced her feet on either side of the lion's head, wrapped one hand under its muzzle and the other behind its rounded ears, then twisted, straining her upper body.

With a crack of its neck, the beast was dead.

Ravenna panted, her heart beating rapidly. She looked around, checking to see if there was another creature nearby, though she knew it was unlikely. Movement caught her attention at the corner of her eye; she spun. Miska was there. But something was off. The world was spinning, and she could not quite find the ground to place her feet.

Ravenna fell backward, tripping over the dead lion. Her head landed on the soft undergrowth. Miska appeared at her side, his eyes wide, his mouth moving. He pressed a hand to her shoulder and throat. Pain bloomed again, and she wasn't quite sure why. Ravenna lifted a hand to touch the spots that hurt. Her fingers came away red.

"Oh," she said, frowning. Then, everything slipped away until the green of Miska's eyes were the only things that remained. After that, darkness.

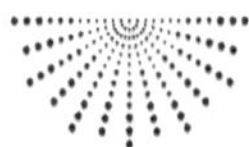

The ride to the borderlands gave Davorin too much time to think. The ten mercenaries that Utheria had selected to go with him were so terrified or in awe of him that they hardly bothered to speak except to each other. Part of Davorin was grateful for the chance to run over his plans in his head. The other part wanted to do anything *but* run over any potential problems that meeting with Seraphina might bring with only his thoughts for company.

So instead, he thought about the problems he had left behind. For one, Lenore was not warming up to him as much as he would like. He had thought they were making progress, but then the incident with Ravenna at the start of the ball had happened and it went downhill from there. Lenore had scolded him thoroughly for making Ravenna show off her wings. Davorin had apologised profusely to the Red Queen and promised to find Ravenna later and apologise. Only the stupid angel—sylph, whatever—had gone and caused a commotion out on the balcony and fled before Davorin could do anything.

Now, she was laid up in the healer's quarters after having gone after and killed a rabid desert lion. That other servant, the one who looked like he was part of the red desert stone, had claimed she saved him, getting in the way of the lion. She had received a set of nasty wounds as a result and, according to Nadezhda's leering tale that morning, had nearly died.

Davorin was not sure whether he should be impressed that the sylph had killed a desert lion, or wary that she was so dangerous.

He chose to be impressed. Wariness would imply that he was afraid of her in some small way. He knew she hated him; that was obvious. But she was also obedient, completely so. Fear was unnecessary.

"My lord." One of the soldiers approached Davorin, flashing a submissive nod. He was leaner than Davorin would have expected of a mercenary, but Utheria knew her people. "We were wondering…what's waiting for us at the borderlands?"

Davorin raised his eyebrows, surprised. "You have nothing to worry about."

"It's just, well, we figure you can handle just about anything but an overwhelming force. And we wanted to know why, then, you bothered to bring us along," the soldier said. Davorin looked closer at the man. He was not only lean, but pale-skinned with dark circles under his eyes. He was nowhere near as pale as Ravenna, nor did he possess the hardness that Davorin had come to expect from the other mercenaries. But there was a cleverness, a sharpness, in his blue eyes that struck Davorin.

"What is your name?"

"B-barrow," the man said.

"Well, Barrow, had you perhaps been anyone else, I would never have answered you. As it is, I think you will be useful. We are going to go meet with my sister, and a show of power is quite useful with her," Davorin said.

Barrow's eyes widened. "Your sister?"

"The Lady Seraphina, wife of Lord Baldur, High Warlord of Southron."

Barrow nearly choked and fell off his horse. Only training held the man in his saddle. Davorin sighed and made a mental note to ensure that these mercenaries were thoroughly loyal to him. Seraphina was insidious and had coerced more than one useful ally away from him.

* * *

"They told me that a Salusian man with twin blades was wandering around my encampment, but I didn't believe them." Seraphina preened as though Davorin had bowed and asked formal permission to enter her tent rather than barged his way into it.

"Hello, sister," Davorin grumbled. He was hot, dusty, and more than a little tired. Seraphina, on the other hand, looked as though she had been bathing in gold. Her tawny skin had become a dark golden-brown. Gold dust adorned her bare shoulders and gold leaf was painted across her cheekbones and up her fingers. She wore a light-yellow robe with wide sleeves that belted under her bust and Davorin suspected that she was wearing nothing else beneath. Seraphina had long ago learned to use her body to her advantage.

"Dear brother," Seraphina extended a hand, but otherwise lay reclining on a plush velvet couch. "I didn't actually expect you to come here after I sent my response to your message. I can assure you that all is well...here."

"Should I even *ask* what your husband's forces are doing here, amassed at the border between Southron and the Red Desert?" Davorin bit out. He sat on another one of the plush couches, ignoring the look of annoyance that resulted. Seraphina would just have to deal with a little dust. "Or would you rather me demand to know what you were thinking, uniting the tribes of Southron?"

"You worry overmuch," Seraphina sniffed. She sighed and sat up, propping her fist under her chin. "Don't you have enough to do with worrying about the Empire?"

"Just because I am not currently in the good graces of the Empire does not mean that I am not doing my best to serve its needs." Davorin ground his teeth. How dare Seraphina, of all people, suggest he was doing anything but working in the best interests of the Salusian Empire. *His* Empire. "Father is still sane enough to manage things with the help of the Council."

"Dagan's death took more out of Father than anyone would care to admit," Seraphina said. Davorin sucked in a harsh breath.

"I have heard nothing that suggests the well-being of the Empire is anything what it should be. My work continues there, even though I am here."

Seraphina waved a disinterested hand. "Come now, brother. We all know just how much you care about the well-being of the Empire. Tell me, why did you kill Dagan again? Oh, yes, because he was going to eventually bring about the downfall of the Empire."

Davorin snarled, a deep, wordless sound that rumbled through his chest. Seraphina, for all her machinations, scheming, and calm expression, blinked. "Dagan was more worried about finding immortality at the hands of mythological monsters than he was with the care of the Empire. He was conquering kingdoms with wanton bloodshed, and the conquered peoples became little more than slaves. If that had continued, then there would have been an uprising within two years. The Empire would have fractured. Our economy is still in tatters. Our peasant work force demands more resources than we can provide, all because Dagan siphoned them away. I mean to do things properly. To build the most powerful nation this world has ever seen. And I won't need mythical creatures to do it."

Seraphina bared her teeth in a loose smile, "Speaking of mythical creatures, I heard that you captured yourself an angel."

It was Davorin's turn to blink. Ravenna's presence in the land was sure to have brought about whispers, but the number of people who had seen her was relatively low. And Seraphina did not have any spies in the Red Palace. Davorin had made certain of that.

"A powerful omen," Seraphina purred. "If you believe such nonsense. What did you do, tie wings onto some unsuspecting girl and parade her around far enough away that people couldn't quite see her?"

Davorin smirked. "Actually, dear sister, that is one thing that hasn't been warped by rumour. She is a true angel. Calls herself a sylph, a winged woman. She is stunningly beautiful. More beautiful than you, even. And extremely capable. She killed a desert lion just last night."

Seraphina curled her lip and stared at the gold leaf encrusting her skin. "Would that I could believe you, Davorin. But magic and magical creatures vanished from this land generations ago. Anyone who still believes in such nonsense is a fool."

"Perhaps." Davorin shrugged. He looked around the opulence of the tent. "Where is Baldur? I would have expected him to be here to greet me."

"Out on patrol," Seraphina said. "He will be here this evening and you can ask him all about his rise to power."

"If he is the leading High Warlord of Southron, what does that make you? His Queen? Or his spymaster?"

Seraphina rolled her eyes. "You assume too much scheming, Davorin. That will forever be your downfall. Baldur managed to unite the tribes of Southron on his own. If he asked for my advice, then I gave it. But it wasn't some ridiculous bid for a kingship. The constant warring between the tribes was going to tear Southron apart. Did you know they had nearly dissolved the Tribal Council?"

Davorin sighed and leaned back. "I'm sorry. I know how ambitious you are, though. It's hard to believe that this could have happened without your scheming."

This time, Seraphina smiled fiercely, her grin nothing short of dangerous. "Just because this happened without my input doesn't mean I won't enjoy the benefits. Besides, Baldur now needs to think about the direction he is going to lead the country. How better to help him than to use my experience with the Salusian Empire?"

"Which is why you're gathered on the border of the Red Desert?"

"This again?" Seraphina huffed. Davorin leaned forwards so his elbows rested on his knees and he was close enough to his sister to see the intelligent gleam in her eyes. Seraphina, for her part, did not blink.

"I have the Red Desert under control," Davorin assured her through gritted teeth. "This gathering of forces has the Red Queen concerned."

"Ah, now we see your real reason for being here!" Seraphina crowed. "Tell me about your lady love? Does she know that you are after her kingdom as much as her heart? Or has the distant Davorin finally fallen for a woman?"

"Don't be ridiculous," Davorin grumbled. He should not have said so much. If anyone would exploit this information, it was his sister. "I am working for the betterment of the Empire."

"Adding the resources of the Red Desert to the Empire would certainly appease Father. And it would prevent Baldur from having to go to war."

"You cannot seriously have been considering fighting the people of the Red Desert?" Davorin had not thought Seraphina that stupid.

"The united tribes of Southron are a far more formidable

force than you realise," Seraphina purred. She traced a golden finger over the embroidery on her yellow robe, almost an absent gesture. Davorin understood far more than that; Southron was more than just dangerous, it was wealthy, also. A more formidable pairing, he did not know.

"I will have the Red Queen as my wife very soon," Davorin vowed. Seraphina smirked, tilting her head.

"As you like, dear brother. I shall give you a month. If you do not have control of the Red Desert by then, Southron will march. I know you are working for the betterment of the Empire, but really, we cannot wait forever."

No, Davorin thought grimly. His sister's ambition, no matter how she downplayed it, would not last that long. If he failed, not only would the Empire be worse off and his father's doubts be confirmed, but Southron would have control of a considerable power. They would be his enemy. Davorin didn't dislike his sister enough to want her dead. Just controlled.

"Very well," he agreed. "One month. I'll send the notice of the wedding by my fastest horse."

CHAPTER TWENTY

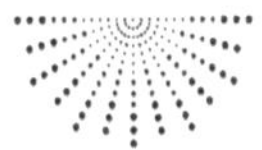

This was not the first time Ravenna had woken in pain. When she had pulled out her feathers as a child, the days after had been agony. When Jazer had branded her, Ravenna had woken with tears in her eyes. So, this was not the first time she had woken in pain, but it was the first time that she had woken with someone else's hand in hers.

Ravenna blinked her eyes open, squeezing them against the dryness. She swallowed and coughed. The resulting spasm of her muscles had her rearing her head back and arching her back up, her wings struggling as they lay pinned under her body.

"No, shh, relax."

The voice was soothing amidst the cloud of agony. Ravenna glanced sideways. Miska was there, wearing the same black tunic vest and breeches he had been wearing…when was it? Last night? A few hours ago? Ravenna did not know.

"I need you to relax. I know it hurts, but you need to relax. Breathe," Miska ordered. He put a hand on her right wing as it beat uselessly against the bed.

She forced herself to take a deep breath, letting her muscles relax a touch and took another breath. After counting to ten, the pain lessened slightly.

"What happened?" she croaked.

Miska brushed her hair from her forehead.

"You killed a rabid desert lion," he said, then smiled at her, gentle and beautiful. "You saved me."

"It scratched me." Ravenna remembered twisting the creature's neck, but she did not remember just how severe the damage was. Judging by the way her neck, left shoulder, and chest were throbbing, she imagined it was quite severe.

Miska nodded. "Yes," he breathed. "I thought you were going to die. Warra had to mix up a special poultice to draw the madness poison from your blood."

"How bad?" Ravenna asked, her words hardly more than a breath. It did not matter. Miska understood.

He turned and fetched a small round object, holding it above Ravenna's head so she could see. It was a mirror, and what looked back at her was not her reflection. Or rather, it was, but harsher, sharper. The top most wound started at the point where her left shoulder met her neck. The three beneath it stretched from the top of her arm across her chest, ending just above her right breast. On her left wrist was a circle of puncture wounds from the lion's fangs.

Miska took the mirror away, trembling. Ravenna lifted her right hand and grasped his, wondering why he looked so stricken. Miska tried to smile, but the water gathering in his eyes belied that. "I should have been more aware of my surroundings. If I weren't so useless, so hopeless, you wouldn't have been hurt."

"I have been hurt before," Ravenna said. "I will probably be hurt again. I'm glad I was there to help you."

Miska scoffed and rubbed his eyes with the back of his hand. He tried to pull the other out of Ravenna's grasp, but she tightened her grip. "It was all my fault," Miska said.

"No," was her simple answer. "It was mine."

Miska recoiled, his shoulders snapping to attention. Ravenna wanted to turn her head away so he would not see her pain, but he would not be able to understand what she said if that happened. She forced herself to keep her head turned towards Miska, though she allowed her eyes to drift downwards.

"I have always been accustomed to being on my own. And then my movements were restricted by Jazer, by Da...by my being a slave. And then here, I could run on my own. It was natural to do so. I should have realised that someone would follow me. Would want to keep track of me."

There, it had been said. Ravenna turned her head away, ignoring the twinge it brought in her wound. She felt Miska brush her forehead gently, pushing her hair aside. She closed her eyes, unable to stop the single tear that fell. Maybe Miska hadn't seen.

He brushed the tear away, too, and then he whispered in her ear, "I did not follow you because I was bid, my dear Ravenna. I followed you because I was worried about you. Because I wanted to."

Miska's lips brushed Ravenna's forehead. It was like a fire had been sparked at that spot and ran down the length of her spine. Ravenna's eyes flew open. She searched desperately for a sign of *something* in Miska, something she could not quite identify. He looked back at her with a sad smile, deep green eyes intent on nothing but her. To her surprise, Ravenna smiled back.

"What are you doing?!"

Ravenna jerked, alerting Miska to the intruder.

He turned on his stool and shrugged sheepishly at Warra.

The old woman bustled in with a suspicious look in her eyes.

"Ravenna is awake," Miska explained.

"Yes, blaggard. I can see that. The question is why you didn't come fetch me the moment she woke!" Warra shuffled over to Miska and whacked him on the back of his head.

Miska winced, but his eyes were sparkling.

"And you!" Warra pointed at Ravenna. "Have you no better sense than to go fighting a rabid desert lion? They're dangerous enough at the best of times. You're lucky to be alive. As it is, you'll be weak for ages."

Ravenna nodded. "Yes," she rasped.

Warra clucked her tongue. "And that fool didn't even give you any water. Miska! Help the girl sit up."

Miska's attention was distracted following the veins atop Ravenna's hands, earning him another thwack to the back of his head. He looked up, wide-eyed. Warra repeated the instructions, her own eyes twinkling fiercely.

Ravenna was not sure she would ever understand these particular humans, but she did like them quite a lot.

Warra saw to Ravenna's thirst and then to her wounds. As she was caring for the long scratches, her snapped remarks to Miska fell away to softer remarks to Ravenna. She was informed she had been asleep for two days. The cuts had stopped bleeding, but if Ravenna worked too hard, they would open up again. Warra applied a poultice, waited for it to dry a touch and then put on bandages as best she could manage. With Ravenna's wings, it was nearly impossible to wrap them all the way around the wounds.

"Now, you're to stay here for at least another day. Then we can see about getting you back to your own quarters," Warra said, shooing Miska away to clean up the mess. "And you're not going to like it, but you're going to have to be very careful before you do anything physical. No running, no jumping, and *no fighting*. Those slices are long, but they're also deep. You need to give your body time to heal."

"I understand," Ravenna murmured. She did, but it did not help that it felt as though the small freedoms she had were being taken away. There would be no more training with Vareis. Maybe she could convince Miska to bring her books from the library. She hadn't gone through all of the journals by Lenore's sylph ancestor, yet. Still, there was the sense of being trapped.

"Hmph," Warra sniffed. "You'll be on your feet before I tell you, back here trying to figure out why you're not healing. Well, don't come crying to me if your wounds open up again!"

"Thank you, Warra," Ravenna said, trying to smile at the healer. The older woman returned the smile graciously and smoothed the bedclothes around Ravenna.

"You saved our Miska, here," Warra said, glancing over her shoulder to be certain that Miska was focusing his attention elsewhere. "We are all grateful. Miska is well loved here. He is a good man."

"Yes," Ravenna agreed, catching her eyes following Miska's frame as he moved about the room, tidying up with a pleased expression on his face. "He is."

Warra nodded, as if Ravenna had confirmed something, then bustled off. Ravenna watched the others' movements for a few moments. She blinked heavily and, before she could see Miska retake his place on the stool beside her bed, fell asleep again.

I LEARNED *from my dear Yvette that some thousand cycles ago, it was considered common for humans to wield magic. She told me that the dragons' disappearance led to a dearth of magic in the land and that now, only some three humans are said to wield magic. Two of those are but names, otherwise lost to the mists of time: Nicaros, Ilucia. The third is called Oterian, a man said to possess the visage of an elf dipped in shadow, with skin as dark as night and eyes like the stars. He is said to have been alive during the Fire Wars and to have convened with the leader of the Stormbringers, Veritus. Stories of the Stormbringers are rare enough on Shinalea, no longer part of our*

history but lost to lore and therefore irrelevant to the Intellecti. I, myself, know only that they were legion and fought on the side of the dragons, for all the good that did them. There is much we can learn from our human counterparts. If only the Intellecti had been open minded enough for...

✳ ✳ ✳

Ravenna tossed the tome aside, thoroughly bored. She had always been a keen reader on Shinalea, absorbing the histories and lessons Tacitus taught her with a fervent zeal. But after having nothing to do for three days but sit in her bed, reading, she was growing more than a little tired of tomes.

Three times a day, Miska came by with a tray of food and drink, Warra trailing in his wake. The little healer allowed Ravenna ten minutes to walk around, use the necessary, stretch her wings and get out some of the energy she had building in her blood. Then, it was back to sitting in bed to eat and regain her strength.

These little moments of exercise were extremely frustrating, not because Ravenna wanted to do more, but because she *couldn't.* She fairly collapsed back in her bed after each interval, her heart pounding and her wounds throbbing. It was frustrating to no end.

"Well, if you hadn't already been weak," Warra had said, clucking her tongue as Ravenna did her best not to glare at the healer. "But you know as well as I that you hadn't been eating properly for at least a month before this incident. You arrived here half-starved, for goodness sakes! Not to mention your training with Vareis. You were strong, but a body can only take so many abuses."

"Yes, Warra," Ravenna had grumbled.

Now, she was more than a little tired of reading about Lenore's ancestor. The former Intellecti seemed to have left

Shinalea not because of some accident, like Ravenna, but because he chose to see what the rest of the world held. He was frustrated with the restrictions of the Intellecti and the sylph society, preferring to do as he wished. Only, he was not often mistaken for a deity or divine being, like Ravenna. Perhaps it was because there was still magic in the world back then. Whatever it was, Ravenna didn't care. She was tired of reading about his complaints regarding the Intellecti and philosophical musings on events that had happened ages ago.

Ravenna sighed and looked around her room, hoping for some entertainment besides the stack of books beside her bed. Lenore kept bringing more, never staying for long, her eyes apologetic and a little afraid. Of what, Ravenna didn't know.

She sat up straighter in the bed and stretched as much as her wounds would allow. Her wings flexed wide, the feathers separating and shaking as the muscles tightened, then relaxed. She flapped once, settling them down again, and nearly knocked over the books. Ravenna let out a sound of disgust and fell back against the pillows.

"You do not look happy." Miska's head appeared in the doorway, an amused smile tugging at the corner of his lips.

Ravenna sighed dramatically.

"Do you know how unnatural it is for a sylph to have her wings pinned down like this? We never sleep on our backs or sit with our wings against a wall. Yet here I am, unable to do anything *but* sit here with my wings pinned, because if I lay on my stomach, the scratches would open up again."

Miska approached Ravenna's bed, carrying a small tray with a large flagon and a pastry that looked like it had been made of slivered layers of butter. "It's a bit early, but Queen Lenore is having a dinner tonight and these were amongst the treats that the kitchen is preparing. I thought you'd like some."

He sat on the edge of her bed, not even bothering to ask her permission. Secretly, Ravenna was glad. She disliked having

Miska, of all people, so formal with her. He finally seemed to have gotten over his aversion to further injuring the person who had saved his life. Now, they could be friends again.

She took the drink and sipped it. "It's cold!" she said, holding it away from her. "And sweet!"

"It's an iced cream drink. There is a tiny ice room deep in the bowels of the palace where we get the ice for the iced drinks and creams. Do you like it?"

She nodded. "I do. Thank you."

He handed her the pastry without a word and she devoured it before she could ask what it was. He tossed his head back and laughed.

"I, ah…I've finished the books," she said after a moment.

His eyes widened.

"I have nothing else to do."

He sighed. "You're bored. I wish things were different. You should be up, training with Vareis and enjoying your days. I should be the one injured and on bed rest."

Ravenna reached out and touched his arm. He looked at her in surprise. "Miska, let's get this straight once and for all. If I had not run out, you would not have been in danger. But if I had not been there and you were in danger, you would have died. You are not a fighter, not accustomed to harming others or to taking a life. I am not a killer, but I would do what is necessary to protect those I care about. It is too late to change things, so you may as well accept what has happened."

Miska tightened his fist, struggling to keep his expression impassive, as though he had not heard her. But he was not as capable of concealing what he felt. He had not Ravenna's ability to conceal her mind, nor her history to enforce it. After a few moments of struggle, he just gave up completely.

Miska stood, tugging Ravenna upwards. She winced slightly at the pull on her wounds, but obliged. She would have done almost anything to get out of that bed. "Come on," he said, not looking at her so he could not see her response and she couldn't read the emotions ranging across his features.

Ravenna was pulled through the open window into a stifling day beyond. The gardens were completely still, there being no wind and no clouds. The sun beat heavily down and even the moisture in the air provided by the underground springs felt oppressive. The palace servants were all indoors and the soldiers in the far training arena were too busy with their own tasks to bother with the gardens. Ravenna and Miska were alone.

Miska, though, did not seem content to stop at the pavilion where they had shared meals. Nor did he lead them further into the gardens to see where plant-life met desert. He instead pulled Ravenna around to the other side of the palace, a place closer to the grand library and quarters for the honoured guests that stayed at the Red Palace. The carvings grew more elaborate, the trees were better groomed and well cared for, as opposed to the other plants which were left to grow as they liked.

Eventually, Miska slowed to a stop, Ravenna breathing heavily beside him. She examined her surroundings as she got her breath under control, ignoring the searching look that Miska threw her way.

They were standing beside a large stone pool, its sides perfectly square, the water disturbed by the gentle trickling of a fountain in the centre of the pool. It was grey with algae, but the shape was unmistakeable. A man, wings folded calmly at his sides, stood with his arms around a woman. Water flowed from a pedestal beneath the statue. These would be Lenore's ancestors, then.

"Are you alright?" Miska asked, steering Ravenna to a shaded patch of grass beneath a tree. She sat, stretching her wings out as far as they would go. The relief in her muscles was stunning, as was the view when she could finally catch her breath. Miska sat across from her, the shade dappling his reddish skin an unusual colour.

"This place is beautiful," Ravenna said, ignoring the concern for her person. "I didn't even know it existed."

"It is Queen Lenore's private gardens. She lets me and the other servants come here, sometimes. I thought you would like to get out of your rooms, maybe. I didn't mean to stress your injuries."

"I'm fine, Miska," Ravenna snapped. She sighed, picking at the bandage wrapped around her wrist. "You didn't have to interrupt your day to come babysit me. I would have been fine."

"What if I said I wanted to spend time with you?" Miska asked, a sharp edge entering his voice for the first time since Ravenna had thrown him to the ground in the library all those weeks ago. She frowned, hardly more than a tightening at the corner of her mouth.

"That is your choice," Ravenna said carefully. Where was Miska going with this conversation? "But you did not have to."

Miska was the one to sigh, now. He shook his head. Looking back up at Ravenna, he said, "Is there anything you need? Some water? Something to eat?"

"I don't need anything."

"Are you sure? I was the one who brought you out here. I should help you if you want—"

"Nothing! I don't need anything. I'm not hot or cold or hungry or thirsty or tired or bored or anything," Ravenna said. She wanted to seethe, but Miska made it difficult. It was the way he watched her so intently, looking for clues into her emotions, her words. All because he could not hear her voice.

No one had ever watched Ravenna like that. Like they wanted to see her. Even Tacitus, as much as she loved him, had, more often than not, listened to her words with his eyes glazed, his mind elsewhere. Or he had sat beside her and looked off into the distance.

But Miska…

"That's your problem," he said, and Ravenna finally realised that he was angry. "You've spent so long pushing away your own needs, dealing with everything on your own, that you don't know *how* to let anyone—me—take care of you!"

Ravenna reached out to touch her fingers to the back of his hand. Thankfully, Miska did not pull away.

"Let me do *something* for you," he said, voice thick.

Ravenna nodded. Even as her mind raced to figure out something she wanted—needed—that Miska could give her. Her mouth went dry, but she managed to get the words out.

"Please," she breathed. "Just…just hold me?"

Her voice sounded uncertain, but Miska would not know or care. He just smiled, moved impossibly close and wrapped his arms around Ravenna. He held her until the shudders stopped wracking her body. And he held her still, long after they had gone.

CHAPTER TWENTY-ONE

*D*avorin spent three days enjoying his sister's hospitality. He had been given a luxurious tent to himself while his mercenaries were quartered amongst the Southron fighters. Barrow had taken to Davorin's request for spy work like a wolf to the hunt. The others did their best, but they had not the unobtrusive looks nor the brains of Barrow. Still, one spy was welcome enough.

For Davorin's part, he spent his time trying to talk with Baldur without Seraphina around. The Southron Warlord was annoyingly difficult on this point. When Baldur was not with his wife, he was out on patrol or running drills. He was strong enough, as far as men went, but his fighters were often the victors. And he laughed a good deal more than seemed prudent for someone of his position. But the fighters seemed devoted to Baldur, would hardly hear a word against him. As for Seraphina, they loved her without reserve.

Some, Davorin expected, loved her in more ways than one. He had no proof on that matter, though, and so had nothing to hold against his sister.

On the fourth morning, he lingered at the breakfast table in

Seraphina's tent. She was dressed in copper that day, her robe seemingly made from the metal itself. She had copper claws tipping her fingers and copper beads woven through her hair. Baldur, on the other hand, wore his same simple tunic and breeches that he wore every day. Today, it sported a slight tear in the hem.

"Brother," Seraphina purred, lingering over the tea she had imported from the Salusian capitol, "don't mistake my meaning. But you have been here far longer than I expected, given your plans with the Red Queen. Do you have any intention of leaving anytime soon?"

Davorin finished his own tea—a fragrant reminder of home that left a streak of anger on his palate—and rolled the cup through his hands. "I will be leaving this evening. Travelling in the desert during the day, especially at this time of year, is hard on the horses."

"I see," Seraphina said. "Well, at least let us give you supplies for you return journey. And a gift for your darling, perhaps? What do you think, my dear?"

Baldur smiled at his wife. He reached out to stroke her hair, jingling the copper beads. "Whatever you wish, my love. I am sure we have some finery around that would suit."

Davorin did not quite understand how these people could stand the syrupy words that they sprouted when within ten feet of each other. He would never be so...weak. "Thank you, Seraphina, Baldur," Davorin said, bowing his head. "I will gladly accept your offer. Any supplies can be delivered to my people. As for gifts, it's not really necessary—"

"Tosh!" Seraphina waved away Davorin's words. "All women like gifts, no matter what they say. I'll send someone by later with a few options."

Davorin shrugged. "As you like." Frankly, he was tired of his sister's company and had many things to attend to. He had lingered far too long already, hoping to glean some further information about Seraphina's plans. All he had for his efforts was further knowledge of the Southron devotion to their Queen and her pet Warlord.

Davorin rose and bowed to his sister and Baldur before leaving their tent for the sweltering heat. This scrubland was not quite as barren as the desert where the Red Palace lay, but it was close. Certainly, the tiny well that served as the water source for the whole camp was barely enough. Davorin found himself longing for the enormous and imposing oasis that was the Red Palace. When it belonged to him, he would happily set it up as an eastern home for the Salusian Empire. Surely even the Emperor could not protest at such a grand acquisition.

He ignored the niggling desire to talk with Barrow and the others and sort out their plans. If Barrow was doing his job right, then the mercenaries under Davorin's command should already know their master's intentions. No, all Davorin wanted was some peace and quiet in his own tent.

He closed the flap of the enormous tent behind him. Not for the first time, he wondered who it was that had been displaced by his presence in the tent. Not even Seraphina would have a wooden bed and reed-and-down mattress lying around for whomever wanted to use it. The floor was covered in colourful rugs and a few furs, to keep the sand and dirt out. There was a chest that served as a table, as well as two chairs.

Davorin sat in one of the chairs and pulled a few charts towards him. They were relatively recent surveys of the Red Desert, detailing the potential resources and advantages of the desert, where a person could find water outside of the Red Palace's oasis, where the armies were stationed, where the entrenched fortresses were. It was incomplete, but even so, it showed a treasure trove of wealth stretching all the way to the emptiness that was the Iron Mountains.

"M'lord?"

Davorin jumped to his feet, stifling a curse. He pulled the

blade on his right hip out of its sheath, pointing it towards the entrance to his tent. A girl, perhaps barely nineteen, stood there with a small chest in her arms, eyes wide and afraid.

"Who are you?" Davorin demanded. The girl, bearing the same tanned skin as Davorin and Seraphina, but with locks the colour of false gold and eyes a bright blue, sketched a nervous curtsey.

"I am Nadira, m'lord," she said, lowering her gaze reverentially. "The Lady Seraphina sent me to you."

Davorin raised his brow skeptically, "Did she?"

Nadira blushed, the colour surprisingly becoming. "She said she had some gifts for the Red Queen and wanted your approval."

Davorin huffed. Of course. "Very well. Set them here." He put his blade away and Nadira stepped cautiously forwards. She set the small chest down on the makeshift table, then tugged her dress. As she did, it tightened and revealed more of her curves. Well, at least Seraphina had bothered to send someone becoming.

"Let's see what my sister thought fit to send to the Red Queen," Davorin said, eyeing Nadira's reaction more than the goods inside the chest. Her sharp intake of breath and the way her eyes widened at the sight of the contents was enough for him. The gifts would obviously impress.

He looked at the multi-tiered necklace with red jewels wrapped in gold, the delicate arm cuff in the shape of a dragon, the fabric that looked to be made from liquid silver, the bracelet with green jewels, and knew that they were the least of Seraphina's collection. But they were impressive enough and would certainly pay for a good deal of resources, if Davorin deemed them inadequate for a queen. Lenore rarely wore such grand things, he recalled. Yet Nadira's awed gaze seemed to be unwavering, suggesting that they were grand indeed.

"Well?" Davorin asked, reaching in and pulling out the emerald bracelet. "What do you think?"

Nadira blushed again. Her fingers reached for the bracelet, only to retreat and rest against her bosom. "Oh, it's so beautiful. I've never seen such finery, but what the Lady Seraphina wears."

Davorin was struck with an idea, and a longing. Since both served his needs, he forged ahead. He reached out and took one of Nadira's hands, purposely brushing his fingers against the bare skin revealed by her dress. She gasped, but that gasp quickly turned into a murmur of delighted surprise when he placed the bracelet on her wrist, doing the clasp before bringing her hand to his lips.

"Beautiful," he agreed, making certain that his eyes never left Nadira's. The girl smiled coyly, twisting her head to expose her neck.

"M'lord!" she said. "I cannot wear a gift meant for your... your paramour!"

He pulled her closer, so her body was mere inches from his. "And look how well she wears it."

It took a moment for the young girl to understand what he was saying. When she did, though, the light in her eyes sharpened and she closed the scant distance between them. Her lips found his easily and she did not protest as he wrapped his arm around her back, pulling her into him tightly.

It was the work of moments to seduce her, but he took his time bedding the woman. As morning turned to afternoon, he considered the price of his sister's emerald bracelet well worth the result. A distraction, a release, and proof that he could still manipulate someone into doing what he wished. Between Seraphina and Lenore, he had begun to doubt his skills. No longer.

* * *

Davorin knew that he needed to get up and finish his preparation to return to the Red Palace, but it was very comfortable in the bed with the bare-skinned Nadira laying on top of him. He traced lines along her back and decided that he might as well get some further use out of her.

"Nadira," he said. The girl stirred, her hair tangled and showing obvious evidence of their coupling.

"Yes, m'lord?" she asked, pressing her lips to his shoulder.

"What is someone like you doing in the service of my sister out here on the borderlands? Surely you could have a better life in one of the more established cities in Southron? Or even the Salusian Empire."

Affronted, Nadira sat up, revealing her nakedness. Davorin shifted beneath her, a wry look colouring his features. Nadira snatched a blanket and pressed it to her chest. "I am useful here! The Lady Seraphina has given me a good life!"

"Yes, but surely it could be better," he said, sliding the blanket aside, tracing lines along her hip. "To be a mere servant in a camp of warriors in a land on the brink of war…"

Nadira sniffed. "I am not a *mere* servant! The Lady Seraphina trusts me. I can get close to people most people would fail to get near. I am talented."

He chuckled.

Her mouth fell open and she scrabbled backward from Davorin, shaking her head fervently.

"I would *never*! Not with you, m'lord! I mean, I was told to do so, but you're so much more than the Lady Seraphina said. You were so nice to me. You haven't hurt me like some of the others. I…I want to go with you," she said, her words rushing together even as tears welled in her eyes. False or real, it did not matter to Davorin.

"You cannot," he said. He climbed out of the bed, looming over her enough to make her shrink, another plea dropping from her tongue. He merely reached forwards to brush a strand of her hair behind her ears. "For what it's worth, I believe you. My sister speaks well, but she is as cunning and cold as a snake. She doesn't care for the well-being of her people, only for power. I know better. An Empire is built on the backs of its people and without their support, it cannot survive. Do you understand me?"

Nadira nodded dumbly.

"Good. Now, my dear," he said, throwing in the endearment he had heard that morning passed between his sister and her husband, "do you know what you must do?'

"I…You want me to stay here. To report to you on the Lady Seraphina's movements. Oh, but m'lord! When will you send for me?" Nadira was on her knees, begging, her fingers grabbing at Davorin's hands in desperation.

"When my business is concluded in the Red Desert," he lied easily.

She frowned at that, another tear falling from her eye.

"You intend to marry the Red Queen," she sniffled.

"Yes. But that is nothing to someone such as you," he said. "Now, what can you tell me about Seraphina's doings here. It seems a bit unusual to linger in the borderlands, away from the central cities."

Nadira hesitated, but the emerald bracelet on her wrist caught her eye and her hesitation lasted no more than a few seconds. She licked her lips and looked up at Davorin eagerly. The artifice of her simpering persona was gone, replaced with a blatant lust for power. "This isn't a war band, for all the High Warlord's patrols," she said.

"There is no mineral here, nor no plant worth having. What could possibly be of interest?" he asked. Whatever it was, to keep Seraphina away from her seat of power was something Davorin knew he had to have.

"Get dressed, m'lord," Nadira said, slipping out of the bed and throwing her dress over her head. "I will show you."

Davorin did as he was told and bit back any questions until she was leading him across the camp to a small, patched tent. She looked around swiftly for watchful eyes, then moved inside. Davorin copied her.

What he found was the whole of Seraphina's treasures laid out before him in a number of plain chests. There were jewels, fabrics, spices, teas, fortunes. Nadira, for all her greed at Davorin's gift, ignored them all. She instead gestured him over to a box not much bigger than his closed fist.

"She was looking for this, and more like it," Nadira murmured, flicking the catch open on the box.

Inside was nothing more than a large animal's fang, broken at the top and ending in a needle's point. Davorin picked the piece up and weighed it in his hand. It had more weight to it than he would have imagined, but it was more than simple mass. There was a strength, a sense of power that filled one's bones. Davorin would have thought it nothing more than a large wolf's tooth, or perhaps one of those desert lion's fangs, had Dagan not lectured Davorin on such things.

Over and over, Dagan had spouted the stories. He would talk of little else—when Davorin could even get a conversation out of him. It was either bloodshed or lore with Dagan. Davorin had thought it a fool's obsession, until now.

"This is impossible," Davorin murmured. But he had breathed those words before, when an angel of untold beauty and an icy fire burning in her eyes stood before him. That had been no more impossible than this.

"A dragon's tooth," Nadira confirmed. "The Lady Seraphina found some old records mouldering in one of the smaller tribe's collections when the unification was brought about. There was a detailed map to the grave site of a dragon. She sent a scout on a whim and he returned with this."

"She searches for more remains," Davorin muttered. Realisation struck him. He closed his fist around the tooth hard enough for it to bite into his skin and draw a few drops of blood. The power in the ancient relic was strong enough to make his head sing. Dragon remains were rumoured to contain vast magical powers. They would grant the bearer power in ways that were beyond reckoning.

If Seraphina gained that power, then Davorin—and the Empire—would fall at her feet.

Davorin smiled at Nadira, pulling her in for a swift kiss. Then, without a backward glance or a goodbye, he ran from the treasure trove and back to his tent. Within five minutes, he was packed and walking to where his mercenaries waited, the chest of gifts for Lenore under his arm. The dragon's tooth was tucked firmly into his waistband. In another five minutes, the whole party was gone from the camp.

Seraphina would not discover his theft for two days.

CHAPTER TWENTY-TWO

"What are we doing?" Ravenna asked.

Miska kept polishing the silver border around a mirror in one of the myriad of hallways in the Red Palace.

Ravenna set down her own rag and touched Miska on the shoulder. He turned and fixed her with a smile.

"Done already?" he teased, though Ravenna had not actually been cleaning. She had been cleared by Warra to spend more time out of bed—as long as she neither ran nor fought. And she had promised the healer to see her if the wounds bothered her at all, and to sit if her strength flagged. Miska had then offered to let her stay with him while he worked, so she would not be bored. Ravenna had agreed.

"Miska, what are we doing?" Ravenna asked again, as if it were not obvious. "I mean, I'm a sylph, formerly a slave. I hardly know anything of your human world. And you have grown up amongst this wealth and splendour and…what are we doing?"

"Ravenna," Miska murmured. He brushed her cheek with his thumb. "Does it bother you that you are a sylph and I'm human?"

It was so much harder to talk with Miska, sometimes. If Ravenna felt uncomfortable with others, she could look away, or turn to face a window and the other person would still be able to hear. With Miska, she had to watch every instance of emotion flicker across his features, no matter how painful because if she looked away, he would not hear. But he needed to hear.

"When I was young, I learned about humans in the vast tomes we have. They don't feature much in our recent history, but the stories we have about them were akin to nightmares. I knew them only as cruel, warmongers who drank strategy and death like wine. Then, I was captured. Everything I had heard, no matter how absurd, seemed to be perfectly true. Humans were monsters."

"Oh, Ravenna," Miska said, his green eyes swimming with pain. He started to pull away from Ravenna, but she grabbed his hand and held it tightly.

"When I was in the Pits, I met these two slaves, Radim and Tekko. They were charged with teaching me to fight, so I wouldn't die immediately when pitted against another slave or a starved animal. I thought they were like the others, revelling in death. But it turns out they were just trying to survive. Then there was Davorin..." Ravenna took a deep breath and shook her head. "The specifics don't matter, only the fact that he is like the old sylph stories."

"We know about Davorin," Miska murmured. "Queen Lenore is on her guard. It wouldn't do to have the Salusian Empire bearing down on us. But she knows the truth."

Ravenna nodded. "Good. But my point is, Miska, the overwhelming majority of humans that I've met have been exactly as they were described. Then I came here. And everything is so different. Lenore actually cares about her people. The servants and soldiers are happy. And you! No matter how I snapped or ignored you or fought you, you were always there with a smile and a friendly word. I *shouldn't* want this. But I do."

Miska, for once, did not smile. He just tilted his head downwards so that his forehead rested against Ravenna's. He closed his eyes. "I want this, too," he said.

Knowing Miska could not hear her, Ravenna took action herself—lifting her chin just enough so that their breath mingled, she kissed him.

Miska was fire, passion. He surged against Ravenna with more force than she would have expected from the mild-mannered man. This was wing-tingling, feather-rustling, heart-pounding fire. It was like nothing Ravenna had ever experienced with any sylph and she knew that she would never want to.

She made a low sound in her throat and threaded her hands through his dark brown hair. Miska's fingers ran along her waist, brushing the feathers of her wings and her stomach. They moved closer together, as if trying to bridge any differences they might have. And between them, an insatiable and impossibly strong fire kindled.

Ravenna did not know how long she had kissed Miska, only that a smirking cough startled her awake. Ravenna jumped back, looking past Miska to see Lenore standing in the hallway, a blushing young serving boy at her side.

Miska, unaware of the cough and unapologetic, turned to see his queen standing there.

He nodded respectfully, but he was not quite able to wipe the pleased expression from his face. "My Queen," he said.

Lenore laughed. She touched the serving boy on the shoulder, "Thank you for bringing me here. You may go."

The boy ran off before anyone could blink. Silence descended on the hallway, with Lenore at one end and Ravenna and Miska on the other. Finally, Lenore started forwards, shaking her head and wearing an enormous grin. "Finally! I wondered how long it would take you to woo her," Lenore said.

"You expected this?" Ravenna demanded. Miska, thank goodness, had his attention focused on Lenore and did not catch her words.

"But of course," Lenore purred. She stopped just before the two and clapped her hands, almost giddy with delight. "I couldn't imagine a better match! Miska is the best man you'll ever meet. And you are all strength and goodness."

Ravenna tossed her head at that. "Goodness? I don't think so."

Miska caught those words. He tilted Ravenna's chin up so she was looking him in the eye. "It's true. You have saved me twice, without thought for your own safety. You worry about people even though you have been hurt so many times. You are bitter, perhaps, and sharp, but you care *so much*."

"Twice?" Ravenna frowned.

"The lion," Miska said, tracing a finger along the bandage that Ravenna still wore. "And in the hallway, with Davorin. You told him that I hadn't overheard him because I couldn't. You gave him the only plausible explanation to keep me from death."

Ravenna blanched, having forgotten about that conversation. It seemed so inconsequential at the time, so completely normal that she had not thought anything of it. Davorin had been the one who controlled her, whether Lenore and Miska thought so or not. He still had a sword poised at her throat, metaphorically speaking, but now perhaps Ravenna could fight back. Perhaps she could make her life here without Davorin. After all, Lenore was already wise to his dangers.

"Thank you," Ravenna breathed. "For seeing me better than I ever have."

Miska pulled her into a hug, his arms encircling her shoulders and her arms wrapping around his ribs. Her wings folded around them until it seemed until they were the only ones in the world.

Lenore coughed pointedly again.

Ravenna pulled away, more slowly this time, and linked her fingers with Miska's.

"I did come to find you two," Lenore said after a moment. Her easy smile fell away and she looked a little nervous, nothing like the grand queen that ruled the Red Desert.

"My Queen?" Miska asked, frowning. "What is it?"

Lenore sighed. She shifted her gaze to Ravenna; the sylph felt her feathers flare out slightly, fear gripping her spine. "What do you know of Captain Nadezhda?" Lenore asked.

Ravenna wanted to spit in disgust. Instead, she bared her teeth like the lion that had mauled her and snarled, "She is a monster."

Miska and Lenore recoiled slightly at Ravenna's harsh tone. Lenore licked her lips and tentatively prodded further. "I would have thought...considering her master, that you would, well, think her..."

"Think her less dangerous?" Ravenna asked, her fire quickly tempering to ice. "Yes. Nadezhda is less dangerous than Davorin. She has none of his cunning and calculating mind. She does not plan for the future as he does, nor does she have the innate grasp of power that flows through his honeyed words. That does not mean she is not a monster!"

"We never said she wasn't," Miska murmured, kissing Ravenna's hair gently. "Your vehemence just surprised us."

Us. Like Ravenna was separate. She knew that Miska did not think of her that way, but the choice of words reminded Ravenna that she was still an outsider. She might have fit there well, but it was not her world. Perhaps it could be, though.

She shook her head and replied to Miska's words with a weak smile. "Nadezhda was the leader of the slavers that brought me to the Pits. She kept me sounder than the others, but she was never fair nor kind. She delights in cruelty and violence. Her desires are base and her mind unchecked. Under Davorin's command, she has become a dangerous tool to wield. Make no mistake, though, she is a monster. Just one contained."

"Perhaps not so contained, now that her master isn't here," Lenore said. The other two looked at her in confusion. Lenore winced, frowning almost apologetically at Ravenna. "She was found snooping around your rooms. Reading the journals of my ancestor. Is there something I should know?"

Ravenna pulled back, her calm expression impossible to maintain. "I would *never*—"

"No," Lenore shook her head. "That's not what I meant. I mean about the journals. Is there something dangerous there that would get back to Davorin?"

Ravenna's wings flared wide in alarm, even as she struggled to think of something that the man could use. She shook her head. "I don't know. There weren't any maps or descriptions of how he could get to Shinalea. And much of the information is outdated, considering it is generations old. I don't think there's anything."

"Perhaps you should come with me, anyways," Lenore said, still frowning. "I've had Captain Nadezhda taken to one of the lower chambers for questioning. There isn't much I can do, as Davorin is my guest and his people are as well. But I must do something."

"You may not want to risk this," Ravenna murmured. Miska brushed his thumb along Ravenna's jaw and lifted her chin. She saw his eyes swimming with confusion, as much as they swam with affection. Ravenna explained. "Nadezhda is second in command to Davorin. If he discovers that his Captain was being held and questioned, he may retaliate. He already wants..."

Ravenna broke off and took a shuddering breath. She could tell these two exactly what Davorin wanted. She could tell them that he thought of her as his property and that he expected her to help his cause with Lenore. She could tell them that he would take the army of the Red Desert and add it to that of the Salusian Empire without a second thought. Lenore's people would be subjugated to a cruel master. But Ravenna found the words stuck in her throat. There was a lingering feeling that if she said nothing, perhaps these people would be safer. Perhaps they would not be swept up in Davorin's insane schemes. The truth was that they would just be more likely to be unable to defend themselves.

"It's alright, Ravenna," Miska said, putting a protective arm around her shoulders. "You don't have to put yourself in danger for us."

"Is *that* what you think this is? My reluctance to tell you is because *I'm* in danger?" Ravenna hissed. She shrugged Miska's arm off and forced him to step back with a flex of her wings. "You are a fool if you think that."

"But I saw him talking to you in the hallway!" Miska protested. Lenore put her hand on his arm, amber eyes shining. "I saw him threaten you!"

Ravenna scoffed. "His threats hold no sway over me," she said. "But they will for you."

Lenore blinked. She shook her head, the tiny braids of her hair swinging along her back. "I don't understand. I thought you had no magic."

"Magic? What does that have to do with anything?"

"How else can you defy Davorin?"

Ravenna looked at the floor, studying the swirls in the marble. In her fear and anger, she had built that man up to be something greater than he was. A pillar of stone, a monster of legendary capability. Even Lenore and Miska had begun to see him that way. And yes, he was powerful. He was cruel. He held no remorse. But for Ravenna, he was nothing more than another human. These people had more to lose by defying him.

"Davorin seeks to marry you," Ravenna said plainly. If she expected Lenore to react violently, then she was mistaken.

"I expected as much, given the attentions he has paid me. At first, I thought he was merely seeking an alliance, such as I have with some of the other smaller bordering lands, but then he brought me you. I don't think I was meant to see you as a slave to free, but as a gift." Lenore tugged at the light fabric of her navel-grazing shirt. She lifted her eyes to Ravenna's.

Ravenna inclined her head.

"I know the Red Desert is wealthy in resources and finances, but no one from the Salusian Empire has paid me anything more than a cursory visit. So what does he want?"

Ravenna raised her eyebrows in surprise, looking between Miska and the Queen. They both looked slightly confused and worried. "You do not know?" Ravenna asked. She received blank looks in response. "Davorin seeks to acquire your army. Your people. He wants to add your fighting ability to that of the Salusian Empire. I don't know why, but I think it has to do with another brother or some failed expectations by the Emperor or something. What I overheard was not comprehensive."

"There was another brother," Miska said. "Dagan. He was killed during his latest campaign to conquer the surrounding lands. But everyone thought that the expansion of the Salusian Empire was at an end. Dagan was the bloodthirsty, ambitious one. Davorin was always seen as more of a scholar, a schemer, than a conqueror. His works in the Empire have balanced many economies of the conquered peoples. And made them completely dependent on the Empire."

"He wants to succeed Dagan," Lenore breathed. Her golden skin grew pale and she staggered for a moment. Miska was immediately by her side, steadying her. Lenore pressed her hands to her stomach, fear written plainly on her face. "He wants to continue the expansion of the Empire. He wants to take this whole land and everything beyond. No wonder he felt threatened by Southron's movements at the border. If his sister is half as ambitious as he is, then she'll be clamouring to get her hands on my lands, too."

Ravenna placed a hand on Lenore's. When the Queen lifted her head, Ravenna's eyes were hard, cold. "Perhaps we should go ask his Captain about his plans."

"Perhaps we should," Lenore agreed, though she still looked ill.

"Maybe we can encourage her to tell her master that the Red Desert is not for the taking," Miska put in. Both women looked at him, saw the hopeful and determined expression shining from his green eyes. Lenore smiled. Ravenna kept her expression blank, thinking that it would take more than sheer will to deter Davorin. But she followed Lenore to where Captain Nadezhda was being held. Her fingers twined with Miska's the entire way.

* * *

Nadezhda sneered as the trio came into the room. She was sitting on a stone bench carved from the wall in a room that looked like it had not been used for anything but storage for years. The guard gave a relieved glance as Lenore, Miska and Ravenna approached, as if he would rather not be there with the woman. Lenore set herself directly in front of the Captain, Miska and Ravenna behind. It was on Ravenna that Nadezhda focused her attention, though.

"So, the little bird found herself a lover," Nadezhda said, chuckling dryly. "What will Lord Davorin say about such a choice?"

"Lord Davorin has no say in Ravenna's choices," Lenore said. Her voice held all of the natural command afforded her station. It slid off of Nadezhda like water.

"Doesn't he?" Nadezhda said. "What gratitude to the man

who rescued her from slavery, to consort with lowly servants. Where are you from, boy? You don't look like any desert dweller *I* know, and you're certainly not from Southron or the Salusian Empire. Though it figures that a flightless bird would end up with an inbred ingrate."

Now it was Ravenna's turn to speak, and she found that all the fire in her belly had turned to that familiar feeling of ice. Her voice was cold and as unfeeling as the bitter winter wind, "This flightless bird is worth more than your pitiful life, Captain. I doubt your master would appreciate you alienating me, considering I am an angel, a divine being, after all."

Nadezhda paled, but still managed to spit, "You're not an angel. There's nothing divine about you. I've seen you bleed."

Ravenna gave a wing-shrug, "Perhaps. But the rest of the world does not know that. And I would imagine that Queen Lenore's reach is farther and stronger than yours."

"Lord Davorin will hear of your insolence!" Nadezhda clenched her hands into fists, but she was wise enough at least not to jump and goad anyone into a fight. Ravenna was still injured, and Warra would have her head for getting into a fight, but if Nadezhda chose to attack, she would not mind taking the woman down a few notches.

"Lord Davorin will hear that you have been snooping around my palace," Lenore snapped.

"He merely wished me to see how Ravenna was recovering after her devastating attack by the lion. He was worried that her wounds would get worse and that she might be forever maimed," Nadezhda said easily. She looked at Ravenna in mock concern. "Should I have ignored the wishes of Lord Davorin on such a matter? He is incredibly fond of you, Ravenna."

"As he is fond of you?" Ravenna asked smoothly.

Nadezhda's eyes flashed dangerously and she turned her head.

Ravenna shook her head in disgust. She was about to say

more, challenging Nadezhda's place in Davorin's world, but Miska twined his fingers in hers again. He had been silent through the whole exchange. He could not have seen everything that Lenore and Ravenna had said, but Nadezhda's reactions would have told him enough.

"Captain, I have no right to hold you, as you have not broken any of my laws and your leader has been welcomed here as a guest," Lenore said regally. "But you have been caught in a place where you shouldn't have been, in possession of items that were not yours. You say that you were merely checking in on Ravenna, to make certain that she is recovering well after her brave actions. But Ravenna was not there when you were, and there is no reason that you should have been present while she was not. Have you anything to say in your defence?"

Captain Nadezhda sneered and shook her head. "I was mistaken about Ravenna's whereabouts," was all she said. "I simply thought to wait for her and read a book to pass the time. You have my *most sincere* apologies about the misunderstanding. If there is anything I can do to make amends—"

"I will let you know," Lenore said. Her posture stiff, she gestured for Nadezhda to leave, then stepped aside. Nadezhda rose and stretched, her stature, as well as her tight Salusian clothes, accentuated her muscles. No matter her words, she was dangerous and everyone in the room knew it. There was just nothing they could do. For now.

"Out of my way, little bird," Nadezhda purred to Ravenna.

The sylph stood her ground for a heartbeat, wanting nothing more than to exact several Dalketh movements on Nadezhda. But Ravenna took a deep breath and stepped aside. Miska squeezed her hand.

"Captain," Lenore said, her voice halting the other woman in her tracks with ease. Nadezhda stiffened as she realised how easily Lenore could command, then turned her head to smile at the queen. "I will be informing Lord Davorin of this incident."

"Yes, of course, Your Majesty," Nadezhda said with falsely sweet words. She looked at Ravenna and Miska with a sneer, then shook her head. She spoke once more, as if unable to resist giving a last barb to the creature she hated. "It's a pity we don't have another of your kind. I'm not so sure what use a flightless sylph will be in any case. But Lord Davorin seems to care for you."

With that, she left the stone chamber.

Miska snorted and shook his head. "That woman is dangerous."

"You were right, Ravenna," Lenore agreed. She turned to look at the black-winged sylph and frowned in concern. "Ravenna?"

Ravenna heard none of this. Her ears had filled with the terrified pounding of her heart, the shrill beating of hundreds of wings fleeing in terror. Her legs felt weak and her throat grew dry as if she had been in the desert for some hours. Ravenna staggered to the bench Nadezhda had recently vacated. Miska and Lenore were immediately at her side, their eyes concerned, their voices buzzing in her ears in indistinct waves.

"Did you hear?" Ravenna breathed. Miska furrowed his brows.

"I don't understand," he said. "What's wrong? Are your wounds bothering you? Should we call for Warra?"

Ravenna shook her head weakly. "Another of my kind. She said that they wanted another of my kind."

"I thought that they didn't know about sylphs," Lenore said. "That's why I didn't press the issue about her reading the journal. Because she wouldn't understand what she was reading, and because you said there wasn't anything dangerous in it."

Ravenna shook her head again. "I told Davorin that I wasn't an angel. That I was a sylph. He didn't care because the rest of the world would only see me as their angel. But—what have I done?"

Miska sat beside her, his eyes fixed on her face even while his hands sought hers out. Ravenna wanted to pull away, wanted to force herself to face the horror of what she had unleashed, without anyone to ease her pain. But she found she could not let go of Miska's hands. Lenore shook her head.

"I still don't understand," she said.

"That journal would have meant nothing to them, to Nadezhda, had they not already known that I was a sylph," Ravenna explained. Her voice was dull, and she felt as if the world was slipping away. "Now they know that there are others. A whole civilisation. And what do you think Davorin will do with that information?"

The Red Queen's eyes widened in horror as she finally understood what had happened. Davorin would never rest once he knew that Ravenna was not the only sylph, was not some impossible oddity that would never be found again. He would do exactly as he meant to do with Lenore's Kingdom. He would seek out the other sylphs and conquer them. The devastation that a human war would have on the sylphs was unimaginable. They didn't know anything about fighting but for their watered down Dalketh that most only learnt as a child, and the few that went out to hunt. Davorin would slaughter her people, and those that survived would endure what Ravenna had endured, and far worse.

"We have to stop him," Lenore breathed.

Ravenna let out a brittle laugh that had even Miska wincing. "Do you think you could stop him? He has an army of hired blades on your doorstep. He has the backing of an Empire. And that is discounting Lord Davorin himself. He will not go down without taking all of you with him. If we fight him, we will lose!"

"You don't know that," Miska protested. Ravenna let out a whimper and buried her head in his chest, wanting that feeling that they had shared such a short time ago. She wanted to be back in that hallway with Miska, none of this knowledge burdening her and weighing her wings down.

"We can try," Lenore said, placing a hand on Ravenna's wing. The feathers shivered at the touch, but Ravenna did not pull away. She lifted her head and knew, by the shock in Lenore's and Miska's eyes, that her calm expression had failed. The true extent of her pain was apparent.

"You will fail," Ravenna said plainly. "Even if you don't, Davorin will find my people, his legendary slaves. And I cannot let my people face this, this *demon* without warning them. Preparing them."

Miska sucked in a breath and pulled back from Ravenna. "You want to go back?"

Ravenna closed her eyes and shook her head. She had thought, until now, that going back to Shinalea was all that she wanted. She wanted to be amongst the trees and the tomes, the stones. She wanted to be back with Tacitus and to feel his warm wings fold about her in comfort like they used to do when she was a child. She had thought that going home was everything she would have wanted. Never had she missed Shinalea so much as when it was taken from her. Then, she had come to the Red Palace. Now she had people—humans!—she trusted and cared for. She had found respect in Lenore and love in Miska. She had seen herself truly for the first time in her life. And she had understood how much more there was to life than enduring the disdain of a people that should have accepted her.

Until now, Ravenna had wanted to go back, though sylph law would have prevented it. Now she did not know what she wanted.

"No," Ravenna said, her voice cracking in grief. "No, I would rather fight here with you. But I cannot."

"Then I'll go with you!" Miska declared. He looked so firm, so strong, and willing.

Ravenna brushed a hand along his cheek, marvelling at the

reddish-brown colour. It was like nothing she had known amongst the sylphs and it was beautiful. What had Miska endured in his life? To be beaten until he could not hear, yet still learn how to function and to thrive. He was happy and kind and intelligent, and he saw deeper into Ravenna than anyone else she had known. He cared so deeply. She knew, without a doubt, that if she accepted, he would walk to the ends of the earth to go with her and help her.

"No, Miska, you must stay here," she murmured.

He blinked and frowned.

"Ravenna," he breathed. She shook her head.

"Your place is here. The people you care about are here. They need you," she said, glad that he could not hear the pain in her voice. Lenore could, though, and turned her head away with tears glistening in her eyes. "You must take care of them."

"I care about you," he snapped. "You need me."

Ravenna's heart squeezed in pain, one worse than anything she had ever felt before. Heartbreak. "I care about you, too," she said, tears choking her voice.

He understood, though. Miska always understood.

"But I don't need you."

With those words and the hurt that they brought to Miska's eyes, Ravenna feared she had lost the only person she had ever truly loved.

Miska pulled away, shaking off her hands and moving out of reach of her wings. He shook his head, hair falling into his face to obscure his eyes.

Ravenna wanted to reach out and hold him, to wrap her wings around him, to keep him close. She forced her hands to remain where they were, settled neatly in her lap.

Miska paced up and down the stone chamber, his breaths heaving as he held back the sobs that threatened to break free. Each step cracked Ravenna's heart further. Once, Miska rounded on her, fury and pain in his green eyes. So unlike anything Ravenna had known, they were human and they should have pushed her away. Instead, she watched and tried to memorise their colour.

Finally, Miska stopped pacing before her. He sank to his knees and looked up at her. Carefully, he brushed away a tear that had fallen to her cheek. "Okay," he said softly. "Okay."

"I don't want to leave you," Ravenna said before she could stop herself. She trembled where she sat, trying to regain the control she had lost.

Miska surged upwards and pressed his lips to hers. He pulled back and smiled a watery smile. "I know. But you must."

Ravenna touched her forehead to Miska's. She swallowed back the tears and the pain, trying to shove them to that dark place where all her other pain lay. But it would not go. That emptiness she had thought as horrid and would now gladly take as bliss, would not come.

Ravenna turned to see Lenore desperately trying to hold back tears as well. The Red Queen was shaking, her own pain written plainly for all to see. It touched Ravenna to know that she had not been alone in her affection. "I'm sorry," Ravenna said simply.

"I know." Lenore grasped Ravenna's hand in her own. "You take care of your people. You warn them. And we'll take care of Davorin."

Ravenna closed her eyes. She knew as well as they that Davorin would be a difficult enemy to fight. All the forces in the Red Desert could never reach their leader in time to defend it against an enemy that had been invited to its gates. If Ravenna left—when Ravenna left—she would likely never see any of them again. She just hoped they would not all be dead.

CHAPTER TWENTY-THREE

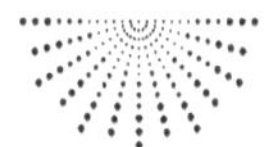

That night, Ravenna stood with Lenore, Miska, Warra, and Vareis at the edge of the Red Palace's boundaries. The desert stretched before her to the horizon, seemingly endless except for the Iron Mountains to her left. The stars shone brightly, and the ground was illuminated silver by the moon. The horse that Vareis held by the reins stomped its foot impatiently.

"If you keep the mountains on your left, you'll make it to the ocean. It's about two nights' hard ride to the ocean. Don't travel by heat of day, or you will die of lack of water before you can even reach the ocean. Then follow the coast south to find the point where the slavers brought you ashore. They like to follow the southern border to get to their precious Market," Vareis spat. She clucked her tongue and gave Ravenna something like a regretful smile. "You're a capable fighter, no question of that. A little untrained and untried, but no one can doubt your capability. Those blades will serve you well. Mind you keep them sharp, you hear?"

Ravenna touched the hilts of the twin blades she now wore

at either hip. When Vareis had gifted her with the weapons, she could not help but be reminded of the blades that Davorin wore. But these, Vareis said, were a special triangular blade that the desert peoples specialised in. Fighting with them required more precision and flexibility as they were lighter and thinner than the heavy swords others preferred. Somehow, the weight seemed to rest perfectly in Ravenna's hands.

"Thank you, Vareis," she murmured. The training master had done more than provide Ravenna with leather armour, arm bracers, swords, and knives. She had given Ravenna back that feeling of freedom and joy that she had lost.

"You keep fighting," the training master sniffed. She thrust the reins of the horse into Ravenna's hands and strode away before her emotions could overcome her. Ravenna bid her a silent goodbye, then turned to the others.

Warra was still bustling about the packs of the horse, putting herbs and poultices into the bags. Ravenna had been lectured long on their uses and applications. Lenore and Miska, though, stood a few strides off. Lenore waited until Warra was done and had bustled off to a distance before stepping forwards.

"Ravenna, you have become one of my greatest friends. If you manage to help your people, consider coming back here?" Lenore asked, looking uncertain for the first time since Ravenna had met her.

"I will," Ravenna said, though she knew that the possibility was slim. Lenore would face great challenges ahead and they both knew that the chance of her winning against Davorin and his determination was low. Still, Ravenna pulled Lenore into a hug and ignored the twinge of pain that flared through her left shoulder when Lenore returned the embrace with all the strength in her slim body. Ravenna ran her hands over the multitude of braids and their fiery colour. "I'll come back for you."

Lenore pulled back, wiping tears from her eyes. She laughed, but the sound was full of pain. "Don't worry about us. The Red Desert has one of the best fighting forces in the land. We can take those fools that Davorin hired. I…I wish I could send someone with you. That you were not going alone."

"I am used to being alone," Ravenna said, smiling.

"But your people—"

"Will at least hear me out before they judge me. I will convince them."

Ravenna knew that was not quite what Lenore meant, that there was more to be said and understood between them, but she forced her mind away from such thoughts. Her path was chosen. She would risk the wrath of her people and return to them. Save them.

And in the meantime, would leave those whom she loved at the hands of Davorin's forces.

That army, Ravenna knew, was dispersed about the land. And fearsome they might be, but those that were close to the Red Palace would hardly be enough. Lenore's kingdom would be ravaged long before they won, and the losses would be great. There was a chance, but it was slim. That did not stop Ravenna from hoping.

"Goodbye, Lenore," Ravenna whispered. "May your wings touch the stars."

"And may your heart stay true," Lenore returned. She kissed Ravenna's forehead gently before stepping back to join Warra. A sad set of sentinels, watching Ravenna's last goodbye. She turned to Miska. He swallowed back his tears.

"Don't go," Miska said, his normally precise speech slurred by grief. It was so strange to Ravenna that when she had first arrived, his words were nothing more than a further aggravation on her ears. Now, she would dream about those words. Carefully formed, deep, soothing. Words said by a man who could never hear them.

"I must," Ravenna said. She looked up at Miska. He ran

his hand along her hair, then caressed her cheeks and kissed her lightly. There was that same fire, that spark that ran through Ravenna's blood and turned her pain to pleasure.

"They don't love you as I do," Miska pleaded. They both knew the argument was futile.

"No," Ravenna agreed. "No one can love me as you do. But they need me. And you, Miska, you are strong and brave and *good*. You must promise me that you will take care of Lenore and the others. And that one day, when all this is over, we will see each other again. *Promise!*"

"I promise, Ravenna." Miska kissed her again, deeply and desperately. "I love you."

He broke away from her hold and walked to where Lenore and Warra stood. Ravenna closed her eyes and took in a deep breath. She mounted the horse as Vareis had taught, and only took a few moments to settle into the saddle, her wings outstretched to balance herself. Ravenna looked back at where her friends stood. Her eyes sought out Miska's. His pain was gone, determination in its place. Ravenna tried to steel herself to do the same, but that feeling of heartbreak was impossible to quench.

She swallowed the lump in her throat. Her voice failed her, but she mouthed the words all the same, knowing Miska would see and hear. "I love you."

Then, without a backwards glance, Ravenna spurred the horse into motion and rode off into the night. She rode towards her home, yet she knew that she was leaving that same place behind. No, the sylphs would never love her as these people did. But, like it or not, they needed Ravenna more. She would have to hope that these humans could weather the storm and that she would see them again.

When Ravenna did look back, hoping to catch one more glance, it was too late. Even the Red Palace was out of view. She swallowed the pain, finally managing to shove it into the dark, and urged her mount faster.

* * *

ABOUT AN HOUR INTO HER RIDE, Ravenna wished fervently that she had practised riding skills during her time at the Red Palace. She found it incredibly difficult to keep her seat when the horse was moving at such a pace. And while her wings were balancing her, the constant adjustment had Ravenna wincing as her wounds were jostled. The horse's movements were relatively steady and the creature obviously knew enough to keep a smooth but relatively fast gait. But what would happen when they stopped to wait out the hot day? Would the horse instinctively lead them towards water or would she have to break out some of the precious supplies that had been provided her. Would it eat the scrub grass that grew sparsely in the desert?

Two hours into her ride, Ravenna's mind wandered from her own plight to that of those she had left behind. Lenore's chances were far from hopeless. The Red Queen had a valuable and formidable army at her service. If she could get word to them to gather before Davorin returned, then perhaps they would win. Davorin's hired blades were comparatively few in number, but they were more dangerous than many predators Ravenna had known. Without the scattered army of the Red Desert, Davorin's forces would likely tear them apart. Would Lenore risk such a thing? Would she sacrifice the lives of her people for that slim chance they could win against Davorin?

Three hours into her ride, Ravenna gave up thinking at all. She just let the horse move in and out of a walk as it took the rest it required. Once, she stopped at a tiny spring near some tall rocks and let the creature drink its fill while she drank hers. She climbed stiffly back onto the beast and spurred it forwards, making certain to keep the Iron Mountains at her left.

The one thing Ravenna refused to think about was the place she was going.

Dawn came too quickly for Ravenna's liking. But she knew that the sweat-slick sides of the horse and her own aching muscles required them both to rest. She aimed for a craggy rock that rose out of the desert like a jagged tooth. Almost as soon as they had reached the shade of the rock, the horse stopped and would move no farther. Ravenna dismounted.

She gave the horse some of the precious water and drank some herself. There were only a few bags of water, as her journey was not meant to last all that long, and Lenore had promised that there were water sources in the desert. From what Ravenna could tell, the dry, dusty land was devoid of all precious water. And the oasis of the Red Palace was far behind. She gave the horse more water, then tied the reins to a stake Vareis had provided. The horse tossed its long head and let out a terrible sound.

Ravenna beat her wings defiantly at the creature. It settled eventually, turning its back on Ravenna to graze on the few patches of scrub grass nearby. Ravenna lay back against the rock, her wings sheltering her from the rising sun. Finally, as the day began to warm around her into the height of midsummer, she closed her eyes and slept.

* * *

PAIN SHOOTING across her shoulder and chest woke her. Ravenna gasped, eyes flying open. Sometime as she slept, she had turned to lay on her injured side and the wounds protested mightily. Warra had said they would not open again, but they were far from properly healed. Groaning, Ravenna turned onto her back and tried to see through the stars that clouded her vision. She took several deep breaths, then sat up.

"It's only pain," Ravenna said through clenched teeth. "It will not kill you."

The horse snickered and tossed its head before it went back to grazing on the few pieces of grass that remained. Ravenna noted that the creature looked hot and tired, despite the fact that it was late afternoon and it had done nothing all day. But even in the shade of the rocky outcropping, the heat was sweltering. Even Ravenna's open-backed tunic and flowing breeches felt too heavy.

After her wounds stopped throbbing, Ravenna dared to take the bandages off. She nearly whimpered at the relief it gave. She could not see the wounds, even if she craned her neck, so she settled for gently probing them. They felt hot and itchy, but now that the muscles had relaxed, the pain was minimal.

Ravenna stood and went to the horse. She dug out one of the poultices from the saddle bags and spread it liberally on the scratches. There was no way she could tie a bandage herself, so Ravenna just let things be. The scars would be worse, probably, for it, but she didn't care. What were some scars compared to her purpose now.

She watered the horse again and ate some of the dried fruits packed in the bags. Then, unable to wait any longer, Ravenna vaulted herself into the saddle and rode off into the distance, the setting sun at her back.

This night's ride felt slower and somehow more frantic than the night before. Then, she had been sure of her plan. She had been sure that leaving Lenore behind was the right thing, that walking away from Miska so he could stay where he was most needed was what was best. Now, she just sincerely missed her friends and hoped that they would rally the troops in time. What awaited her was still not to be considered.

The horse was also not nearly as fleet as it had been. It still alternated between a brisk walk and its faster, jarring pace. But the walks lasted longer, and the faster pace was hardly long enough to speed their journey. Ravenna tried to stop once or twice as they came across precious places where water trickled, or to try and rest the beast. Eventually, though, her need surpassed her concern for the horse and Ravenna just kept pushing onward. It would never have made it back to the Red Palace, in any case, and though a quiet part of her mind twinged at the sacrifice, most of her knew it was necessary. The blank emptiness that had come with snuffing out her pain and her longing to be in a place far behind left only her rational mind and her need in its place.

The horse's steps faltered near dawn. It stumbled. Ravenna leapt from the saddle to avoid being caught underneath the creature as it fell to the ground. The beast screamed as it fell, its flanks heaving for air. Its nostrils had foam rimming them and its coat was sweat-dark.

Ravenna cursed. This thing would carry her no farther. She undid the saddle while the horse lay on the ground. The supplies she had been given barely fit into one of the smaller bags, but Ravenna kept all she could. Then, leaving the horse to breathe its last or live as it may, she continued on foot.

Some luck was on her side. Less than an hour's walk had her hearing water as it rushed onto the shore. Sparse scrubland had turned into scraggly pine trees and enough greenery to support birds, small animals and the like. Another few minutes and Ravenna found herself shielding her eyes as she looked at the sun rising over the water.

"Shinalea," she murmured. After all this time, it felt so strange to be beckoned home.

For the first time since Ravenna took to the road, she wondered just what would meet her when she went back.

She had lost track of the time that had passed since her leaving. Had it been a moon? Two? A season? A cycle? It felt a lifetime. Would Tacitus still be researching his ancient sites, having to fly to the sites on his own now that Ravenna was not there to do the research for him? What of Desarra and Crispinus? Had the dark sylph joined the Lords of the Wing? Had Desarra found whatever acceptance she had been looking for now that Ravenna was gone?

Legs trembling and wings shaking, Ravenna decided that she would rest there on the shore before searching for the beach where she would depart back to the island. She hoped the low boat that the slavers had used was still in place. She hoped that she would recognise the place where she should depart and that she could cross to the island easily. Ravenna knew how to navigate by the stars, but she had never crossed the ocean under her own power.

"Enough," Ravenna snapped to herself. She scrambled down the rocks to the beach and stopped as her feet met sand. This was not the desert sand that had plagued her for the last while. This was ocean sand, littered with shells and the remains of sea plants. This was familiar.

Ravenna settled into the sand in a shallow cave, out of reach of the tides. And, as the sun rose higher into the sky, she closed her eyes and dreamed of a people left behind. Only, they were not graced with wings and amber-fire eyes.

* * *

A FURTHER TWO nights passed before Ravenna had travelled along the coast long enough for the landscape to look familiar. She hadn't even been certain that she would remember the place at all; at the time of her capture, she had been traumatised and terrified. Her memories were tainted with those overwhelming emotions and she struggled to push them aside and find the information she needed.

Eventually, though, Ravenna stumbled her way south to a place that was like a whisper of a memory. Her food was almost gone, and her water supplies had run out completely. Ravenna was exhausted and every climb over a rock or boulder had her wings stretching for balance and pulling at her wounds. The saltwater that invariably found its way onto her skin did not help. The pain became a constant background drone that she ignored. All that mattered was putting one foot in front of another until she found the way back home.

Ravenna stumbled forwards and was too slow to catch herself. Her wings instinctively moved so that Ravenna would roll with the impact, but she still ended up on her back, exhausted. The sun had set completely and now she was looking at the world by moonlight. The moon, three-quarters full, was bright enough to cast the beach into silver. The trees looked like shadow and starlight. The sand was bright and luminous. And the boat seemed made of silver.

The boat.

Ravenna scrambled to her feet. Her feathers trembled with joy. The boat. The boat!

This was the same shallow-bottomed sea craft that had taken her from Shinalea. The slavers had left it behind, and here it was. Some divine being must have been looking down on Ravenna, for fortune had never been so kind. She had a chance of reaching her people, of warning them about the terrible things that were coming.

The things that had already reached her precious Miska and Queen Lenore.

Ravenna slammed those thoughts down under an impenetrable barrier in her mind. She focused instead on digging the boat out of the sand that had washed up around its sides. It was sun-bleached and there was rainwater gathered in the bottom, but it was sound, and it would do what she needed. There were even oars still there to take her home.

She did not pause to find something to drink or take a moment to eat. As soon as the boat was free, Ravenna pushed it into the water with all her strength, her shoulder muscles wincing in pain as the wounds stretched across them. But the boat took to the water. Ravenna pushed it out past the waves that tried to carry it back to shore, the saltwater lapping at her clothes. With a single beat of her wings, Ravenna jumped out of the water and into the boat. She pulled at the oars and was on her way, her thoughts focused only on what lay ahead.

She did not look back once.

CHAPTER TWENTY-FOUR

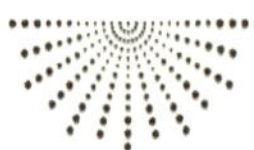

*D*avorin arrived at the Red Palace the dawn after
Ravenna had left, though he was not aware of that.
All he knew was that there was power in the impossible artefact
he carried with him, just waiting to be explored. And he had a
whole palace of people with which to test it.

His fighters peeled off as soon as they reached the encampment, going to see to their mounts and recount the tale of their
journey. Davorin rode a little farther into the camp, a slight
smile touching his mouth while he assessed the strength of his
mercenaries. Even so early in the morning, they were already up
and practising or seeing to their weapons and preparing for the
day. One of the younger boys that they kept about to run
messages spotted Davorin then dashed off into the camp, likely
to fetch Utheria or Nadezhda.

Davorin did not want to talk with either of his commanders.
He wanted to sit alone in his room in the Red Palace and
examine the dragon's tooth. He had not dared pull it out on the
ride back from the borderlands. Those travelling with him
might have seen. Quick-eyed Barrow might have seen; if anyone
could understand what it was that Davorin carried, it was

Barrow. But still, the power that Davorin carried at his belt! He did not have that magic thrumming through his blood as before. Just the thought, though, was enough.

"My lord!" A voice called out to him, forcing Davorin to stop halfway to his tent and face the intruder. Nadezhda was jogging towards him. Her cropped hair had grown out slightly in the time since they had been in the desert. It suited her no better than the short hair. Davorin curled his lip but dismounted from his horse.

"Captain," he said wearily. "Is there a reason you demand my attention just as I was going to get some proper sleep?"

"I wanted to catch you before you went to your Red Queen," Nadezhda said. She passed the reins to Davorin's horse off to a waiting soldier, then practically dragged Davorin into their command tent. This early in the morning, the large canvas marquee was completely empty but for the large table in the centre of the room.

Davorin wrenched his arm free of Nadezhda. "What do you think you are doing?!" he hissed, his hand flying not to his blades but his belt. "To assault the Firstborn Son of the Salusian Empire, Heir Apparent to the—"

"Heir Apparent?" Nadezhda broke in, scorn lacing her tone. "That's news to me. Did you learn this while you were cavorting with your sister?"

Davorin bit back a sharp retort, knowing full well that it would do no good. Nadezhda was a creature formed by Dagan's hand. She was crude, but effective. And Davorin needed her to cooperate with him. For now. He took a deep breath and forced his composure to rise. He would play with Nadezhda just as he did with those fools in his father's court. It would not be long now before he no longer had to hide behind his mask of politeness and interest. The world would see him for who he was.

"You overstep your bounds," Davorin said cooly.

Nadezhda flinched.

"Go ahead, Captain, tell me what was so important that you had to drag me across the camp to tell me. Tell me why you decided to test your authority by telling me what to do."

Nadezhda's eyes flashed to the ground and she pressed her mouth together. If Davorin was not mistaken, there was a hint of fear in her eyes. Good. She had never been cowed by Dagan, not in all the years those two had trained together. Davorin had at least accomplished that better than his brother. And he had the dragon's tooth, something that Dagan would have killed the Emperor for.

"My apologies, Lord Davorin," Nadezhda murmured. She glanced up at him. He met her gaze evenly. Nadezhda licked her lips and turned to face the table so she wouldn't have to watch Davorin's scrutiny of her words. That was a bit worrying. "You should know that I worked to follow your orders while you were gone."

"My orders?"

"To keep an eye on Queen Lenore and that fool Ravenna. Make certain that she wasn't subverting your plans with the Red Queen."

Davorin nodded. "Ah, yes. And did she try to subvert me?"

Nadezhda licked her lips. "Not exactly. I don't know if she said something earlier, but that woman and her servants have always been nothing more than graciously polite. But they watch you carefully. I couldn't get much time with that stupid sylph. So, I looked around her room. I found a book."

Davorin sighed. "A book? Captain Nadezhda, I trusted you to keep an eye on my interests in the short time I have been away. You were meant to further my cause with Queen Lenore, you were meant to keep an eye on Ravenna, and you were meant to make certain that my soldiers were ready to fight at a moment's notice. Yet you tell me you have found nothing but a book?"

"Trust me, my lord," Nadezhda growled, baring her teeth like some fell dog, "this is a book you will want."

Davorin rolled his eyes but gestured for her to continue.

"It was written by another sylph," Nadezhda explained.

Davorin started, taking a step closer to her to see if she was telling the truth. Surely, she would not play that sort of trick on him. Surely, she was as loyal to him as she had been to Dagan. Why, then, would she say something so outrageous?

"*Another* sylph?" Davorin demanded. "I thought Ravenna was the only one. A creature otherwise lost to the mists of time."

Nadezhda shook her head. "It was some generations ago, but it was most certainly written by *another* sylph. And that is not all. Apparently, there is a whole civilisation of sylphs. They live completely isolated from us, and they don't do anything but study and hunt and have their little society, but they exist. And what's more, they *fly*."

It was impossible. Ravenna was an oddity, a woman of untold beauty with wings like the night. She was the spitting image of the divine beings that served as messengers and warriors to the gods, the angels. Religion taught that they were beings of air and magic and that they were the bringers of signs to the devout. Ravenna was not an angel. But she looked like one. And now to learn that there were more, that there was a whole people made up of these creatures? Davorin's rule would never be contested again if he could have these beings on his side.

Nadezhda coughed. Davorin turned back to his Captain, noting the gleam in her eye. "There's more," she said simply. "They were the Stormbringers."

Now Davorin did stagger. He had to rest his hand on one of the chairs around the table in order to gain his balance. The angels were religious symbols. They mattered only to the devout and those who wanted to ask the gods for guidance. The Stormbringers, though, they were warrior legend. They were a symbol of strength and power to any who had picked up a blade. They were the legions who fought against the Darkening alongside the dragons. They were the undefeated army who swept on their enemies from skies churned dark by their wings. Their prowess was unmatched and their reputation vivid. If they could be taught to fight like Ravenna…

To have them at his back? Davorin could conquer the world.

He thought again of the tooth at his belt. It had been impossible but two days before, yet here he stood, holding a piece of dragon lore. Ravenna's existence had been impossible. Magic was a tale to tell children, a fool's belief.

But it was all real.

Davorin would use every piece at his disposal to acquire a legion of Stormbringers. He would conquer them, this modern collection of sylphs who had forgotten their heritage just as surely as their existence had been lost. He would conquer them, and he would break them, just as he had with Ravenna. Then, he would train them to fight for him.

"Bring me Ravenna," Davorin ordered. He was so caught up in this vision of a future where he held the magic of legends in his hand that he missed the fear that flickered across Nadezhda's expression. He did not miss, however, the hiss that she gave. Davorin focused on her, saw the hunch of her shoulders and the wariness about her. "What happened?" Davorin growled.

"I was caught in Ravenna's room," Nadezhda said. She fidgeted, brushing her fingers along the worn creases of her leather armour as though that would protect her as it had before. "The Red Queen brought Ravenna and that idiot servant to question me. They knew about the book."

Davorin's image of the future cracked before his very eyes. He put his hand on the spot where he carried the dragon's tooth. When he spoke, his voice was cold. "I ask you again, *Captain*. What. Happened."

This time, Nadezhda's words were barely a whisper.

"Ravenna is gone. Left to warn her people. I was not in time to stop her or know where she went."

"Oh," Davorin said, voice mild. He pulled the tooth from his belt and ran it through his fingers as though its mere presence was comforting. He fitted it in his fist, the point curling outward like some terrible dagger. "Is that all?"

Without waiting for an answer, Davorin seized Nadezhda by her armour. He pulled her so close that he could taste the fear in her breath. He saw every tiny flaw in her face, every inch of fear that shone in her eyes. Before she had time to whimper, Davorin drove the dragon's tooth into her neck.

The tooth pulsed, power running through its magnificent shape. Nadezhda clutched at her neck, but no matter how she scrabbled, she could not pull the tooth out. She gurgled something at Davorin. He sneered at her and released his hold on her armour, letting her fall to the ground to writhe in pain. Blood began to spatter the ground where Nadezhda coughed it up and where it welled around the fang.

Then, almost as if touching blood had called back some long dead power, the tooth began to pulsate. It glowed first white, then red, drawing power from the dying woman. Davorin felt the surge of power in his own body, a song that drowned out any other sound and made his very bones tremble with power. Magic.

Davorin threw back his head and laughed. At his feet, Nadezhda lay unable to move as the tooth did its terrible deed. Her skin changed from its healthy tan to something sickly, then to a red that was like blood mixed with water. Her veins showed blue against her skin, darkening until they were nearly black. Around her eyes, the skin peeled to form scales in that same pale red. Her fingernails curled into claws. Her teeth elongated. And finally, when it seemed that Nadezhda could go no further without losing all trace of humanity, the tooth pulsed once more and melted into her wounds.

Davorin could still feel the magic of the dragon's tooth running through him. He knew that if he forced the song to change, then Nadezhda would stand. Even as he thought the change, she stood. Her eyes were bloodshot and reptilian, no longer even slightly human. "Face me," Davorin ordered with relish.

She turned to face him, bowing at the waist. "*My lord,*" she rasped. Her voice echoed with some other creature's voice, deeper, throatier.

"Who are you?" Davorin asked, though he felt he knew the answer. It was in every note of the song that thrummed through him.

"*I am the one long dead. Long forgotten. I am Bane and Fear and Rage. But you know this as well as any other, for you freed me from my prison.*" The creature that now possessed Nadezhda raised its head and fixed Davorin in its greedy gaze. "*You freed me, Master. You name me.*"

Davorin smiled. "I shall call you Dagan, after my dear departed brother."

The false Dagan bowed its head, a perverse jerking motion that had once been smooth on Nadezhda's features. "*What would you have me do, Master?*"

"We are going to raze this palace. We are going to find Queen Lenore and make her bow to me," Davorin purred. He sucked in a breath, heady with the energy rushing through his body. "And then we begin the hunt for the sylphs."

Dagan threw back its head, the black veins throbbing, and let out a shrieking battle cry. It and the chuckle that escaped Davorin's mouth were both blotted out by the harsh music that pounded in his head, whispering of power yet to come.

CHAPTER TWENTY-FIVE

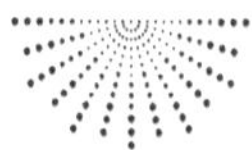

avorin called Utheria to the tent and not ten minutes later she scrambled inside. Her eyes were wide, but she stood with the proud posture of any true warrior. She spotted what was formerly Nadezhda standing in a corner and licked her lips nervously.

"My lord?" Utheria asked. "We heard screams…has Nadezhda not performed to your standards?"

Davorin smirked. It was telling that his soldiers did not even bother interrupting him when there were screams of pain and death in his tent. Did they think him cruel or just exacting? Neither much mattered to him provided that they actually did what it was he wanted. He would worry about his reputation later. For now, all that mattered was acquiring the power necessary for him to make his next move.

"Nadezhda has sacrificed herself to my cause," Davorin explained smoothly. "She was eager to reunite with my, ah, brother's spirit and so gave her body to host him."

Utheria gaped. "T-that's witchcraft! Calling spirits back from the dead is for priests! Isn't it?"

"Surely, Utheria, you understand that the priests are only

using powers borrowed from other beings. After all, they worship somebody, do they not?"

This time, the young leader of Davorin's mercenary army had no words. She dropped instead to her knees, fear and awe plain on her face. Davorin stepped forwards, forcing her to lift her chin to look up at him. He took in the way her leather armour contoured with her body, how her curved blade sat in its sheath on her back, how like a soldier she was. The look she wore on her surprisingly pretty face suited her, Davorin decided. One of awe. Of fear.

"Rise, Utheria," Davorin said. She did, scrambling backwards to keep from being too close to her lord. "I see you understand, now?"

"Yes, my lord," she breathed. "What do you need of me?"

It was a request that went beyond her current role as leader of the mercenaries. And perhaps Davorin would make some use of her later, when he had time to marshal his forces and make certain that his victory was guaranteed. For now, though, he just said, "Gather your forces. We are taking the Red Palace."

"I thought you were going to marry Queen Lenore. We would lose a goodly number of people if we openly attack."

Davorin rolled his eyes. "Lenore will have me," he assured her. "And as for losses, just don't attack openly."

His commander faltered, caught between her loyalty to him and her experience as a warrior.

Davorin sighed and waved his hand for her to speak.

Utheria shuffled her feet in a most childlike gesture. "Their forces have been gathering since last night. There were reports of four riders going out to summon the armies to the Red Palace. I thought it was because she had accepted you..."

Davorin cursed and slammed his hand on the table. Utheria flinched. The creature called Dagan did not, merely turned to look at Davorin with eagerness in its eyes. That look, that desire for blood, was so much like the actual Dagan that for a moment

Davorin was taken aback. But no. He controlled this dragon reincarnate. He was finally in control. And he would take the Red Palace.

"All I need," Davorin ground out as he bit back a grin, "is for you to get me through the door and to the queen. Fight for as long as you can. It won't take long."

Utheria shifted her feet again. "And you are so certain that—"

Davorin rounded on her, fury burning in his eyes. The song that pounded through his head grew to an impossible roar. With a snarl, Dagan leapt from where it stood and brought its claws across Utheria's face. She let out a yelp and jumped backwards, one hand covering the scratches, the other pulling her blade from its sheath and pointing it at Dagan.

Davorin stepped in behind her and wrapped his arm around her neck. He released some of that thrumming power into her and Utheria let out a scream. After a moment, she fell limp, unable to even think about fighting back.

"You are being well paid," Davorin growled. "And you are fully aware of my abilities and my plan. Yet you *still* question me?"

"N-no, lord," Utheria said, her voice barely louder than a whisper. "I obey."

Davorin released her.

Utheria fell to the ground, gasping for breath. When she could breathe well enough, she straightened and fixed a wide eye on Davorin as he towered over her. He curled his lip. "Then get up and rally your soldiers."

Utheria wasted no time as she clambered to her feet and rushed out of the tent.

Davorin let out a wordless snarl as she vanished, then spun to face the dragon's spirit. "Was that magic, what I just did?"

"*You were the one who performed the act,*" Dagan said, smiling through the Captain's lips, revealing pointed fangs. *"You should be aware."*

"Give me a straight answer," Davorin snapped. "Was that magic?"

Dagan inclined its head. *"It was a manifestation of the song. In times long since gone, that was one name for the act."*

Davorin nodded, clenching the hand through which the magic had flowed. Magic! To think, in this age of magicless beings, stuck with much of their history lost and their civilisations constantly bickering over absurdities, he was a wielder of magic. With the false Dagan at his side and a legion of Stormbringers at his back, he would be unstoppable. He would be immortal.

"Come," Davorin said, forcing his thoughts to the task at hand. A person could only accomplish one thing at a time, no matter how far thinking they were. And right now, he had a queen to subdue. "We are going to take the Red Palace. Keep anyone from killing me, but don't kill more than you must. And leave Queen Lenore to me."

Dagan bowed at the waist, pressing a clawed hand to its chest. *"As you like,"* it purred.

Davorin put a hand on the blades at either hip and breathed in deeply. He heard the song pounding through him, full of terrible potential. He opened his eyes and started towards the Red Palace. The mercenaries were stirring beside him, most of them already forming into their ranks. They were more disorganised than a proper army would be, but it would serve for now. They followed Davorin as he marched through the garden towards the steps of the elaborately carved palace, trampling plants and ignoring the cries of the servants as they did so.

The steps of the palace were already swarming with the soldiers that were garrisoned there. They had obviously been waiting for Davorin because their weapons were already drawn and their expressions were determined. Davorin simply drew his blades and shifted them to sit more comfortably in his grasp. They were not the standard curved swords that many of the Salusian Empire favoured, but the shorter, heavier leaf-shaped blades made of true steel and bone. They were not out long before they sang with blood.

Each stroke against the soldiers of the Red Desert was like swatting flies. Davorin had so much power running through his body that his blows felt twice as strong, his movements faster. He sliced through the arm bracer of a young man who fell to the ground screaming as he held his stump against his chest. Another strike had Davorin blocking a poleaxe to his head and returning a stab to his opponent's chest.

Dimly, Davorin was aware of the beast, Dagan, moving around him with graceful ease that such a terrifying creature should not have possessed. It seemed that with each stroke of Dagan's claws, each kick and block and strike, the music running through Davorin's head pulsated. Soon, Davorin's own movements were coordinated with the song.

Then, there was no one to meet his sweeping blade and Davorin faltered. He was breathing heavily, far more than he should have been. Dagan, on the other hand, stood calmly by as if it had not even broken a sweat. Davorin turned to look behind him and saw the mercenaries were spreading out, taking on the other soldiers that had come to their comrades' aide. A few followed behind Davorin, ready to help fight their way to the Great Hall, where Lenore would likely be waiting.

"Why am I so tired?" Davorin murmured to Dagan. The creature raised one of Nadezhda's brows, the scales around its eyes stretching grotesquely at the motion.

"To use the song properly, one must know its ways. Or you will simply burn up in the process, trying to control something far beyond you."

"It will kill me?" Davorin demanded, straightening. He put

his blades across Dagan's throat, ready to end the creature to save himself.

"*No. But you should perhaps not use it to augment yourself in battle,*" Dagan said, as if doing such a thing were easy.

Davorin closed his eyes, concentrating on the song. It surged forwards, wanting to break free and flow through everything in Davorin's path. He felt blood running from his nose and his head began to pound. Davorin snarled and forced the music back, forced it to quiet. As he did, he heard Dagan let out a sigh, almost of relief. Davorin quickly held onto the tune that seemed to connect him to the dragon's spirit. He opened his eyes to see Dagan looking calmly at him.

"When this is over," Davorin said through gritted teeth, "you will teach me to master this magic." He rubbed the blood away from his nose, leaving a smear of red in its place. Davorin gripped the hilts of his swords tighter, then turned and strode into the Red Palace.

The interior of the palace was much quieter than the raging battle outside. In fact, it was almost eerie in its emptiness. Davorin looked behind some of the carved pillars and doors. Only once did he see anybody, and it was no more than a serving girl who scurried away with a terrified squeak as soon as she saw Davorin. So, the Red Palace was not empty, but nor was anyone putting up any resistance. Had he been tricked?

"Come out, Queen Lenore," Davorin spat.

Dagan gave him an odd look but said nothing.

Finally, he reached the enormous doors that led to the Great Hall and the most likely place where Lenore was hiding. Davorin pounded his fist on one door and, to his surprise, it swung open.

The sight that met him made his blood pound in his ears and not from fear. Queen Lenore was indeed sitting on her throne, her gaze imperious and her posture regal. Arrayed before her were at least twenty soldiers, all wearing leather armour reinforced with metal plates, their weapons gleaming and their eyes hard. At the sight of Davorin, they raised their weapons.

"I see you've arranged a proper welcoming reception." Davorin smiled darkly at Lenore, twisting his blades in his hands. The soldiers nearest flinched as he did so, and he chuckled. Their anger was a facade. It would crack into submission soon enough.

"Do you think me a fool?" Lenore asked, her voice hard. She shook her head and those ridiculous braids swung as she did, the gold beads clinking together. It was interesting that she felt the need to dress in her finest while waiting for Davorin to return. In the end, he cared nothing for her riches or beauty, only for her kingdom, her armies. "I know why you came here. And I have had enough."

"So have I, my queen," Davorin said, sneering.

It was then that Dagan entered the room. Wearing Nadezhda's form, the dragon spirit was far more graceful than the Captain had ever been. It seemed that the fight on the palace steps had finally settled the creature into its host's body. One of the soldiers nearest, a large woman with a long-handled axe, dropped her weapon at the sight of Dagan. A few others shuffled away. Davorin watched Lenore's reaction, horror and revulsion plain in her eyes.

"What...that was Captain Nadezhda," she said. Her hands tightened on the curved arms of her throne, the knuckles turning white against her golden skin. Her eyes flashed and in that moment, Davorin knew that he had won. Now it was merely a matter of discussing terms.

"It was," Davorin agreed. "But is no longer. I have brought magic back to the world. This is the result!"

Dagan bowed, pressing its clawed hands to its breast in a mocking gesture. It straightened and fixed the Red Queen in its gaze. *"It is my honour to serve the Lord Davorin,"* the creature said, its double timbre echoing through the stone chamber. More soldiers stepped backwards, fear now obvious in their visages.

"What have you done?" Lenore breathed.

Davorin raised his brows questioningly. "Why, I have only done what is best for the Empire. As I am doing now."

"You delude yourself if you think *this* is best for the Salusian Empire, or anyone," Lenore said. She tightened her mouth into a thin line and said no more. But Davorin wasn't finished.

"You know nothing of my plans," Davorin said with a shrug. "But I don't need you to understand. I only need you to comply. So, what do you say, Queen Lenore. Will you consent to marry me and become part of the Salusian Empire? Will you spare your people the suffering of a prolonged war and instead entrust them to someone who actually cares about their wellbeing?"

Lenore curled her lip in disgust. She lifted her chin and looked down on Davorin with enough venom to make him seethe. "You? Care about their wellbeing? You are nothing but a cruel monster who is interested only in blood."

Davorin snarled, some of his control over the music in his head slipping. The ground under his feet cracked and spidered out towards the soldiers. They stepped back in alarm, eyes wide. "I care *nothing* for blood! I am not Dagan!"

"You are *exactly* like Dagan," Lenore said.

Davorin snapped. As he released the song into his blades and surged forwards, rage fuelling his steps, the dragon reincarnate began fighting as well. The creature seemed to revel in the drops of blood that spattered the floor as it sliced at those in its way. Their weapons were snatched from them, their lives forfeit if they fought back. And leading the charge was Davorin. He didn't hesitate to kill when before he might have at least spared them to preserve some sense of mercy. Twenty soldiers had stood in his way. After only a few minutes of fighting—every motion enhanced by the magic he now held, Davorin was at the base of the throne.

Lenore was on her feet, eyes wide in alarm. She had a single dagger clutched in her hand, as if she thought that it would do any good. Davorin held his arms out wide, the blades still held but not threatening. He advanced on Lenore until he was close enough to see her swallow down a scream. He didn't have to look behind him to know that the entire Great Hall was carnage. That there wasn't a single soldier still living. He could feel it.

"I would change your answer," Davorin said in a low voice. He bared his teeth at Lenore, feeling some of the spattered gore from dead soldiers dripping down his chin. "Do you really want to subject your kingdom to this?"

Lenore swallowed again, this time fighting against tears. "If I agree, you will spare my people."

"I do not seek slaughter," Davorin said. "I seek only to bring people to a better life, in the Empire. I take care of my people. But if they fight…If *you* fight, then I will burn your precious Red Desert to ash until it is a place devoid of life. There will be nothing left to defend. No one left to save."

Lenore closed her eyes. A single tear slid down her cheek and she nodded. "Very well," she said, her voice even. She opened her eyes and fixed Davorin in a look that was pure fire. "I will consent to marry you."

"You have made the right choice," Davorin said. He reached out and ran one of her braids through his fingers, frowning at the texture. She would have to wear her hair loose, instead of this absurd fashion that was neither soft nor inviting.

He turned away from her to look at Dagan who was waiting patiently in the centre of the room. The creature was covered in blood, none of the liquid belonging to it. It looked no different for all the gore, the blackened veins still protruding and the reddish scales around its eyes glimmering fiercely. A quiet part of Davorin looked at the death that he had caused and quailed at the thought. He sought peace under one banner, a better life for all, not carnage or conquering for the sake of blood. And yet he had waded to his bride's throne through a stream of red.

It does not matter, Davorin thought. The song surged through his thoughts and drowned out any doubts. It pounded in his veins, the rhythm beating in time with his heart. It was power and strength and it would make him a god. Dagan had been obsessed with immortality and now Davorin had it in his hands. He would master it. He would control it. And the entire world would be his to shape.

Davorin turned back to Lenore and saw her expression fall as she took in the carnage fully. She would never love him, he realised, but she would do as he bid. That would have to be enough. "Dagan," Davorin commanded, his eyes never leaving the face of his queen. "Go and tell the others that Lenore has consented. The Red Desert is mine."

Lenore's mouth opened and mouthed something, though her voice was silent. Her face streamed with tears. Davorin didn't know what she said and he almost did not care. Almost. This was the best thing for everyone. He would convince Lenore of that. And if she did not comply? Well, then he would crush her people before her very eyes.

For now, though, he would make the desert his. Then, he would go searching for the army of sylphs to fly at his back. No one would ever doubt him again.

Davorin settled on the throne, Lenore standing beside him, her limbs trembling. The chair wasn't comfortable, and it did not display the wealth that the Red Desert could command. But it suited Davorin. Yes, it suited its new king. Davorin, Firstborn of the Salusian Empire, Heir Apparent to the Throne and King of the Red Desert. It suited him very well.

CHAPTER TWENTY-SIX

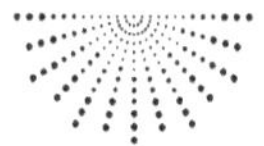

*R*avenna was not quite certain how she came to be on the island. The rough pebbles beneath her stomach seemed soothing compared to the heat that bore down on her back from an indifferent sun. Her wings were outstretched, the longest primary feathers getting wet in the waves that soaked through her clothes. Her throat was so tight from thirst that it was difficult to breathe and every part of her ached. Somewhere in the back of her mind, she knew that she had made it across the ocean to the home of her childhood. There was something she had to do; she just was not certain what.

The familiar beating of massive wings stirred some undying instinct in her. Ravenna pushed herself upwards with the last strength into her arms, her wings helping her pull herself into a sitting position. From there, she staggered to her feet. The world spun around her, green trees mixing with a too-blue sky. She spread her wings for balance and reached for the blades on her hips. She was inches from death, yet Ravenna knew she would never flee again. She would fight.

The sylph landed before her, his charcoal-ash skin dark

against the bright orange tunic and flowing breeches he wore. He had a knife strapped to a leather band around his hips, the hilt and belt both finely decorated with gold. His wings were a slightly darker shade than the gild and they were broad enough to black out the sun.

"May I lose my feathers! Ravenna, is that you?!" The sylph took a step forwards, shock written plainly on his face. Ravenna drew the swords, holding them before her in the Dalketh position that her body knew, even this close to the black.

"Don't come closer," she hissed, narrowing her eyes. "Who are you?!"

The sylph paused, feathers trembling at the sight of the swords. But he obviously saw that Ravenna was in no position to defend herself, because he took another step forwards. No matter how much she wanted to fight, Ravenna's arms were shaking too much. She was too tired, too thirsty, too hungry. She would be bound again, forced to do the bidding of others. She would rather die, but her body demanded that she live.

Ravenna fell to her knees, unable to stand any longer. "Who are you?" she repeated, rasping out the words in a desperate plea. Her swords were still gripped in her hands as the sylph stepped forwards and knelt before her, his eyes wide as he took her in. She could not let go of the swords. Of the last piece she had of Lenore and Miska.

"I-It's me, Crispinus. Wings, Ravenna, you've been missing for *moons*. A whole season. What happened to you?"

Crispinus. The name was familiar. It struck a chord long buried in Ravenna's mind. She swayed as she tried to remember, nearly falling once more to her face. Instead, Crispinus caught her in his arms and immediately launched them into the air, his massive wings beating with a strength that Ravenna would never know. She kept hold of her blades even as they flew, her own wings limp with exhaustion. It was only as they passed over the Aerial City that Ravenna remembered.

Crispinus. Crispin. Strange, that the arms of her former torment should be so gentle.

* * *

"Tacitus! You should not be here; you are too weak." The speaker's voice drew Ravenna from the depths of sleep. She tried to open her eyes, but they remained stubbornly closed. Perhaps that was alright. She was still so tired.

"Kratos, if you try to keep me from her, so help me I will tear pages from your tomes!" The other voice spoke. This one was deeper, sharper, yet touched with a weariness that seemed wing-deep. It was like a favourite song to Ravenna, something that reminded her of everything that was good and welcoming in the world. She longed to see its owner.

Blinking, Ravenna forced her eyes open. They were crusted over from sleeping too long. She lifted a weak arm and brushed the barrier away. Slowly, her body came to proper wakefulness. She was lying on her back, her wings spread wide beneath her in a bed properly designed for their care. Her throat was still sore, but it no longer felt raw and ruined. Her left shoulder ached slightly, but not as badly as it had done. And the rest of her? Well, it was nothing so bad as what she had known before. She would recover.

Ravenna pushed against the bed with her wings, forcing herself upwards. She groaned with the effort and was nearly ready for collapse when she found herself in a sitting position. Immediately, the rotund form of Kratos was before her, his wings wide in alarm. "You should not be sitting up! You are injured!"

"I'm fine," Ravenna said, trying to push him aside.

"But you have wounds in so many places and I need to—"

"I'm fine." Her words were made of the same steel that she had carried with her.

Kratos squeaked in alarm and stepped aside. Tacitus—her Tacitus—was revealed. Since she had been gone, Tacitus had grown as weak as Ravenna had strong. His wings were ragged and drooped, their ends brushing the floor. His limbs were too thin, and he looked as though every breath were a struggle. But at seeing Ravenna, his amber-fire eyes brightened and he glided forwards to sit on the end of Ravenna's bed with ease and eagerness.

"My child," Tacitus murmured, extending a hand. It shocked Ravenna to see that tears were forming in the older sylph's eyes. She never thought he cared that much. "You have returned to me!"

Ravenna covered his hand with her own, her mind too full to marvel as she used to that their flesh was so differently coloured. What did any of that matter, now? She looked up at Tacitus, unable to smile, even to take joy in being reunited with her heart-father. She felt a slight glimmer, deep inside her, but it was soon overtaken by the void of fear and duty and emptiness.

"I would not have returned at all, had I a choice," Ravenna said. She knew the words were harsh. Tacitus flinched away from her as if she had driven a knife through his heart. "No, Tacitus. I love you as much as I can. But you know as well as I the truth."

Tacitus bowed his head, tears flowing freely. "I know," he choked out. "This place was never good for you. If you had stayed, it would have stifled you. But...*why did you leave me?*"

Ravenna gave a wing-shrug, her expression as flat and calm as ever. "Had I choice, I would not have."

"You speak in riddles." There was accusation in Tacitus' gaze. Like Ravenna was still his ward and disobeying him. She blinked, her icy gaze unyielding.

Tacitus looked away. He gave a sigh and his wings shook with the effort. "I am dying, Ravenna."

"Yes," she said. It was obvious. That pillar of strength that had made her life worth living was crumbling. But to Ravenna, it had fallen the day she was captured by humans and taken away. There was nothing she could do to regain that state of relative innocence and happiness. Tacitus would never understand to see her take on the role that she must now accept. Perhaps it was better this way.

"It was my greatest wish that you should find your way home to me, so that I might give you my blessing before I die. And now you have come."

"Yes," Ravenna said again. She could see the confusion plain as day in Tacitus' eyes. He did not understand why she had not come back the same as before. He had wanted her to return as the separate but happy sylph that she had been, his heart-daughter who needed him. She was not that. Not anymore.

Tacitus reached once more for her hand. Ravenna took it, squeezing what strength she had into his frail fingers. Tacitus smiled faintly and shook his head, his dark golden hair falling into his eyes and obscuring their pain. "I do not know what tragedy befell you, nor where you went, but no matter what changes may have occurred, you are Ravenna. You are my heart-daughter. No matter what you do now, know that you have my blessing. Anything that is mine, is now yours. All of my personal tomes. All of my legacy. My standing as an Intellecti. It is yours. I love you, Ravenna. I always will."

Ravenna bowed her head. "And I love you, Tacitus. May your wings touch the sky."

"And your heart soar free."

Tacitus rose and walked away, his steps no longer graceful or glad. He looked back at Ravenna from the door to the healer's wing in the Stone Tower. For a moment, she had expected to see the red stone of a palace in the desert. Instead, she was faced with dark grey blocks that had kept her isolated from the world.

A shadow passed over her face. Tacitus nodded at the sight, then turned his back on her. Ravenna knew that it would be the last time she saw him.

Not two heartbeats passed before Kratos was standing beside Ravenna's bed, his eyes full of fear and confusion at what had just passed. "Ravenna…what *happened* to you?"

She looked down and saw that she wore a simple top tied around her neck, the back open for her wings. Her trousers were ones that she recognised as her own, probably fetched from her old room. They were loose around her waist and showed the brand from Jazer openly. The scratches on her shoulder and across her chest had healed fully, but they were red and ugly scars. The saltwater from her sea passing had probably not helped. Ravenna could see a few more scars and scratches from where she sat, and she knew that there was the long wound on her back between her wings. She looked nothing like the unblemished sylphs that lived in Shinalea. The worst injuries they ever received were from hunting accidents. No wonder Kratos was horrified.

Ravenna threw her legs over the side of the bed and made to stand. "I need to see Queen Mariala."

Kratos was immediately by her side, supporting her with his wing across her back and his bulk under her arm. Ravenna threw him off. She was weak, but she could stand perfectly well. She staggered to the table on the far side of the room while Kratos gaped at her. On the table's surface, looking salt-worn and a bit grimy, was her sword belt. The blades themselves had been replaced in their sheaths.

Ravenna picked it up and tightened the belt around her waist, keeping her breeches cinched tight, making her feel slightly more secure. She turned to find Kratos with his wings pressed close to his sides in fear. "I need to see Queen Mariala," Ravenna said again.

The other sylph gulped and looked away. "She…she is dead. The Choosing is set for this next week."

Ravenna would think about the death of her benevolent grandmother later. "Then I need to speak to the High Council."

"Y-you can't just demand to speak to the High Council!" Kratos squeaked. Ravenna lifted a hand to touch the scratches that ran across her chest. Then she rested her hands on the hilts of her twin blades.

"Trust me," she said flatly. "They will want to hear this. It is to do with the Stormbringers."

Kratos let out a little laugh, the sound high and nervous. "That's a myth. A child's story to keep away nightmares."

"Are these myths?" Ravenna growled, pointing to her wounds. She turned around and showed Kratos the very obvious scar down her back. "Is *this* a myth? Send for someone to take me to the High Council. *Now!*"

Kratos let out a squeak but ran do to as he was told, launching himself out of the window without another word, leaving Ravenna alone in the healer's chambers, chest heaving. Not three minutes later, a shape darkened the window. Crispinus.

"Ravenna," he said, bowing his head in greeting. "Are you recovering wel—"

"Take me to the High Council," Ravenna demanded. Crispin raised his eyebrows. For a moment, he looked like the sylph who would gladly torment Ravenna for the enjoyment of Desarra and himself. She was different from him and therefore a worthy target. Then, he faltered. He took in her scars and the way that she stood with her shoulders straight and her gaze firm. Ravenna knew that just as sure as Tacitus had not known who she was anymore, Crispin was losing something similar. He had always seen himself as superior to her. Now, she knew that if he were to demand a fight, she would win, even in her weakened state.

Crispin bobbed his wings in acknowledgement and approached Ravenna. She allowed him to slip an arm behind her neck and another beneath her knees. He carried her in his arms easily, but now there was a wariness there. Her own wings seemed to fight, battling against the feeling of helplessness as Ravenna was forced to allow Crispin to fly her to the heart of the Aerial City.

The stonework beneath her had not changed. The city was still beautiful, a work of masters and home to the beautiful sylphs. As Crispin carried her, Ravenna could practically see the stirring of wings. She would not be hard to miss, with her stark black feathers and hair, her skin still moon-white after a season in the desert. And to be flying in Crispin's arms, too. Briefly, Ravenna wondered where Desarra was, why her own sister had not stopped her mate from coming for her.

It did not matter. Desarra's thoughts were immaterial.

Crispin alighted in a stone courtyard adorned with plants whose bright colours and artistic shapes were carefully cultivated to show control and decadence. Ravenna shook her head as Crispin set her down.

"What is it?" he asked carefully. He knew better than to ask the reason for her visit to the High Council. But his curiosity fairly burned Ravenna.

"I wonder who will care about keeping these plants perfect when war reaches us," Ravenna said. Crispin recoiled, his wings flaring in alarm. Ravenna raised her brow and shook her head again. Everything was going to change.

She turned away from Crispin and strode into the chamber that housed the High Council. It was an ornate room. Every piece of possible stone had been carved into feathers and whorls, some pieces holding glittering pieces of crystal, some decorated with pictorials of the sylphs' proud history. All of it meant to be a symbol of the High Council's influence. All Ravenna saw when she viewed the sylphs sitting in their half-circle was a bunch of over-preened fools, unable to see past their desire for power.

It was telling that they waited for her. But the murmurs passed back and forth between the seven members halted as soon as she entered, as if they had not expected that which walked through the doors. Surely, they knew of Ravenna's return. And that she had been gravely wounded. By her reckoning, she had slept for nearly two days. So why did they eye her like a hawk among sparrows?

"Ravenna," the leader of the High Council addressed her. He sat in at the peak of the half-circle, his peers arrayed on either side. She thought his name was Strygis. A sylph of golden skin and golden wings, he was plump and arrayed in the finery that his station afforded. The way that the other sylphs seemed to defer to him in this situation told Ravenna that he ruled by force. Oh, what little he understood.

"Councillor," Ravenna nodded. She did not bow, as would be expected of her, but kept her back straight and her wings spread.

"Why did you seek an audience? We should be discussing whether or not you should even be allowed to return to Shinalea! After all, you have been to the Mainland. You know our laws," Strygis sniffed.

Ravenna chuckled.

"Oh, yes. I have been to the Mainland. And I would still be there if this were not so pressing," Ravenna scoffed. She placed her hands on the hilts of her swords, the movement already familiar though she had not even fought with the blades. A few of the High Council flinched.

"What is so pressing that you break one of our most fundamental laws?" Strygis asked. His fingers flexed, as though imagining what he would do to punish Ravenna for her insolence. She ignored the movement, instead addressing the whole Council.

"Humans," Ravenna said. There was a gasp from a charcoal sylph, her wings bristling. Another let out a surprised curse. Strygis merely pressed his lips together. Ravenna sighed and pointed to the long, thin scar on her arm. "I received this when human slavers—those who capture others to sell into service—came to Shinalea and captured me. This is where they branded me. This is where they cut down my spine..."

She told her story swiftly and concisely, emphasising the injuries inflicted upon her, glossing over those humans she loved. Miska did not even make it into her story; she found it too painful. Instead, Ravenna painted a picture of a cruel and furious race who culminated in Davorin, a conqueror who was seeking the Stormbringers of ancient times. The sylphs. She gave her evidence from the journals and made a spectacle of her scars. If she had been able to feel anything but determination and emptiness, then perhaps Ravenna would have been disgusted by the picture she was painting. Not all humans were evil. Not all were cruel. She *loved* a human with all her heart and yet she would not let his name pass her lips.

Finally, when Ravenna's tale of her escape across the desert to warn her people came to an end, nothing but silence remained. The High Council stared at her, unable to form reactions into words. If they thought about arguing, then there was the evidence of Ravenna's story written on her skin. If they thought about declaring her banished, there was the steel at her hip. They knew she would not have returned if it were not important and the truth was staring them in the face.

"They do not know where to find us," one sylph said after a moment.

Ravenna raised her brow. "Do you honestly think that will stop them? This island is less than half-a-day from the mainland. I was *captured* by humans right on these shores."

"You can go back! Lead them in a different direction!" Another sylph nodded eagerly.

"And if they find you while I am attempting to lead them astray? What will happen, then? Will you just fly off like a flock of startled crows? Or will you die?"

Strygis pounded his fist on the table.

"You should not have returned! You doom us all!"

Ravenna said nothing for a moment. She looked at each council member individually, meeting their gaze until each flinched away. Finally, she spoke, her words quiet though they rang through the chamber. "We were doomed the moment we lost that which we were."

"How could this have happened?" The dark female sank into her wings, the feathers fluffed in fear.

Ravenna did not lower her gaze. "The moment the law to exile those who ventured beyond our shores came into being, this was the only possible result. We could not remain hidden here forever. And when the humans did come, they would have forgotten us. We would have forgotten them. Both of us, lost to myth and the mists of memory. Our isolation will prove to have been our undoing."

"You brought this upon us! The humans would remain ignorant if not for you!" Strygis leaned forwards, wings flaring overhead.

"Perhaps," Ravenna said softly. "And perhaps not. They found Shinalea without my assistance. Either way, I have come to warn you. To save you. Send a scout if you doubt me!"

Silence echoed in the chambers. The High Council would not even exchange glances.

Ravenna nodded. "If you will not send a scout, then you must trust me. Trust the scars that I bear. If you do not prepare for this, then you will die."

Strygis looked to the council member on his right, then to the one on his left. Neither said anything, though the charcoal sylph flicked her eyes to something below the table. Strygis shook his head furiously. The charcoal sylph whispered something fierce, jerking her head towards Ravenna. She could feel them staring at her scars. She lifted her chin and spread her wings, hands resting on the swords at her hips. Strygis glared at the table, but with another whispered word from the sylphs at either side of him, he nodded.

These sylphs were terrified, Ravenna saw. It was for the best, she knew, but she had never seen such fear on any of her people's faces before. It was like having the last remnants of happiness from her childhood torn from her. Ravenna's chest ached for it, but she showed no sign of her pain. They would face much worse in the times to come. Enough that there might not be much left.

Strygis watched Ravenna, meeting her gaze. He flicked his eyes to each of her scars, lingering on the brand at her hip. Finally, he took a deep breath and reached beneath the table, removing something and setting it out for all to see.

Ravenna took a step back, shock coursing through her. This was a diadem made of gold-wrought feathers. It was the Crown of Wings, the symbol of the Queens and Kings of the sylphs. And they were offering it to Ravenna.

"Help us," the female sylph to the left of Strygis begged. She reached out to push the golden crown closer to Ravenna. "*Save* us."

Desperation bloomed in their eyes as they pushed that gold-wrought feather crown towards her. Ravenna knew that they were begging her silently to take the crown, to lead them, to save them. Only one had the courage to ask outright.

She curled her lip and turned her head away from the crown. "No."

"N-no?" Strygis asked, voice quivering as he realised all his splendour and influence and supposed power would do him no good, now.

"No," Ravenna repeated. "I do not love you well enough for that."

"But —"

"I will not be your Queen." She gave them a hard, sharp stare. "But I will fight your war."

Then, she turned on her heel and left, her wings fluttering slightly behind her. Silence followed in her wake.

EPILOGUE

*R*ock slipped under Miska's feet, making him stumble and fall. His thin leather slippers had worn through and he could feel the rocks digging into his feet. He kept onwards, though, only one thought on his mind.

I have to find Ravenna.

It had been three days since he had run from the Red Palace, fleeing for his life, and to find someone to save those he left behind. He had come upon the Great Hall, determined to see whether or not the soldiers could have saved Lenore from Davorin. They were twenty against one man. Surely, they could have defeated him easily? But the carnage that he had seen through the open door…

Miska shivered, only partly from the cold. He remembered the look of despair on his queen's face. He remembered how she stood facing the door with Davorin beside her, his gaze fixed on her face in a triumphant grin. Lenore had seen Miska. And she gave him the only command that could have enticed him to go. She had told him, "Run. Save us."

Miska had not even bothered to pack any supplies. He just fled the Red Palace, the place that had been his home since he was a child. He left everything he had known behind to go find Ravenna. Surely Ravenna, the love of his life and the strongest person he knew, could save Lenore. He had to find her. He would bring her and that army of Stormbringers that Davorin wanted. But the sylphs would be fighting against that bastard. Then Ravenna would grind him into dust.

Only…Miska wasn't certain that he was going the right way. He had not seen Vareis' directions to Ravenna properly. He had only noted the part about the Iron Mountains. Was the path to Shinalea over the mountains?

He had been wandering in the mountains for nearly half-a-day and was completely lost. His feet began bleeding and the farther he went, the more he shivered. This was cold, terrible, bone-breaking cold. And these trees! They were tall and spiny, with no resemblance to the lush trees in the gardens surrounding the Red Palace, or the scrubby plants of the desert. They made everything look the same, and their web-like, exposed roots obscured the sharp rocks underfoot.

Miska tripped and fell, grasping at a branch. He could feel it crack, even if he could not hear it. He straightened and tried to catch his breath. Tears stung at his eyes as he realised he did not even know the way back to the desert. All around him was unfamiliar terrain with no sign of water or food or people.

Miska missed Ravenna. If she were here, she would know what to do. She had read all those books. Surely, she knew how to navigate. And she would know what to do about the crawling feeling on the back of Miska's neck. It was almost like he was being watched, but not by an animal. No, this presence was intense and intelligent and it scared Miska desperately.

Miska felt a tremor in the earth. He started running, fear pumping through him, pushing his steps onwards. He did not care about the fire that burned through his bleeding feet. He did not care which way he was going. He just had to get away.

A hole in the ground yawned in front of Miska. He mistimed

his jump and fell instead, tumbling down a slight slope. His head slammed onto the trunk of one of those horrid trees and the world spun before him. Miska rolled onto his back, groaning. He looked up and knew, then, that his life was at an end.

He would never see Ravenna again.

Lenore would die and the Red Desert would be left to the hands of Davorin.

He had failed.

Miska whimpered as the dragon's head drew closer. Its step made the earth tremble, its bright white scales shimmering in the sun. Miska saw its jaw moving and, for once, he was glad that he would never hear. He was not sure he could have borne the noise that heralded his death. Miska felt his head throb again and he closed his eyes, slipping gladly into darkness.

His last thought before he succumbed to the black was of the strong and beautiful Ravenna. He hoped she was alright.

* * *

End, Book I

ACKNOWLEDGMENTS

The amount of people that are involved in making a book is actually quite large. I would like to thank all of them for the support and help that has gone into *The One Who Could Not Fly*, because without you, none of this would have happened.

Firstly, there are my beta readers, whose comments made this book so much more than it was. I gladly took all that you told me and did my best to improve it. I hope that it meets your standards. I would also like to thank my editor, Vanessa, for putting a lot of time and work into this piece. I would especially like to thank Fay Lane, who put together the most beautiful cover with short notice. You are an absolute genius.

Then there are the people who have been eagerly awaiting this first book of the Wing Cycle, who believed in me and thought that this would be a great next step in my adventures in writing. To Michael Evan who waited patiently through the frustrations. To my readers, who did not press me. And to my dad, who listened to me rant and rave when everything was falling apart, and helped me take initiative to move forwards. To all of these people, I say thank you.

"There are far, far better things ahead than any we leave behind."
— C.S. Lewis

ABOUT THE AUTHOR

E.G. Stone is an independent author who has been writing, quite literally, since the age of six. Since then, E.G. has improved rather a lot and has written (so far) twenty-two full-length novels, various short stories, a screenplay, snippets of poetry, and various blog entries that may or may not make sense. E.G. enjoys writing in many different genres. The favourites are science fiction, mystery (preferably of the murder variety), adventure, fantasy — basically anything where the world isn't quite what you would expect. When not writing, she is off musing about the workings of languages, both real and created, or wandering around and experiencing new people, places and things. E.G. reads voraciously, perhaps to the point of slight-insanity. She also is enjoying making a go of this writer thing full-time. Weird, nerdy, perhaps a little crazy, she is having a grand old time writing, reading, reviewing, interviewing, and causing trouble.

9 781734 796506